CLARION III,

THIRD IN A SERIES WHICH THE CRITICS HAVE ACCLAIMED—

"These people have something to say, and they are ready to use any means—any at all—to say it, and they just don't seem to give a damn if Mommy sees it."

—Theodore Sturgeon

"This, friends, is the SF of the future, by the writers who are going to write much of what we will be reading a few years from now."

—Crawdaddy

"There are a lot of fresh viewpoints and attitudes displayed by these upcoming talents."

—Publishers Weekly

"The most valuable book [*Clarion*] yet written about science fiction."

—National Review

Other SIGNET Science Fiction You'll Enjoy

☐ **CLARION II edited by Robin Scott Wilson.** "This, friends, is the SF of the future, by the writers who are going to write much of what we will be reading a few years from now."—**Crawdaddy** (#Q5056—95¢)

☐ **THERE WILL BE TIME by Poul Anderson.** Only a natural-born time traveler stood between man and a future which could destroy human civilization. (#Q5401—95¢)

☐ **THE FALLIBLE FIEND by L. Sprague de Camp.** Could a rational, literal-minded demon survive in an irrational world of men? (#Q5370—95¢)

☐ **THE CITY AND THE STARS by Arthur C. Clarke.** A tense story set millions of years in the future, when one man sets out to unite Earth's sole survivors, two isolated nations ignorant of each other's ways. (#Q5371—95¢)

☐ **THE WEATHERMAKERS by Ben Bova.** Harnessing weather was the goal, and the man who could perform this miracle was Ted Marrett. But the opposition he faced was almost overwhelming and his greatest opponent was the weather itself. (#Q5329—95¢)

☐ **OPERATION: OUTER SPACE by Murray Leinster.** A television producer, his secretary, and a psychiatrist find themselves trapped inside a spacecraft, being hurled far beyond the confines of the Solar System toward a planet inhabited by bizarre creatures—a volcanic world strangely similar to Earth. (#Q5300—95¢)

THE NEW AMERICAN LIBRARY, INC.,
P.O. Box 999, Bergenfield, New Jersey 07621

Please send me the SIGNET BOOKS I have checked above. I am enclosing $______________(check or money order—no currency or C.O.D.'s). Please include the list price plus 25¢ a copy to cover handling and mailing costs. (Prices and numbers are subject to change without notice.)

Name______________________________

Address____________________________

City______________State__________Zip Code__________

Allow at least 3 weeks for delivery

CLARION III

An anthology of speculative fiction and criticism

Edited by

ROBIN SCOTT WILSON

For Herman King and his fellow university administrators, who have made the Clarion Experiment work.

SIGNET TRADEMARK REG. U.S. PAT. OFF. AND FOREIGN COUNTRIES
REGISTERED TRADEMARK—MARCA REGISTRADA
HECHO EN CHICAGO, U.S.A.

SIGNET, SIGNET CLASSICS, SIGNETTE, MENTOR AND PLUME BOOKS
are published by The New American Library, Inc.,
1301 Avenue of the Americas, New York, New York 10019

FIRST PRINTING, OCTOBER, 1973

1 2 3 4 5 6 7 8 9

PRINTED IN THE UNITED STATES OF AMERICA

We are pleased to announce the winners of the NAL prizes for the best stories from the 1972 Clarion Writers' Workshop (at Michigan State University and the University of Washington):

1st prize: "Mist, Grass and Sand" by VONDA McINTYRE (does not appear in this book)

2nd prize: "Road Map," by F. M. BUSBY

3rd prize: "The Teardrop" by DVORA OLMSTEAD and "Everybody Loves: In a Circular Motion" by MEL GILDEN

Honorable Mentions:

"When Pappy Isn't There" by LIN NIELSEN

"Asclepius Has Paws" by MILDRED DOWNEY BROXON

"Servants" by DAVID WISE

"Say Goodbye to the World's Last Brothel" by ROBERT WISSNER

Contents

Introduction

This is the third volume of what appears to be a continuing annual collection of fiction written by men and women—most of them rather young—who have attended one or another of the science fiction workshops collectively termed "Clarion." The first three sessions of the Clarion Workshop were held at Clarion State College in Pennsylvania in the summers of 1968, 1969, and 1970. In 1971, two workshops were in session, "Clarion East" at Tulane University and "Clarion West" at the University of Washington in Seattle. In 1972, Vonda McIntyre's "Clarion West" was again held in Seattle, and Jim Sallis' "Clarion East" moved to the Justin Morrill College of Michigan State University, where Professors Leonard Isaacs (biology) and R. Glenn Wright (English) were co-directors. At this writing, both workshops show increasing signs of permanence.

In five years and seven sessions, the Clarion Workshops have enrolled about 150 beginning writers. They have been taught by sixteen writers: Terry Carr, Avram Davidson, Samuel R. Delany, Harlan Ellison, Frank Herbert, Damon Knight, Ursula K. Le Guin, Fritz Leiber, Judith Merril, Frederik Pohl, Joanna Russ, James Sallis, Robert Silverberg, Theodore Sturgeon, Kate Wilhelm, and this editor. They have produced something on the order of 28,000 pages of finished typescript, each of which has been patiently read and carefully criticized by the workshops' staffs and participants. Out of all of this have come a hundred or so stories and novelettes in print, a half-dozen novels (that I know of—it is increasingly difficult to keep track), and a couple of dozen well-established literary careers.

I feel as proud as any new father, recognizing—as any honest father must—how very little I had to do with these new careers, how very blessed with talented people the workshops have been, how great has been the role (to continue the metaphor) of the motherly muse of us all. I will not strain the image further with a dissertation on my own relationship with Mother during these years, except to note that my work with Clarion—as workshop director, as anthology editor—is at a close, and I am re-reading the *Kama Sutra* with a gleam in my eye.

I suppose that—apart from the success of students who have become friends, the enthusiasm of friends who have become colleagues—the most satisfying aspect of the Clarion experiment has been the demonstration that a significant number of people are able to bridge the dreadful gap between the humanities and arts on one hand and science and technology on the other, a gap, I believe, that threatens the continuing viability of our society. For three centuries, we have been fractionating the old *quadrivium* and *trivium* that once comprised human knowledge. We have divided and subdivided until the U.S. Office of Education's list of "Conventional Academic Subdivisions of Knowledge and Training" contains 572 entries.

Some of us are doing our damnedest to put it all together again, to see science and technology as a humane occupation with humane implications; to see humane studies in the context of a world dominated by science and technology.

This is the peculiar genius of science fiction.

Winnetka, Illinois, 15 November 1972

Road Map

by F. M. Busby

F. M. Busby ("Here, There, and Everywhere"— Clarion II) *is a retired communications engineer who has sold ten stories in his first year as a free-lance writer. His first novel,* Cage a Man, *will be published by The New American Library later this year. Before going into the dot-dash business, Buz was a farmhand, cabdriver, two-time Army vet, auto mechanic, baker's assistant, teletype repairman, college student, surveyor's assistant, comptometer operator, and inept janitor.*

Of this story, Buz writes: "I've long been fascinated by the idea behind 'Road Map' and have never understood why it should follow the 'rules' that are claimed to govern it. So, what if it didn't? And what if—?"

He woke, hungry. The waking was sudden, not like his usual gradual drift to consciousness; he was fully alert. He opened his eyes and saw blurred masses of bright color—he couldn't bring them into sharp focus. He tried to bring his hands up to rub the sleep away. He couldn't do it; he felt the texture of cloth under his hands and vaguely saw them move, but something was wrong with his control, his coordination.

For a moment he was close to panic. Then he thought, Whatever it is, it doesn't hurt—and I can feel and move; there's no paralysis or numbness. Searching for an explanation, he wondered if he'd had some sort of surgery, and was suffering aftereffects from the anesthetic.

He couldn't recall planning or needing any operation, but temporary amnesia might be another side-effect. The thought encouraged him—rather, the realization that his mind was working well enough to think of it. Deliberately, he began to test his memory of the basic facts about himself: name, age, marital status, state of health—the lot.

Ralph Ascione, age fifty-eight, two years a widower—he paused to weather one of his still-frequent bursts of missing Elizabeth, and caught it short of seeing her death again.

Health good, so long as he took care of his heart. Thought of that organ also gave him pause, but he decided his symptoms were nothing like those of his one serious attack. The mental recitation continued; the facts were all there: height, weight, home address, date of his son's imminent wedding, and all the numbers that specified the life of Ralph Ascione. His memories were sharply defined and readily accessible. The only thing that eluded him was any explanation of his condition.

What more could he learn of it? He listened, but heard only vague sounds that told him nothing. His mutinous hands brushed nothing but cloth. His tongue touched bare gums; where were his dentures? The air smelled of hospital; that part of his guess was probably right.

He squinted and tried to focus his eyes. If he were seeing at all correctly, his bed was a cage, at least five or six feet high—but open at the top. He considered the possibility of insanity but rejected it; the discrepancies that disturbed him were physical. And he didn't *feel* sick. . . .

Below his middle was warm wetness; whatever his ailment, it included incontinence. He felt depression; maybe his state was worse than he had thought.

A new sound came; in the blurred distances, something moved. Vaguely seen, a huge face loomed over him and made soft, deep clucking noises. Then he understood.

Reincarnation, by God! They'd always said you don't remember; well, somebody was wrong. Either he was the exception—some kind of fluke—or else all babies remembered at first and lost the recall later. He didn't want to lose his. He ran a few facts through his mind again; no, they weren't fading. . . .

He was surprised at the way he absorbed the shock so easily. Before he could flinch at the loss of his lifelong identity, something inside him grasped eagerly at the prospect—a whole new lifetime!

But his thoughts rioted in confusion, so that he hardly noticed the way his mouth sucked instinctively at the bottle or the warmth and gentleness with which his bottom was washed, dried and rewrapped. The cuddling and petting calmed him; first his body relaxed, then his taut awareness. He could think again.

The question of age puzzled him. Remembering his son's earliest days, he was almost certain he was at least a week past the newborn state. Perhaps, he theorized, consciousness could not emerge until the effects of birth trauma subsided. It didn't matter, but still he wondered. He'd like to know his birthday, he thought, and the year.

The year! He'd always been curious about the future, wanting to live to see as much of it as he could. Well, sooner or later he'd learn what part of it was now his lot.

The nurse talked to him and made crooning sounds, but at first he couldn't force his ears and brain to shape the sounds into intelligible words. Then slowly, like becoming accustomed to a thick dialect or accent, he began to understand. And then he received his second shock.

"Sweet baby," said the nurse. "Oh, she's a sweet, sweet baby!"

His mind froze, his self-image fighting to keep its place as the nurse returned him to the crib and left the room. He recognized what was happening within him, he dove deep and found the concept of himself as a person first and everything else second, and the struggle eased. Well, came the thought, that's fair. See how the other half lives.

He could not think of himself as a she; he sought but could not find any feeling of *she*ness. His bodily sensations were too diffuse to tell him anything; from the internal feelings at his crotch he could have been male, female, hermaphrodite or completely sexless. His hands were no help; even if he could have controlled them, he was too well swaddled.

Intellectually there was no need to confirm the nurse's words; surely she knew and said the truth. And certainly it hardly mattered at the moment, and wouldn't, in a sense, for some years to come. But inside him was something that clung stubbornly to the concept of maleness and refused, without proof, to give it up. Inside him, against his will, raged conflict.

He'd have to wait and see, he decided. Either his inner attitudes would shift naturally, guided by glandular balance, or he'd have to work at adjusting to the new, the totally unexpected situation. He was pleased to find that he was not consciously resisting the inevitable; he had no desire to begin his new life with a built-in basis for neurosis.

Sensation brought his self-congratulation to a halt. He had wet himself again, and more than that. Without conscious intent, he began to cry, loudly. The noise he made was out of proportion to the mild protest he felt; he wanted to laugh at the incongruity. But what the hell, he thought; it's the only game in town. And eventually the nurse came and changed him again. He concentrated on the way it felt to be laved and patted dry, and was fairly certain that the warm washcloth encountered no protrusions. The nurse had not lied to him.

What would it be like, then? He thought of the women he knew well, of what he understood them to be like. He wondered if he understood them at all, or they him.

Elizabeth understood him, of course, sometimes better than he knew himself, and from the start—their agreement to marry came quickly and with few words. Elizabeth Wilson was so young as to need parental consent for marriage, but she was free of the gaucheries he expected from such youth. She seemed so much a part of him that when, rarely, she became truly angry in a disagreement, he acceded to her wishes almost automatically, out of sheer surprise. One time: "No! We will not take the morning flight. I can't be ready until afternoon." When the morning flight crashed without them, half-joking he accused her of precognition. "If I could see the future, Ralph, I wouldn't have led clubs into dummy last night, and cost us the rubber."

A part of him, and he a part of her. No wonder he missed her so much.

He thought of his mother, widowed when he was twelve—of how her warm love became overly protective for a time. ". . . wear your galoshes; it might snow . . . shouldn't you wear a sweater under that light jacket? . . . I'm not trying to choose your friends, but there's a lot of talk about that girl . . . Of course you can live on campus if you wish, but I'd feel much better if you stayed here and drove to classes . . ." Her touch on the reins was light but ever-present. Then one day, after much thought over a long period, he told her it was time he began making his own mistakes—the storm was less than he had feared, and afterward they could be friends. But as a woman, he realized, he knew very little of her.

His sister Cheryl? Happy child, then spiteful brat and runaway hellion. With Cheryl, the breakaway drew blood, and the later reunion was equally painful. Then, her life stabilized, she was a good friend to him and Elizabeth.

He could put little importance to the other women who crossed his life. No great loves, and after adolescence, no great hurts.

His thumb found its way to his mouth; the sucking pads in his cheeks worked diligently, but nothing came to swallowing but his own saliva. The crying reflex blurred his thought; he held it back for a moment, thinking: Elizabeth is really all I know of women.

He visualized her; the picture in his mind changed from scene to scene, from time to time. And then, crashing through the defenses he'd neglected, came the bloody, mangled thing that had died in his arms.

It was good to cry, mindlessly, for nothing more than nourishment; he purged himself as he fed, and then slept.

Time was strangely extended; his experienced mind knew he'd begun consciousness only a few days ago, but his body emotions insisted the period was much longer.

He still found it difficult to accept the reality of his tiny female body; its size was also a dual, contradictory thing to him. And perhaps, he thought, when I can make my mouth and tongue say words, I can get the feedback to become "she." Meanwhile, he waited and learned, and wondered.

His vision improved, and the movements of arms and legs. He could see and sometimes touch the plastic toys that hung close to his face, and make them rattle. Once he stuck a thumb in his eye. It hurt, but the motion had been slight and random, and did no damage. Usually he could bring thumb's comfort to mouth at first or second attempt.

Governed by his body's needs, he slept much of the time.

Bowels and bladder were a minor outrage, out of his control. They voided, and his will had no effect. The boy began to handle it in about a year, he thought. Without much prodding. I wonder how old I am.

He thought more about his son Carl, regretting that he hadn't lived to see the boy remarried. But perhaps Carl was still alive at the start of this new life, and someday he could see him again. What a strange meeting that would be! And what a thing it was, to have fathered a genius. As a child, his son seemed to learn by instinct. Later he had no need of adolescent rebellion; he was always amenable but never subservient. Quite a boy, and quite a man . . .

Thought of fatherhood gave way to pangs of hunger. He cried and was answered.

He was fed by breast as well as by bottle. Bottle was more efficient but breast comforted him warmly; instinct did not always make him sleep after bottle. He wondered who his mother might be, and where he was, and when; he liked the blurred glimpses he'd had, of her smile. He was fairly certain that he was in the United States and near his own time; the language hadn't changed, the little he'd heard of it. And he knew he was Caucasian and of a relatively affluent family, for he could see his skin and knew the cost of private accommodations. And where, he wondered, was his own father?

Nothing was said in his hearing to answer the questions that still plagued him. Very well, he would wait. In him, content and patience grew, but not at the expense of memory or purpose.

One day, feeding at breast, he heard a new male voice. "Hello, dear, I couldn't get back any sooner. You're all right, I see?"

"Oh, yes!" He heard the sounds as much through his mother's chest, one ear close to it, as through the air. He strained to hear what was said, but sleep was upon him, and a thought: That's my father; I wonder what he looks like.

He woke, being lifted and laid into a smaller resting place. Then he was jounced in walking-rhythm, felt cold air on his face—then he was set down. Doors closed, ear-hurting; he was in a confined space of dead air. Noise came, and bad smells, a pattern of harsh movement. His memory knew the bounce of city streets and the stench of vehicle exhausts. His young body knew only fright and discomfort.

Lifted again at the end of it, his place-of-lying moved and swung in strides—more cold air, and then warm—until it was again set to rest. The light was dim, but he could see, leaning over him, the faces that were now his mother and father. His memory prickled but did not speak.

"Well, now," said the father-face. "Welcome to our home, Betsy Wilson."

Unease tugged at his gut; he strained to see more closely. The faces were so big to him, and strange. Both were smiling; suddenly an old picture superimposed on what he saw . . . and then he knew.

He was not in the future; he was more than fifty years deep into his own past. These were Elizabeth's parents. He was Betsy Wilson, who one day would become Elizabeth Ascione.

He thought—when he could think again—no wonder she knew me so well!

If only I can remember as well as she had.

But of course she would, for she was herself; there had never been any other. Ralph was the earlier segment of her conscious life and she the later—though the two ran, had run, would run, parallel through the years he had lived and she was now to have. And with knowledge of her personal identity came acceptance of her sex.

What will it be like, she wondered, to meet him—see him—and *know*? He had never known; there had been no hint. What if she told him? She hadn't; could she? Probably not; he wouldn't believe it. Only after her death had his hard-headed materialistic view of the universe begun to broaden.

Her death! She had forgotten that there are drawbacks to living in known time. The freeway horror that lay two years back in her memories also waited for her, fifty-two years ahead. Oh, God! If only I hadn't outlived myself. Then I wouldn't know. I wouldn't know . . .

But was the future predetermined in such detail? Did it run on tracks, or could it be changed? She had to find out. She had no way to do it now, and wouldn't for years; she simply didn't know enough details of her early life. Oh, a few things, from mutual reminiscences, but nothing she could think to use as a test. For the present she could only wait and think, and learn.

The fierce vitality of her young body would not allow depression to hold her for long. Time enough later, she thought, to try to rattle the bars of time, and evade or accept a death more than half a century away.

Then she realized—it would be her second death in that remote decade. And she couldn't even remember Ralph's. . . .

"Look, dear," said her mother. "I think she's trying to laugh."

Learning and achieving seemed slow to her, but instinct combined with mature knowledge and purpose to make her development precocious; her parents occasionally remarked on it.

First she needed to communicate. Not by speech—that was months away, and she shouldn't introduce it too soon, for fear of being considered a freak or prodigy. She used crying and movement; deliberately she cultivated different tones and cadences to ask for food, to be changed, to be held and cuddled. For the latter she also worked to make her arms reach out when her mother or father came near. She found that snuggling *was* essential to well-being—the psychologists were right—the contact, the warmth, the rocking and soft-voiced crooning had a definite physical effect, and for best vitality she needed it. Luckily, her mother seemed to feel the complementary need, and satisfied it often.

The infant Elizabeth grew, became a toddler. Overt sexual development was years ahead, but she began to notice that it *felt* differently, to be a girl. She couldn't remember male infancy; those recalls were buried nearly six decades deep. But being Elizabeth did not feel the same as being Ralph. She had no words to describe the difference, and she knew why; words derive from shared experience. She decided the distinction was something like that of being right- or left-handed: no "better" or "worse," but merely two states of being.

When the time came for speech, she was ready; she practiced, when she was alone, to train her tongue and lips. She knew better than to go too fast or use adult vocabulary, but she would not stoop to babytalk. Her camouflage was not perfect; occasionally she caught puzzled looks on her parents' faces.

And once her father said, "I know what it is, honey. Betsy always has just the right word. She seldom makes mistakes." After that she took pains to err more often. But not too often; she had her pride.

The one thing she did hurry, camouflage or no camouflage, was toilet training.

Early along, she worried about the problem of adapting fifty-eight years of male experience and habit to a pattern of acceptable female behavior. The worry was waste; she found as she came to walk and speak that her parents gave a constant flow of clues, with and without words, to what was expected of her. The less she relied on deliberate thought, the more she relaxed and responded naturally to them, the easier she found it to be a convincing Elizabeth. Yet she did not lose herself in the role; her memories were intact, with their commentaries on the ways of her life.

Now, she thought, I see what Women's Lib was complaining about. Role-training? Every minute, and in ways they don't even realize, consciously. But she herself had no complaint; the role was necessary to the years and the life she would have. And so far as she knew, Ralph hadn't tried to press her into any mold. She'd had many activities, anything she said she wanted, outside the homemaker's sphere. Of course, it might look different from this side, when the time came. Wait and see.

Ralph had not much enjoyed the jungle-law years of small-boyhood; Elizabeth was glad to be spared a rerun of the experience. She found the world of small girls utterly new: sometimes delightful, sometimes appalling, but generally fascinating, as she learned it. Staying in character became more difficult; slips of knowledge that her parents would not notice were grossly apparent against the bright clear light of misinformation firmly shared by her playmates. When in doubt or in no doubt at all, she learned to stay out of the line of fire. As when Sharon-down-the-block, three years older, explained the facts of life to Betsy and a group of her agemates . . .

"You get married and the minister does something, and a baby comes out your bellybutton."

"Right in church?" "I bet it hurts a lot." "*Does* it hurt, Sharon?"

"I dunno," said Sharon. "Kathy didn't say. But anyway, we don't *have* to."

Maybe you don't, thought Elizabeth. But I think I do. . . .

Except for occasional rediscovery of something long forgotten in the times she was reliving, school became a dull and boring ache. The prison of childhood stretched ahead, interminably. She had forgotten the way childhood's thought and speech can remain the same for so very long. Sitting through hours of repetition, varied only by the wrong answers that led to still more repetition, she longed to come to grips with a future she could put to test.

She had put in abeyance her need to try that future, to attempt to change it, she'd kept busy learning and practicing her role. Now she looked for a checkpoint of some kind, for a handle she could turn. Occasionally she tried to do something she was fairly certain Ralph's wife could not have done as a child, but the results were never conclusive. There seemed to be an inertia, along with her own trained wish and habit, that kept her from doing anything that might make her seem unusual, or shock or hurt her parents. So when she was ten, she watched thirteen-year-old Sharon pass for twenty-one and acquire a small arm-tattoo in the carnival tent, the drunken man's hand so steady, as his mouth was not. But she could not bring herself to follow suit, even if the man had allowed it.

Impatiently, she awaited the onset of adolescence; she was in no hurry for sexual development as such, but she felt prisoner of the static ways of childish glands, in herself and in her associates. The world of little girls had lost its charm for her; changes in minds and personalities would be welcome. She knew how banal the teen-age mind could be, but at least it would be a different banality, and could interest her for a time.

Still, menarche at eleven caught her unprepared; signs at chest and pubis had not seemed so far advanced. But one day at school her skirt was wet where she sat. Her role-playing body panicked. Drawing upon earlier knowledge, she excused herself and walked home. Well, it was time for that talk, the one her mother had begun several times but never completed. She entered her home.

"Mother?"

"Yes, Betsy." Elizabeth, like all her friends, changed her nicknames frequently; nonetheless, her mother always called her Betsy. "I'm in the kitchen here."

Sitting on a high stool, Mrs. Wilson peeled potatoes at the kitchen sink. She weighed more than she had earlier or would a few years later, more than her daughter would ever weigh. Her hair, bleached lighter than the brown of Elizabeth's, was piled in a loose upsweep that drooped alarmingly on the left side. "Yes, dear?" she said.

"I've started, Mother." Elizabeth turned to show her stained skirt. "I'll rinse it with cold water. But you'd better show me how those things work, the ones you use."

She knew her mother would cry and embrace her, and she did. Then, the skirt rinsed and the flow controlled, the two women sat in the kitchen, the older with coffee and the younger, bathrobed, sipping milk.

"Betsy, I've never got around to tell you much. I should have, but . . . well, what do you know already? I mean . . ."

From sounds heard clearly, late at night, Elizabeth knew her mother enjoyed sex well enough; she simply couldn't talk about it. The problem was, how to make things easy.

"I know how not to get in trouble like Sheila across the street last year. I mean, I know what it is they do." No point in discussing the ovulation cycle—she wasn't sure her mother knew how it worked. And contraceptives? Forget it.

"That's good," said her mother. "I'm so glad we had this nice talk, Betsy." Another embrace; Mrs. Wilson wiped her eyes.

"Yes, Mother. So am I." She went to her room; it was time for homework.

Her mother wasn't stupid, she thought, nor ignorant. She was merely a product of her times. Elizabeth opened her notebook, then closed it, lost in thought. . . .

Unless she had lied to Ralph, she came to him virgin. And she wouldn't have to lie; she knew him too well. So what if—was this her chance to test her future?

She thought about it. There was no hurry; she would wait for her body to ready itself more fully. There was still nearly half a decade, before Ralph.

She had chances to do things she *hadn't* done—knew she hadn't done—but she didn't, somehow. Once she watched Sharon and two other girls, giggling over a newspaper picture of a fashion model, cut each other's hair into an imitation of the scalplock worn by the girl in the picture—but she went away with her own hair intact. The three were suspended from school and pictured in the local press, but not she. Now why, she thought, didn't I? It would have been harmless enough. . . .

At fourteen, crushed under sixteen-year-old Ricky Charlton in the back seat of his car, she wished she'd chosen an easier way. "Please, Beth!" In the heat, sweat trickled down her sides. She'd guessed Ricky to be a good choice for her gambit, but his hand on her labia was clumsy and downright painful. She'd have to be the one to make sure the condom was worn properly; Ralph had used them, sometimes.

And from Ralph's experience she knew she couldn't acquiesce too soon; Ricky had to believe he alone had won, could have won the goal. That was the way boys thought, at his age in this time. She had her reputation to think of, at school.

Too soon or not, neither of them could take much more of this. Silently she consented, and helped him fit the necessary appliance. Against his heedless urgency, she tried to arrange them both for better comfort.

Alongside the car, a series of explosions; someone had thrown a string of firecrackers. When it was done, she waited. "Ricky?"

"I don't know—it won't—it's your fault! Why did you make me *wait?*"

Oh, the hell with it.

She met Ralph when she was sixteen, he twenty. As the time neared she thought of those days, over fifty years past on the one hand and rapidly approaching on the other. At times she found herself remembering scenes between them from her own viewpoint; the phenomenon worried her—was she losing her firsthand memory of Ralph's lifetime? Then she realized that her mind was composing the events from a mixture of memory, empathy and extrapolation. As well as anticipation . . .

Tom Gilchrist, a stocky good-humored boy of her own age, escorted her to the "social" at the neighborhood dance hall. It was their third date—and, as she recalled, their last; their friendship was only lightly tinged with romance. At the entrance they paid admission—Dutch treat—and were given nametags.

They danced, talked, sipped sweet insipid punch. Constantly she looked to find Ralph Ascione; if she could remember where in the large hall she first met him, she would find that spot and stay there. And when she saw him she did not recognize him.

She saw the nametag, yes. But he so young, ears leaping out from the thin face, hair cut and slicked in a fashion she'd long forgotten seeing above that face, was almost a total stranger.

How had it gone, before? Seeing the person she had been, she could not remember. How old? Twenty? But he was turning away, she had to make her move.

"I think I know him, Tom." Pointing. "I should say hello."

Young Gilchrist obliged; he touched Ralph's shoulder, turned him and brought him to her, and read the nametag as he saw it. "Ralph Askeony."

"No," she said, "it's Ash-*own*." Yes, she thought, that's exactly what she said to me.

Ralph smiled as he took her hand. "How did you know that?"

Constantly, within the limitations of her school and his work, they were together. To be with my earlier self, she thought—and I know, and he doesn't. I wish I could tell him; that would break the pattern, that ends with me lying in my blood as a baby lies in its wet—only, so much more of it. . . .

But he couldn't possibly believe; I know. And there will be other ways. There is time; my world can't outwit me forever.

And one day he will know. This day, when he is me. But that is *now*. No, it's all too complex. . . .

She gave herself to the situation and found it charming, trying to recall events from his viewpoint so long-ago to her, watching his reactions from outside him and remembering what he felt, seeing her as she was now. She knew her own beauty both from inside and outside.

The years between dimmed but never vanished. As before, she was not certain as to how the decision of marriage was reached so quickly. Her parents were startled, but agreed with surprising readiness.

Had ever such a marriage been? She knew him, and as if in reflection he seemed to know her as well. She had indeed come virgin to him, but from his period of their life she drew comparisons that confirmed the joy she found in their sex together.

She could share his hobbies—spelunking, rockhounding, ham radio—she knew them from his life. And the companionship, the talking—I talk to myself, she thought—yes, but I love that self and its answers.

She found she had to be careful not to answer questions before he asked them. It was not that her memories over fifty-plus years were so detailed, but that empathy built upon her recalls, almost to a semblance of precognition.

Absorbed in her present, she forgot to expect pregnancy. And she realized that since meeting Ralph she'd also forgotten to look for ways to test the shape of the future. How many chances she'd wasted, she couldn't know. Well, there was time enough yet, and now was no time to take risks with a small life for the later sake of her own. No, not now.

Tiny events, she thought, are less certain. What if I have conceived a daughter? Then—God, no! I can't give up Carl. We both loved him so much.

That night and several more, her sleep was troubled.

Pregnancy was more difficult than she expected, but she didn't complain. One day she realized that her reticence, seen by Ralph as sign that all was well with her, had misled her into expecting an easier time. She could almost laugh, but came to dread the birth itself.

It was neither as easy as she hoped nor as bad as she feared. At the last moment she was put under by the anesthetist; she could not recall clearly the moment she saw the baby and felt it laid onto her collapsed belly. Relaxed, still to a great extent under the effects of the drug, she heard Ralph's congratulations and reassurances from a far distance. There was something . . . why couldn't she remember?

She had complications, dangerous and painful. The sedatives did not allow her mind to clear. Dazed, she came partially awake at intervals, to be allowed to cuddle her baby. Was it Carl? She could not summon energy to ask.

One day she awoke almost fully, knowing, somehow, that now she would live. The baby was brought to her. "You can nurse the little one now, Mrs. Ascione." What a sweet ache it was!

Then the baby lay at her side, her arm around it and its hand tightly gripping her finger, then relaxing, rhythmically. No, not quite rhythmically. In fact, not rhythmically at all.

Squeeeze, squeeze. *Squeeeze, squeeeze, squeeeze. Squeeeze.* Pause. *Squeeeze,* squeeze, squeeze. Squeeze, squeeze. Squeeze. Pause . . .

Something . . . old memories surfaced. Squeeze, *squeeeze.* Dot-dash. Morse code! The sedatives had given her strange thoughts before this. . . .

The patterns resonated with Ralph's memories. Letters, words, came to her.

. . . not die . . . freeway . . . more years . . . I know . . . as you will . . . hello myself . . .

Elizabeth hugged herself to her, still wondering if it were daughter or son she held.

But either way, she thought, I know where I'm going.

Everybody Loves: In a Circular Motion

by Mel Gilden

Mel Gilden ("What About Us Grils?"—Clarion) *was born on Franz Kafka's birthday in 1947 but tried to work in a department store anyway. He describes himself as a "Big Hebrew Writer Fella" and claims his interest in science fiction stems from his mother, whose own mother used to read Jules Verne to her in Yiddish. He has never written a story involving chicken soup except once, and it remains satisfactorily unpublished as far as I know.*

He likes to write about sex. He works in his bathroom in order not to disturb others with his typing. He would like to preface this story with a sign: "Symbolism Ahead: Drive Carefully." It's okay with me.

The first girl was golden.

Dundee brought in the passionate red coupon he'd cut out of the local paper, and with a bravado he did not feel, he shoved it across the desk at the man on the other side.

"Yes, sir," the fat man with the distinctive black beard said. "Popsicle ladies, on sale now for only two hundred credits." He winked. "The first one is free."

"And you're sure she'll really love me?" Dundee said.

"Love you!" the man roared. "Hell, she'll love you more than Helen loved Paris."

"Well—"

"More than Cressida loved Troilus."

"Listen—"

"More than Juliet loved Romeo."

"Sir—"

"More than Iseult loved Tristram."

"But—"

"But me no buts, my boy. It's guaranteed! We're defrosting

her now. And when she comes out here, she'll be done to a golden turn. Special massagers rubbing down her nubile young body, leaving just enough ice in her to want melting." He clapped Dundee on the shoulder so hard, Dundee had to hold onto the counter or fall over.

"Now, if you'll adjourn to the waiting room . . ." The fat man with a beard like a covey of ravens motioned with both hands through the artificial silken curtains, through the sound shield, through the misty caverns of love, into the waiting room.

The waiting room was an Arabian fantasy hung with tapestries and silks. Pneumatic pillows floated on deep pile carpets with erotic designs, and the air smelled of sweating bodies, tired after doing something other than running the mile.

Small dust clouds puffed up around his feet as Dundee walked to the sultan's chair. He sat down and it creaked a warning. After a while he noticed things about the waiting room he hadn't seen before.

Up in the corner, where a blue sash crossed a pink tapestry, a spider was at work busily trying to suck the life out of a fly still struggling in her silk net. Dust lay like a gray skin on billows of satin hangings imported all the way from New Jersey.

Three notes on the flute, recorded and slightly ragged from many repetitions, blew and Dundee stood up. Curtains parted and a girl dressed in more than oriental splendor walked—did I say walked? Was I so crude? Drifted perhaps—into the waiting room. She was, as the fat man had promised, golden. Her hair was gold like sunlight, and her body was gold like toast. Oriental splendor covered her here and there but only to emphasize a breast here or to decorate a smooth thigh there.

She ran to Dundee and kissed him. Their tongues fought. She pushed him away and said, "I love you more than Helen loved Paris."

Dundee tried to kiss her again.

"More than Cressida loved Troilus."

He held her close but her guaranteed—not to mention fervently declared—love had to wait for the end of a transcribed message of interest to us all.

After she proclaimed her love Dundee led her out the back door of the waiting room and took her home.

Passion galloped like white horses through Dundee's body, and that night the large economy-size bed was wasted on two bodies that took up only one space. The morning after, Dundee lay with his arm around Helia (he'd chosen the name more for its poetry than for its fidelity to a dead language) and thought of all the beautiful golden times they would have together.

Later they talked.

"I want to go to the movies tonight, dear," Helia said.

"What have the movies to offer that I can't? Don't you love me more than Helen loved Paris?"

"Of course, my darling," she said, nibbling his ear. "But John Wayne is riding into the sunset this evening at the Bijou."

He gently stroked her belly, letting his fingers diddle in the triangle of hair beneath. "The man said you were guaranteed."

"And so I am."

They'd taught her the *Kama Sutra* and the *Ananga Ranga* and she gave Dundee what he expected of her.

In the evening she went to the Bijou. The bad guys fell to John Wayne's avenging bullets and he rode off into the sunset. When Helia got home, Dundee was asleep. And because she loved him more than Cressida loved Troilus, she didn't wake him.

The next day they were making love on the kitchen floor and were interrupted by a neighbor—female, ugly, but with a nice build—who came to borrow a cup of sugar.

They argued about where to go on the weekends, who they should invite to parties, what to have for dinner, and Dundee discovered, much to his surprise, that he was jealous of John Wayne.

His jealousy it seems was not unfounded, because a week later Helia ran off with the Bijou's projectionist, a rather short lumpy man who owned a complete collection of John Wayne films.

Dundee received a note from Heila saying, "We make love in front of the movie screen. I've found the Three Mesquiteers is best for my orgasm.

"PS, I'll never tell who the masked man was."

The next girl was incendiary.

In the corner of the waiting room the spider was still

working on the fly. Or was it a different fly? No matter. The fly was open and the spider was sucking out his life.

The enormous man with the coalsack beard had been sympathetic when Dundee'd told him about the void in his love life. The man laughed and said, "That'll be two hundred credits."

Dundee voiced his memory of a guarantee.

"Of course they're guaranteed to love you more than Juliet loved Romeo. It's not that she loved you less, but that she loved John Wayne more. Speaking of more, you owe me two hundred credits."

Dundee found it was customary for the customer to pay in advance. He laid his money down on the counter, betting his wit and charm against the whimsy of the second girl. He said, "You're sure this time?" He counted his fingers along with his change. The fat man with the distinctive black beard did not look like the kind of person he could trust easily.

"Sure?" the man behind the stomach, behind the beard, and behind the counter roared like, as they say, a lion. "Of course I'm sure. I told you my women are guaranteed, didn't I?" He leaned forward and shouted at Dundee. "You aren't hard of hearing, are you?"

"Not that I recall," Dundee said.

"You're one of our steady customers, and so we're defrosting a special one for you. One so fair that milk looks dingy gray even when it's been homogenized, pasteurized and dry-cleaned. A snow queen with a secret warmth all her own—with hair of fire, and a smile like an open hearth." He spun Dundee around. "Await her in the waiting room."

Dundee was in the sultan's chair waiting for his own personal Ann Boleyn. He wondered, fleetingly, if she was a virgin. Off with her head! A head with hair like fire. Three notes, tattered like an old rag, sounded on the flute and the Snow Queen floated into the waiting room. Dundee was there on the clear ocean of erotic carpeting—the *Titanic* ripe for collision. They met and history did not repeat itself because the iceberg (so cool and intimidating, floating with nine-tenths of its body submerged) met Dundee and melted. Dundee explored nine-tenths of her body, submerged beneath sheer silver silk decorated with diplomatic sequins. The Snow Queen moaned and said, "I love you more than Iseult loved Tristram."

Dundee, wiser because of many intimate experiences, let

her catalogue how much she loved him without interruption and took her home.

She looked at the living room. It was done tastefully in redwhiteandblue, and spangled with stars. She—our lady of Shangri-La—looked at the living room and said, "You know, the couch should really be over there."

And that was only the beginning.

They moved furniture for three days straight, and on the intervening nights Dundee fell asleep while the Snow Queen massaged his back.

On the morning of the fourth day, after the Snow Queen had stretched luxuriously so that her small but adequate breasts stared in cyclopean wonder at the ceiling, she said to Dundee, "I think today we'll start on the den."

Dundee said, "The den can wait."

The Snow Queen said, "No it can't. My parents are coming today."

Dundee got up and said, "I'm going to get some casters for the piano."

"A real he-man would lift it."

He started for the door, but she grabbed him and said, "I love you more than Roxane loved Cyrano. Even though you are a weakling." She then made passionate love to all his available skin surfaces, a thing he would have enjoyed three days ago, but now was too stiff to appreciate. When she was done, Dundee said, "I'll be back soon."

He went to his real estate broker and sold his house at a two-thousand-credit loss. The motel room he stayed in was small and not entirely pleasant—the faucets dripped and the upstairs neighbors had children who kept pogo sticks—but the furniture was bolted to the floor.

The third girl was chocolate.

The fat man with the distinctive black beard laughed as he took Dundee's two hundred credits. He said. "Really, you've got to stop mating like this."

Dundee was paying the man two hundred credits (a second exciting payment of who knew how many) so he did not feel obligated to laugh. Dundee had a suspicion he was being taken, and would not have come back if it hadn't been that his friends had promised him such a wonderful destination. His friends had chipped in part of the two hundred credits and Dundee wondered if they were the chips and he the old blockhead.

"You'll be surprised," the fat man said. "Imagine a woman, sweet as candy. A bon-bon of a girl, you might say. Imagine—but I told you it was to be a surprise? Off to the waiting room." He pushed Dundee through the various portals of passion and into—

—the sultan's chair. It was incredible that Dundee had come there a third time. He remembered Helia fondly and his palms sweated as if she were really there. The Snow Queen was an aching back from a winter ago, melted and no longer to be feared, but not forgotten. The spider was sitting in the center of her web. Off on one of the spokes was the hulk of a fly, dead and dry. (Like the *Titanic*, a hulk dead and wet at the bottom of the sea? But the jest goes too far.)

The flute played a note and a half. Somewhere Dundee could hear tape slapping against its own machinery.

His surprise. She was the color of milk chocolate but with a more intriguing shape than any Mr. Hershey had yet thought to market. Dark hair was piled in wiry tangles, naturally, on her head. Large almond eyes looked at his through jungle mists, and as she slipped (after many years of stepping carefully through overgrown empty lots in a particularly poor part of Harlem—after many years of eating the thick smells of tenements where she lived—after all this she got hungry for better clothes, better food, better place to ply her oldest profession) forward, she said in approximately the fashion Dundee had expected, "I love you more than Desdemona loved Othello."

She said no more, and held her body against Dundee's. Minutes later they parted and she said inevitably, "I love you more than Margaretta loved Faust," and ran the speech to its fated conclusion.

Hagar was disappointed at the apartment because she had learned to judge men by their bank accounts and she had figured Dundee to have a more glamorous context. (The pogo stick was only part of the problem. The place reminded her of a tenement she had once frequented and hoped to forget.) Dundee thought it better not to explain about the Snow Queen. You can't teach an old affair new tricks. Dundee was a new trick for Hagar and he knew she had expected something better.

Dundee took a shower—a considerate thing to do considering the Snow Queen hadn't given him time to bathe because she liked the smell of his sweating and sweat-laden body (a perversion Dundee could never understand), and besides it would have taken time away from her rearrangement. A certain musky male odor had been building up ever since and he thought he should, at the very least, start fresh. The smell would explain Hagar's unease at being near him in the car.

She was in bed under a single white sheet and her chocolate-brown (or is black preferred? I was never any good at politics) body gave it a topography that Dundee was eager to explore. Dark brown like earth. Hagar, the earth-mother. Would copulation between an earth-mother and an earth-father beget an asteroid?

Dundee crawled in beside her under the white sheet, and after filling one hand with breast (Guaranteed! Wild and untamed!), he tried to kiss her, but at the penultimate moment—with hormones gushing like Niagara and conquest clear in his mind—she pulled away and extracted, with apologies, a small gray wrinkled ball from her mouth and stuck it on the bedpost.

"I jus' can't get enough a that tutti-frutti," she said.

With reservations, he kissed her and discovered that the tutti-frutti had, as he'd expected and feared, left its mark.

Dundee lay flat on his back and stared through the dark at the ceiling. On the floor above, the leaky faucet accompanied the pogo stick in a rhythm resembling the samba. He said, "You love me more than Hero loved Leander, don't you?"

"Sure, honey. It's guaranteed," she said.

"Then go wash your mouth out." He knew there were many popular brands of mouthwash in the medicine chest. She would be able to find one—the red one for lovers, or the pale gold one for salesmen, or the green one for grandmothers and teachers—that suited her. The red one for lovers would be the most appropriate, but women were unpredictable and Dundee really didn't care.

"Sure 'nough," she said. She pulled the wad of gum off the bedpost with a small click and stuck it in her mouth. Dundee watched her walk, ass swaying to some wild African beat she'd learned from Duke Ellington, to the bathroom and listened to her moving bottles of mouthwash around.

While she was gone, Dundee cut two little eye holes in his pillow case. (The scissors came FREE with a sewing kit he'd gotten at a supermarket grand opening. He'd never gone back there again.) When Hagar got back into bed, she put her gum back on the bedpost and, just as an experiment, Dundee kissed her. The tutti-frutti smothered the peppermint mouthwash, reminding him of the Halloween he'd gotten 4,286 pieces of gum and chewed them all in one afternoon.

Dundee put on the pillow case with the two jagged holes, and said, "How would you like to go to a meeting with me tomorrow night?"

Unexpectedly, she laughed, and Dundee had to get indignant (just for the sake of the charade) and explain that he wanted to seduce her in front of the membership of his "club"—he said club as if it were in quotation marks just to show it wasn't really a club at all—to demonstrate white male supremacy.

She agreed, saying, "I love you more than Manon loved des Grieux." But she put the gum back in her mouth and wouldn't let him kiss her any more.

The next one had a distinctive black beard.

"What did you do then?" the fat man with the distinctive black beard asked.

Dundee said, "The next day I took her to a deserted part of town and left her in an abandoned corset factory tied up with elastic."

"The police will be after you."

"No matter." (There was sexual freedom in Denmark if he could believe the porno flicks. He mentally went over his passport for signs of undesirability.) Dundee said, "I've had enough of this. Make good your guarantee or I'll let the police find me and I'll tell them all about you. I'll become a martyr to better business." Dundee stared hard at the man, hoping to frighten him, but the man only smiled modestly and clucked his tongue.

Dundee said, "I want a plain down-home girl with no interest in John Wayne, moving furniture, or chewing gum."

"Spoken like a man," the fat man said. He opened a big metal book with chromium hinges and ran his fingers down columns on page after page. "Aha!" he cried at last. "I have just the thing for you: a small-town girl brought up on the farm with nothing but pigs and chickens. Her one claim to fame is that she's written a book on animal miscegenation. But you wouldn't begrudge her that."

Dundee had been the victim of too many female faults to begrudge an otherwise perfect woman such a small thing as that. She would appear to the cheers of a silent but no less vocal majority, wearing a corn belt grown in America's heartland.

Dundee allowed his black-bearded benefactor to guide him to a room he had never been in before. It had the look of a hospital. (He remembered from when he'd had his appendix out. The place smelled of alcohol that was no good for drinking and had white walls.)

The fat man opened a thick metal door and a blast of cold air slapped him (would the Snow Queen never leave him alone?) all over.

Much later, after colored lights and voices with mellow urgency, he heard three notes on a flute and ran across an erotic carpet in a room hung with dusty silk and said to the very plain woman he found there, "I love you more than Romeo loved Juliet."

The Ursula Major Construct or, A Far Greater Horror Loomed

by Ursula K. Le Guin

The complex was an arrangement of report material resting on a rectangular mat of treebone pulp. Four upward motilities sat on the mat in an approximate square whose sides were parallel to the corners of the mat.

"Commencement," said Silp, letting an eyestalk droop to touch one of the two motilities nearest him. Made of clear brown earthenware, they were cylindrical at bottom, tapering from their middles to narrow openings at the top. Dead bushbones protruded from the opening, extending over nus head in provocative pattern. Extrusions from sacred gum-trees hung on short extentions from two of the bushbones. "Theme," nu said. "Org/nonorg duality, death atop."

—*The Harshest Critic,* David Williams

The clarion was an arrangement of about two dozen varied perplexities resting on a rectangular mat of anomalous organic fiber or on supports of different shapes and heights, in the living room of Austin Hall. One inward motility sat on the mat in an approximate knot, smoking hard. Its thoughts were not parallel to anything.

"Teacher," said one of the perplexities, "we have only criticized and utterly destroyed eight rather poor short stories this morning. Whatever shall we do this afternoon?"

The inward motility emitted a cloud of smoke and rose, creaking slightly, to a height of 64½ inches from the floor.

"You will go into my room," it said. "You will find a Construct in my room. You will look upon the Construct as long as you desire. Then you will write a story about it."

"Death," said all the perplexities in unison. "Death!"

"Is that lettering?" Frank asked.

"It looks to be—almost like a billboard back home," Jack replied.

Flanking the board were two giant urns, one on each side, with treelike branches extending from their tops, a similar branch connecting the two upright branches.

"If I didn't know that we're on another planet, I'd say we were looking at a football goalpost," Frank mused.

—*The Ursula Major Construct,* Doug Kinnaird

The campus of the University of Washington was tranquil in the peaceful calm of a midsummer morning. Scarcely the chatter of a distant squirrel scampering in a giant madroña or the wheeze of a remote sophomore jogging in sweat-pants disturbed the primeval quiet of the great Northwestern forest.

Strangely enough, it was not raining.

Between the foliaginous barriers of tangled undergrowth concealing the narrow footpath which ran between the Hall of the Macmahon and the House of the Austin, a slender figure sped lightly forward, and occasionally backward, never a twig crackling beneath its moccasined feet. An observer, had there been one to observe, would have been puzzled at the behavior of the solitary figure, which seemed, had there been one to seem to, a woman. From time to time she bent down swiftly and all but stealthily to pick up a stone, a stick, a bit of detritus from the pathside, then, clutching the treasure, paced swiftly on. Had the vicinity contained a hidden scientist he might, depending upon his field of discipline, have characterised this activity as nesting behavior, or as compulsive neatness.

Arriving at the back of Austin House, the wigwam of her forefathers, the mysterious female cast an alert glance in all directions and sped rapidly, yet with furtive gait, toward the trash pile awaiting the arrival of the trash collector in a secluded area. From this she plucked a used plastic cup, two large used rubber washers, a length of used steel wool, a used sandpaper polishing-disk, half a used plastic box, and other items of a like enigmatic, yet sordid, nature. Carrying the augmented hoard with some difficulty, the slender, but no longer young, aborigine returned stealthily to the path, passed between the privet hedges of the sacred enclosure, and vanished into the wigwam of her forefathers.

Strangely enough, it was still not raining.

"What," spat Ursula, "am I going to do?"

"I," sneered Lin, "do not know."

Sprawled dangerously in an armchair, Vonda surveyed the other two with eyes like .625 steel-jacketed Mauser dumdum bullets. Lazily, she spoke.

"What," she drawled, in a voice as quiet as the bolt of a Derringer snicking home, "is that for?"

"What?" hissed Ursula. Sweating and scratching her grimy T-shirt she looked at the steel spoon attached to a length of string to which Vonda's steel-gray eyes were riveted. She nervously twitched the spoon between her powerful fingers. "This? It's to eat pudding with."

Suddenly, a rocketing chord of scintillating harmonies exploded like the Super Duper Screeming Meemie Dazzler that caps the Fourth of July firework exhibition in Muncie, Indiana, from the guitar which Lin held cradled negligently in the crook of her muscular arm. "Shit, man," she murmured, softly.

"Where," insisted Vonda, with dangerous quietness, "did you get it?"

"Found it on the floor in the living room last night," Ursula snarled, flexing.

Suddenly uncurling with pantherish litheness Vonda exploded from the armchair and shoved her face up against the older woman's. "What," she breathed, barely audibly, "are you going to do with it?"

Eyeball to eyeball, they glared tensely.

"Make 'em," sang Lin suddenly, to a rippling chord as dark as rum-laced molasses on a hot summer night in Chattanooga, Tennessee, "write a sto-ory about it. Make 'em write a story about an old spoon on a string."

Silence.

"Yeah," exhaled Vonda, softly.

"Yeah," agreed Ursula, wonderingly.

Suddenly, smiles slashed the three, lean, bronzed faces.

"Yeah!"

The sunglasses stood. "What was it?"

Alex shook the tip of his flame. "I don't know. So strange."

The sunglasses laughed. "I never understood weird things."

"Neither have I," said Alex. Abruptly, he giggled and changed into a bright orange rubber ball and bounced down the sidewalk. The sunglasses strode after him.

—*Pedestrian Alex,* Bruce Taylor

THE SINKING OF THE TITANIC

Dr. Carroll observed that the story, such as it was, was being told backward, an effect which might of course be produced by the mandala in the Institute bathtub, or which might be purely subjective, an illusion of the kind which since the death of Marilyn Monroe not infrequently accompanied the New Wave as, growing older, it crystallized, became brittle, and finally broke into coruscating fragments of a certain epicene beauty. He was indifferent.

The thick, gray paste that enveloped them didn't come high enough to do any more than entrap them, but when they looked up, a far greater horror loomed.

"Look out!" Jack screamed, as the giant silver spoon came down to scoop his companion far into the air.

—*The Ursula Major Construct,* Doug Kinnaird

The janitor came in. He was a man of about fifty with a cast in one eye. His manner was reserved but friendly; his ostensible purpose was to empty the waste-paper basket.

The Construct now occupied the entire center of the room, part of it built up from the floor and part of it hanging down from the light fixture, like a stalagmite and a stalactite growing together over the eons in a cavern, so that he certainly couldn't ignore it; but he was too formal to say anything about it. He said, "This is a class of young writers you've got here, is it?"

There were moments when the Class of Young Writers, who lived in the hall overhead, might have been taken for a Troop of Young Chimpanzees; but it takes more than noise, hair, climbing out the windows, etc., to faze college janitors. They have seen it all already, seen it all. And they are equally used to the peculiar modes of behavior of professors, and to ignoring them too. But there is no doubt that this janitor was a little curious about the Construct.

One could take the easy way and assume that it was Modern Art, but it had a somewhat purposive look, which took it out of the Art category. One had a feeling that it was *for* something. The styrofoam cup, the spoon tied to a string, and the long trailer of steel wool like a gray beard, all dangling from the light fixture, could be explained as a ridiculous kind of mobile; but the arrangement of the four beer bottles and the bathtub plug, the placing of the dead branches and the rubber washers, and particularly the almost hieratic central position of a large dead mosquito-hawk, lent the whole thing an altarlike quality that hinted at religion; while the card neatly lettered in an unfamiliar alphabet and propped against the plastic box seemed to suggest a museum exhibit, not so much an art museum as a Museum of Science and Industry, implying that the whole construct was, in some sense, conceivably a machine.

"I am making the kids write a story about that," I said.

"About that," said the janitor, in a neutral tone. He was a man of great natural tact. He now considered the Construct for some while, as if my explanation, insufficient as it was, had given him the right and freedom to do so. Because it was impossible to be sure which one of his eyes the cast was in, I could not tell what part of the Construct he was looking at; indeed sometimes when I thought he was studying the Construct, he may have been studying me.

He smiled. "I bet you get some pretty funny stories," he said.

An orgstring descended from the white bowl at the apex of the dome. Silp fastened the string around nus remaining eye. The orgstring tightened, pulling num upward till nus tail swung just above the highest bushbone.

"Die in agony," chanted the Critics. "Whole dualer die in agony."

"Die in agony," said Silp. "Die . . . agony . . ."

The Whole claimed num, and nu surrendered to it.

—*The Harshest Critic,* David Williams

Report to the Central Bureau
By: Agent 66.02 Y
Subject: Number 228, Sector 30
Technique: Exhibition of Construct
Number of Participating Examinees: 26 (1 A-subject, 25 B-subjects)

Number of Examinees eliminated by nonparticipation in experiment: 20

Results Obtained:

I. Active participation of A-Subject.

Description of results:

Behavior eagerly cooperative but erratic, not evincing full understanding. Evidence of empathic reception: qualified. Evidence of intelligence: uncertain.

II. Active participation of B-subjects.

Description of results:

Group B-1: Three short mentifacts, all giving evidence of insanity, were produced by the subjects called "Kinnaird," "Williams," and "Taylor."

Group B-2: Two longer mentifacts were produced by the subjects called "Shirley" and "Broxon." These mentifacts[1] are highly enigmatic. They are considered examinable, and are herewith reproduced in the *Journal of Exozoic Memorabilia, Clarion III,* for general examination. Their connection with the Construct is covert but indubitable.

Conclusions: On the evidence of these mentifacts, the Agent feels justified in requesting that Surface Purification be postponed, at least until thorough examination of the mentifacts by professional mentifact-examiners shall have definitively proved the absence of intelligent life-forms on Number 228.

[1] The "Shirley" mentifact is known as "The Word 'Random,' Deliberately Repeated"; the "Broxon" mentifact is called "Asclepius Has Paws."

Asclepius Has Paws

by Mildred Downey Broxon

"Bubbles" Broxon is a twenty-eight-year-old former psychiatric nurse who was reared in Brazil and now lives in a houseboat on a lake in the middle of Seattle. With her on the boat, reputed to have the strangest decor on the dock, is a husband, an Alaskan cat, and a large, neurotic female boa constrictor named Sigmund; you know, just another one of your typical science fiction writers.

"Asclepius Has Paws" is one of two stories inspired by Ursula Le Guin's trash construct. It would seem that Mrs. Broxon has plenty of inspiration at home for further flights of fancy.

He assumed the friendly/gracious stance, but curved his tail to indicate superiority. He was not conceited, he told himself; he was merely aware of the worth of a Chief Therapist. Posture was symbolic at his next destination. He flattened his ears back and closed his eyes for transmission.

Not Arnada Center; no awed, clustered greeters, no sun-bright blue, no Reception. What?

Cool green plant-thoughts, quiet brown rocks, alien memory traces. An Error? He opened his eyes.

Yes. Green plants, good air; carbon compounds in the atmosphere; industry? Dull rock and mineral thoughts, partly covered by memory traces. An Error. He waited patiently for transmission to resume, not moving from his place.

Errors were not uncommon. Some travelers complained, claiming inconvenience and distraction, but he rather enjoyed them. After all, they only lasted a few moments, moments that permitted tantalizing glimpses of unfamiliar places.

Transmission had not resumed. This was unprecedented delay. He would complain. No, better yet, he would let Reception complain while he stayed aloof.

Mirth. He pictured the furor his nonappearance would cause. He dropped to his haunches and rested on gloved forelimbs, waiting. While he waited he listened.

A stream gurgled nearby, wanting only to run downhill, downhill, downhill. A long, wary thing slid along the bank, hungry and watchful. An airborne flyer, also hungry, watched the ground. It swooped, grasped the long thing, and flew off with it. The flyer felt success and thought of hungry young; the long thing felt talon-sharp pain and terror.

He curled his tail around him and listened, instead, to the plants. "Warm, bright, reach, grow toward bright, closer . . ." One lay on its side with a broken stem: "Die, stop . . . failed."

He began to worry. What if there had been a serious malfunction? With worry came anger. How could he do his job if simple transport was unreliable? He had planned only a brief stay at Arnada: a few suggestions, some questions answered, evaluation of technique, perhaps a demonstration or two—and then he wanted to go home. This tour had taken too long already. He was tired and missed his family.

His mustache quivered and his ears flicked forward. A hunter—no, two—hunting for sport, gaming. Animals; more intelligent than the flyer or the long thing. Curious, he looked toward where they would emerge from the underbrush.

They burst into sight, yelping.

Hate hit him. He ran.

"Cat. Chase cat. Teasing, taunting cat. Fun. Make him run up tree. Bark at him, walk away. Leave him afraid to come down. Fun."

But he wasn't a "cat." And he couldn't climb trees. Damn, why did he have to match one of their archetypes? What was a cat?

He listened to their cat-thoughts. Memories of scratched nose: claws. Memory of bitten leg: sharp teeth. Cat: jumper, runner, climber.

Claws, he thought, running. Teeth. Carnivore teeth. I don't have claws and fangs; I have manipulative forelimbs and flat grinding molars. And I'm out of condition.

The animals drew closer, run as he might. He felt their incredulous joy: the stupid cat was passing up good climbing trees. They were gaining on him.

"Then what?" one pursuer wondered. The other remembered a frenzied snarling pack, rending and snapping until the hated cat was nothing but scattered bloody bits of flesh and fur.

He shuddered. He might perish here on this unnamed planet.

The underbrush cleared. He was on a path.

The animals slowed slightly, obedient to a vague recollection, feeling a nagging guilt. There was something they had been told not to do.

He listened to their confused thoughts, hopeful. "Told" implied authority. If he could find that authority . . .

Traces of weary home-thoughts, hunger, on the path, sharper and clearer than any traces before. Memory grooves worn deep. Home-thoughts, people-thoughts. Safety/help?

Farther down the path he saw a large white cube-shape, an artifact. The traces on the path said home, showed anticipation now.

He ran to the artifact, found an opening. "Hot tonight, close it in the morning—" the thought was still there, though it was already afternoon. These dominants forgot things too.

He gathered all his strength and leaped, his gloved hands grasping at the sill, his hind legs scrabbling for a hold on aluminum siding.

The animals leaped and snapped. Sheer terror boosted him in.

He fell in a heap on the floor, panting. His fur was mussed, his heart was pounding, his feet were cut and bleeding, and his protective gloves were a ruin.

He took them off and smoothed his fur.

No strong thoughts here now. A captive plant stood dismal and trapped. A small flyer looked through metal bars at the window.

The room was huge around him. There were traces of dominant thoughts: he could identify three personalities. One had left recent traces: home/glad/hunger/lonely. A young male. He followed the traces across the floor into a room of food. Carnivores, again: fear lay in body-pieces in the cold box, lurked canned on high shelves.

He followed the memory-traces out again. They changed into Out to play/Run!/Fight! and went out the door. He looked up at the knob. It was too high. He wouldn't be able to open it.

There was no one home. He wondered if, being carnivores, they would eat him when they returned. Surely not? He could speak to them, perhaps perform some small service in return for shelter from the animals outside.

He practiced indignation for the benefit of the search party that must even now be checking his route.

Best to learn all he could about those who lived here; with

carnivores one had to work fast, establish a relationship that made one more valuable as company than as food.

He prowled about the house, sniffing chair legs and walls. One of the remaining personality-traces was fresher and more prevalent than the other. It felt adult female. He could taste boredom, dissatisfaction, depression. From the traces, this personality must spend more time in the house than the third—adult male, also bored, dissatisfied, and depressed, though the imprint was the same as the memory-traces on the path outside that had said home/relax/warm.

There were anger networks between the adults and the child, and between the adults themselves. Anger/frustration. Old angers, old quarrels, razor-sharpened by time. And under the scars, affection.

He moved from the living room into a sleeping room, adult. In drawers were wearing things. One emotion-packed article drew his attention. He struggled to open a heavy drawer. These people were much larger and stronger than he.

He pulled out a filmy red item. A wish: She'd look pretty in this. She likes pretty things. Maybe it will inspire her. An answer: Can't you take it back? I never wear anything like that. I couldn't sleep in it; I'd slide out of bed. Besides, I'd look like a tart. Really, how could you? Dejection/disappointment/resentment.

Diffuse emotions in another drawer: white and colored cotton, smells of sun and starch. Duty/pleasure in cleanness; care in sewing on lost fasteners; hot, boring work. Arranged carefully in drawer; wish for appreciation. Answer: none. Taken for granted. Hurry to dress and leave, escape to work.

He stood on hind legs to look at the bed: disappointment/rejection/shyness/resentment. He dropped back to all fours.

Symbols. All the objects were symbols. If he was right, these people could understand him, could even profit from his stay. They hurt. He could heal.

He paced the floor, excited. Perhaps a whole new world. Not consulting; helping! His services were needed, and needed sorely, if these people were representative of their kind.

He no longer felt angry about the Error. He hoped the search party would take a little longer to arrive, at least until the housepeople came home.

Meanwhile he set to work.

He roamed the house looking for symbolic objects small enough for him to carry. In the child's room he found a shabby stuffed toy that said dependence/security/love. It was perfect, a triple harmonic. He dragged it into the front room.

From the adults' room he brought an ironed shirt and a polished shoe that said service/cherish/adorn (resentment-love). He returned for the red nightgown: hunger/please/joy (resentment-shame).

In the kitchen he found an apron: clean/duty/create (slavery-boredom) and a tall enameled machine for washing dishes: gift/help/guilty (household drudge-bore). It was too heavy to move, but necessary to the composition. He carried the other objects into the kitchen.

Arranging them was a complex task, but he was an expert. One emotion-object led, by its size and shape, to another; their placement led to a pattern of emotions offered and answered; relationships were explained in a composition in which the whole was, indeed, greater than the sum of its parts.

This was the beginning step in therapy: awareness of the others' emotions, recognition of conflict, beginning understanding of relationship/causality, clarification and acceptance of unstated thoughts, unadmitted feelings.

The housepeople could not help but stop and look, to observe, to question; and in so doing they would begin to soothe their hurts.

For he found he liked these people. Under all the hurt misunderstanding/traces affection still lived, affection and wonder at how things had changed, tiny, nagging suspicions of not being totally blameless.

And, under his pride of professional achievement, he heard himself wryly reflecting that if he helped them he might not be eaten for dinner.

He crouched on still-bleeding paws and waited. Eventually a thought approached, resentment-toned: "Said he'd cut the grass, ran out to play, have to do it myself, Jim won't help me, tired, tired."

The door slammed.

A woman walked into the kitchen carrying a bag: fear/food and plants.

The fear-memory from the food, the fear of being killed and eaten, made him cringe, but he stood his ground. He too was a predator: did not plants have feelings? How then could he judge others?

She put down the bag and looked at the emotional construct.

ANGER.

Good, he thought, she understands. He stepped forward, weary and hurt, eager to explain.

"Look at the objects," he said. "They have meaning for you, often many meanings. There is a relationship . . ."

"Goddam sloppy kid," she said aloud. She didn't hear him at all. "What's his game now, piling junk on the kitchen floor?"

She saw the nightgown. RESENTMENT. ANGER. SHAME.

He stepped closer. "You are angry," he said. "Beneath that anger is another emotion. Feel it."

She noticed him. "And bringing home animals! After all the times I've told him! Lousy mangy cat probably messed up the house all afternoon." She picked him up by the scruff of the neck.

"No, stop. I am not a cat. Please shelter me. I will be rescued soon. Meanwhile, I can help . . ."

She opened the door and threw him outside. ANGER, FRUSTRATION. Her eyes, he knew, were full of tears. Was something in her realizing—were her feelings changing—success?

But he had initiated only the first stage of therapy. So much remained to be done—and had he, in fact, done anything?

He could hear the animals close, very close. He knew they had been waiting. Now they had scented him. His feet were sore; without his gloves he could not run fast. There was nowhere to hide.

He looked toward the house. He could see the woman through the kitchen window, bending down, looking at his construct.

"Help me! Help me!" he cried.

The animals burst into the yard, barking. The woman looked out the window and turned away.

Forsaken, he crouched and waited. At least he would die bravely.

She opened the door.

"Shoo! Bad dogs! Go home!" She flapped a towel at the animals; they cringed and slunk away. SHAME. GUILT.

He collapsed on the ground, shaking. The woman scooped him up under one arm and carried him into the house.

"Poor old cat," she said, patting his head. "The dogs almost got you. Maybe you are house-trained after all; I didn't see any mess." She put him down on the living-room floor and went back to the kitchen. He walked to the door and watched her.

She was looking at the arrangement again, talking to herself as lonely beings do.

"What a weird assortment of things. What could Billy have been thinking of?"

She bent to pick up the articles. "There's the nightgown Jim gave me," she said. "It's kind of pretty at that. Poor man; I must have hurt his feelings." She paused a moment. TENDERNESS. REGRET. REPARATION?

He exulted. Success! A beginning emotional change! And when the rest of the family came home he could proceed with therapy. It was so long since he had treated individuals. He had forgotten how much he had missed personal contact.

He was stepping forward to speak with her, to tell her who he was, when he vanished.

At Arnada Center they mentioned how abstracted he seemed and apologized for his unfortunate transmittal Error. They could not know how he hungered for a needing world, a world he could never visit again, a planet whose location was unknown, a planet where he had left a work uncompleted.

The Word "Random," Deliberately Repeated

by John Shirley

John Shirley grew up mostly in Oregon, where he was hated for being skinny and peculiar. He worked on or edited a number of underground papers before realizing that "all politics is self-centered, self-corrupting, hypocritical, and bigoted." He writes: "I have played the various roles of hippie, bum, student, criminal, egotist, fool, lecturer, euphemism, acidhead, and writer." He hopes to write surrealist speculative fiction. He is clearly well qualified by background and talent to do so.

His story is one of two in this volume inspired by Ursula Le Guin's "totally ad hoc and irresponsible gimmick," a collection of string and sticks and dead bugs and plastic cups and steel wool gathered by Miss Le Guin in a fifteen-minute walk across the University of Washington campus and assembled in her room as "The Ursula Major Construct."

"Garbage in, garbage out" (GIGO), says the computer programmer, which is why few programmers are artists.

He was tired of the library. The faint, echoing words of the librarian were shaped like the books they passed through. He lingered in the scant poetry section.

No one reads poetry at this honky university, he thought. Lots of dust on the book covers. They haven't been checked out in ages. Except for an occasional harried coed, maybe, looking for a saccharine ode to roses.

He leaned his large athlete's frame against the lonely shelves and remembered the canyons of eastern Oregon.

He closed his eyes:

He and Maria were drunk together. It hadn't been too hard to seduce her. You can't seduce someone who doesn't want it. They lay balmed in the smell of sage and sequoia. They rolled off the blankets in search of new touchings and caked their bare sweaty skin with dust, dust still warm from the sun that was laying torch to the sunset.

He remembered the desert and Maria often because of one special peculiarity in the incident: afterward, they had not regretted it.

They washed and sobered themselves in a canyon stream. But neither made a move to dress, though the air grew chill. With most, it was quickly over and followed by an embarrassed silence and a scuffle to get dressed. But not with Maria. They had sat together, close for warmth, watching the desert sunset burn the outline of the hill in the sky. He thought about school, about the team-letters ceremonies and the obsequious smiles of the principal at *his* star athelete. He tried not to think about the phony cheerleaders that he had pretended to like. No one had understood when he refused to go out for football that last time. They had berated him for trying to start a poetry club—that was for women. Had Haggart become a faggot?

But he loved The Game and the feel of muscles that were so much a part of his responses that they jumped as his thoughts did. He loved to feel the pain of pushing his metabolism to its limit and the feeling of growth afterward. And, as Maria pulled him again on top of her, he thought of the sexual elasticity of contact sports and the orgasmic swell of Making It, of Scoring.

The desert evening draped them, pressed them closer together. They moved against each other like clapping hands at a pep rally. He came, and his climax struck the same note as the last rays of the sunset that illuminated the hillside above them. As he reared and shuddered over her, his vision seemed to coalesce; then sharpen. The randomly placed boulders of the hillside were scattered seemingly without pattern, edged and shaped without purpose. He had never noticed any organization in the morose shapes of the desert or the crumbling wind-swept canyons. But now, they seemed to shift, falling into astonishing coherence. Each boulder, each stone and gnarled bush became elaboration on a central theme. They had relationship, and in that fragmented orgasmic second, they came together as though in an order codified to an alien intent. The image was burned into his mind as the desert sun burns stark its landscape.

He opened his eyes:

The image of the broken layers of rock and shale, of torn igneous lumps and gouged ravines was still strong. He looked at the directly purposeful arrangement of the books in the library, and suddenly felt the desert image transposed over them.

They were the same.

He looked at the objects lining the shelves and allowed himself briefly to forget that they were books. And he laid aside, for the moment, the knowledge that this was a library, ordered according to the Dewey Decimal System. He saw the books stripped of anthropomorphic associations. They were alien objects, new and unidentifiable, bound together on the shelf apparently at random. Some were tall, reaching almost to the next shelf; some were thick and fat, three times the width of most; others were short and thin. He could see no pattern in their visual arrangement. They progressed with three high and thin ones, went to four low and thick ones, shifted to pamphlets. They were colored at random, with random tint and texture.

He laughed, loudly, A scuffle of feet. Something on two spindly limbs swathed in green cones of cloth waved a gangly wrinkled upper limb at him and flapped its lips. It said something he chose not to hear. He looked away from the thing and back to the wild chaos of straight ravines filled with rectangles. He stopped playing the game.

They were ordered again. Dewey Decimal System. You can look up anything you want in the card catalog.

He ignored the librarian who was whispering angrily at him for ignoring her.

He caught a glimpse of himself in a window as he left the building: tall, broad chest and shoulders, typical athlete's stance, short parted black hair, blue eyes that looked back from the reflection like a separate person would. His face was distinctly Aryan and his chin always stubbled. He wore a blue shirt, jeans, and tennis shoes. Big deal, he thought. I wonder if something that'd never seen a human before would see a purpose in the way I'm put together?

The campus was emptier than the desert. All the buildings were cast in the same ugly gray concrete mold, mottled by little holes where the metal supports for the forms had been. The long naked windows that stretched uninterrupted from top to bottom concentrated thin transparency on him as though he were an ant burning under a magnifying glass.

There were a few stunted trees set in pots on the concrete like tiny patches of healthy skin remaining on a leper.

There was no fertility in the passing self-involved faces. There was no ambition in the cement. Haggart debated with himself as to whether he should go to class. Sociology. Where they tried to make the fluid movements of societies as concrete and predictable as their campus casement.

Forget it, he decided. He started, hearing a feminine voice call after him. He turned, half expecting to see a smooth dark chicano face, dark-eyed Maria. But it was Leslie. Blonde hair, hot pants, trite questions in philosophy.

"Where you going?" she asked.

"Home. Where you going?"

"I was going to find someone to skip class with. Need a ride somewhere?"

"Why not someone to explore the South Seas with? A pirate."

She laughed, though she didn't really think it was funny. "Come on. I'll give you a ride."

He followed. He looked at the doll-like symmetry of her profile. She's really pretty. Uses make-up well. Big tits. So how come I'm not attracted to her? All the beautiful women in this goddam university, I should be—

"Here it is," she said, interrupting his thoughts. She unlocked a red Grand Torino and got in. Her parents probably paid for the car, he thought. And they paid for her tuition and room. And whether they know it or not, they pay for her birth-control pills. And so they pay for me.

She drove easily from the parking lot and into the street, steering with one hand. Very casual. Very cool.

"How do you like the philosophy class?" she asked, trying to spark the conversation. He didn't have an answer. He didn't give a damn. Finally, out of habitual politeness, he answered,

"She proselytizes. Everybody swallows it. She pushes her Zen on everybody, tries to make Plato sound like a narrow-minded ass."

"You're right," she said. She *would* say that. "Zen is fun to play with, but it doesn't have any pragmatic value. I mean, wow man, the philosophy has to serve the people; otherwise you've just got an excuse for an autocrat to . . ."

He stopped listening. Pieces of a poem began to fall together in his mind as he watched the autumn-yellow trees flash by. Some of them had lost part of their leaves already and they bared limbs as if they wore short-sleeved shirts. He interrupted her and asked for a pencil. She gave him a puzzled sideways look, then indicated the glove compartment and fell silent. He found a scrap of paper to write on.

> At this speed, not really *auto*,
> trees revolve
> like children on a carousel;
> arms, branches, outstretched.
>
> Negro-white teeth
> break the edges of
> stomach-stretched by-carbonation-clouds
> into film-negative clownfaces.
> The clown faces would continue laughing
> even if we had an accident.

"What's that?" Leslie asked when he finished.

"Just some notes. Reminding myself of something."

She pulled up in front of his apartment house. "Well," she said in a mock sigh, "here we are." She looked at him, obviously expecting to be asked in "for a joint or something."

He almost asked her, then realized that he really didn't want to see her, that if he asked her in it would only be because one is always careful not to waste an opportunity that might be unavailable later. But he said only, "See ya." And climbed quickly out of the car and walked up the steps.

He stopped at the top step and remembered the desert in the library.

He heard Leslie drive off.

He walked back and down the road a block to a small park where he began to pick up odds and ends of litter that lay in the grass. In a few minutes he had enough. He walked home, but just before he reached his apartment the uncomfortably familiar voice of Benny Clummworth rumbled from behind.

Benny was a serious athlete. He had no other real interests. Clummworth had come from the same high school that Haggart had, and he lived a few doors down. He was one of the jocks who had given Haggart a hard time for "going with a Mex." *Yer hair gets greasier every day,* he'd shout at them in the hall. Haggart had ignored him. No one understood why he didn't challenge Clummworth to a fight. Just as no one had understood why he had to drop out of athletics.

Clummworth's presence made Haggart think of Maria again, and he wondered if he'd broken up with her for her sake as he'd claimed or for the sake of his status. Haggart's thoughts were jerked back to the present by Clummworth's insistent snatching at his arm.

"Whatcha doing?" Clummworth asked as though he were building up to a monumental witticism. "Picking up litter for the sanitation department?"

Haggart gave him a cold stare.

"Come on," Clummworth persisted. "Whatya gonna do with that shit? Cans and beer bottles and sticks and stuff—"

"Make a mobile," Haggart lied. "Or a sculpture or something." That was closer to the truth. He shook his arm loose from Clummworth's tightening grasp. The bulletheaded jock laughed.

"A copy of the Venus de Milo?"

Haggart turned his back on him and walked to his apartment, careful not to drop anything. It was a three-room flat; bedroom, kitchenette, bathroom. The walls were bare but the floor was a litter of books and papers. He went into the bedroom, dropped the things he carried, and sat down heavily on the bed. He expelled a great gust of air and lay back, covering his eyes with his arms.

Maria had been like the desert, simple but potent. She had looked more appropriate when she had wandered with him over the rugged, shrub-grown hills than in the sterile schoolhalls. She had little education, but always understood what he meant when he said it simply. Calm and resilient like the desert. He tried to shake memories of her out of his head. He stood and stretched, felt young muscles complain with the need for exercise. With a last, puzzled glance at the odd array of artifacts on the floor he grabbed his swimming suit and towel and walked swiftly out of the building and four blocks to the YMCA.

Forty-five minutes later, exhilarated by a brisk swim, he sat at the edge of the pool, staring at chlorinated ripples. The shouts of other swimmers came to him across the water, vibrating slightly, as loud as if they shouted in his ear—HEY IF YOU DIVE ON ME I'M GONNA—and—IF YOU SPLASH ME AGAIN BOY—and, in answer—I'LL SPLASH YOU, MOTHERFUCKER, TILL YER SO GODDAM WET YER PANTS COME OFF AND YER NOT WEARING NOTHING BUT WATER!

Haggart looked up. Something the last shouter had said . . .

wearing nothing but water. A random splash covered Haggart's face with water. A mask of water. Something tugged at the edge of his understanding. He got up, walked carefully over the slick wet tile to the diving board. He waited his turn, but when it came he hesitated, still thinking of the library and splashing water. Randomly splashing water. Someone yelled in his ear:

"Hey, let's *go*! You waiting for the board to dive off of *you*?"

Startled, Haggart ran out on the board and jumped, coming down sloppily on the end and springing out and up in poor form. He might hit the water wrong, and slap it with his face. The first part of the dive had been clumsy. But at the last moment he snapped his legs straight and arched his back, cutting the surface cleanly.

It came to him underwater, as he was yet a knife sheathed in frothing bubbles. He had started awkwardly, diving askew, righted himself—making purpose out of aimlessness.

He surfaced quickly and swam to the side.

A half-hour later Haggart came back to his apartment, almost running up the stairs. He unlocked the door and entered hurriedly, kicking books aside. What the hell, he thought. They're just random rectangles. He laughed at that. He thought of the term paper abandoned last night and of the overwhelming feeling of purposelessness that possessed him whenever he entered the college. I'm going to find out what it is, he thought. Where purpose comes from. I'll be wearing nothing but a mask of clean water.

He went to the things he'd left on the bedroom floor and took inventory. Four or five sticks, some string, pipecleaners, some cardboard, sandpaper, a fingernail clipper, a tin can, a small block of wood, two beer bottles and a spoon. He went to the bathroom to get tissue, came back tearing it into small strips. He put the tissue in an open can after winding sandpaper around the can, and let paper ribbons spill out like hair. He put the sticks in the beer bottles and used them to support two others to make a small gate of wood that arched over the other things protectively. He hung a string from the ceiling light, attached pipecleaners to that, and wound up a spoon in them. He hung a styrofoam cup from the string and a length of steel wool that hung down like Spanish moss from the cup. He was putting things together at random, but thinking all the time of the desert and the ragged, weather-carved cliffs that were somehow linked together. In a half-hour, he had an anomalous shape that was at the same time anachronism and affinity. He was sweating with the deliberate effort to randomness. He had caught himself several times making a recognizable symmetry with seemingly unrelated shapes. Random. Got to be random. No pattern. He finished, putting the bottlecaps in as a finishing touch.

He sat back and *closed his eyes*: Tried to forget having ever seen the shape he'd made. He felt his mind blank, opened his eyes. Random impressions: A gate. A gate under a rocket (the cup) that had just run out of fuel and was spewing a trail of smoke (the tail of steel wool). A paper-fountain (the can with strips of tissue emerging) spilling over granite facing (sandpaper). The fingernail clippers that stretched from the upper edge of the sponge to paper below looked like a jackknifing diver in midleap. The beveled block with the paper and the bottlecaps looked like a car. A car passing under an arch by a waterfall that flowed into a pool into which someone dived.

Maria died in a car accident in a place like that.

Run off the side of a cliff by a drunk under an arch of wind-shaped desert stone. The car had crashed into the water, and she had died from impact before she could drown. Maria masked in water.

He shut his eyes and cried out:

A feeling like an icy hand on his face made him look up again. His attention was drawn to the outlines made by random twisted shapes; they seemed to delineate the space between the objects in the random construct into the features of a face.

"Maria," he said.

"Thank you, Ronny," her calm voice said. "Thank you for the mirror." Her voice resonated with hollow reassurance. "I needed a mirror so badly in this place. Nothing here reflects. I couldn't see myself . . ."

Her voice faded into the lines of jagged sticks and cups and blocks.

Random lines. A mirror.

Why?

by Theodore Sturgeon

Why answer the Clarion call, anyway? What is a busy writer—most especially a full-time science fiction writer with Atlas's own load of responsibilities on his back and neck—doing taking a week off to teach at a Clarion Workshop? It's more than a week, of course; one has to supercrowd a crowded schedule beforehand, one has to recover—perhaps convalesce is a better word—afterward. Yes, Virginia, there is an honorarium, but you may be assured that it doesn't come to anything like the amount one could make by staying home, especially if one worked as hard as a Clarion teacher. And a Clarion teacher does work hard. At MSU the class started at nine and broke for lunch more or less at noon; after lunch the kids drifted in for conferences, they were with me during dinner, they came back to my room afterward, and sometimes the last one left at two-thirty a.m. Any idea of pursuing one's own work during that week can be abandoned. It isn't just the time and concentration involved; it's the example of the kids themselves. They are deadly serious. For most of them, attendance at Clarion represents a most important investment; in some cases, a sacrifice. I have taught elsewhere, and have come to expect the attendee who comes for almost any other reason than to be serious about the course—the one who wants to wear it like a lapel-badge, the one who thinks it might be a good way to get laid, the one who hasn't read the descriptive literature and thinks it is a course in children's drama or some such, and bitterly and noisily resents it, every hour, every day, the one who takes writers' courses the way others take amphetamines, not to learn or progress, but just to pursue some personal and unsharable high, and the one—more often than not a very sweet little old lady—who has written one story back in 1948 (and mind you, it's a good story) and is now bringing it to the sixteenth consecutive writers' course to have it read and admired, and who will never write anything else. But at Clarion I have seen virtually none of this.

They work hard. These kids, almost without exception, mean to work, and they do. (I must interject that my use of the term "kids" is a convenience. They are not all youngsters, and they are not childish. Some of the best may be childlike, but that's something entirely else.) I remember one who came to my room very late on Monday to discuss the biology of an extraterrestrial creature, which for story purposes must be warm-blooded and winged. We worked out its skeletal structure and the first draft of the story appeared in class on Wednesday—which meant it had been done in time to be Xeroxed and distributed on Tuesday afternoon. It was workshopped and appeared again in class on Friday, completely rewritten, and by my standards, ready to sell; and it was no short-short either. I can't write that well, that fast.

And there's the one (you learn the back-story of these people, willy-nilly) who already was a selling writer, who was supporting a wife and child, and who decided that whatever corners he had that needed knocking off could be handled at Clarion; and so he and his wife scraped the bottom of the barrel to send him to MSU for the course, and arranged their lives so that she would work for a year while he wrote full time. Now that is no hobbyist. Happy ending: he's selling well; I'd mention his name but my function here is not the revelation of personal matter, save my own. I got into a lot of personal matter. Some of it would tear your heart out. There is no way I could possibly express the wide and deep admiration I feel for these kids as a group.

Clarion has been criticized as advertising itself as a science fiction course which doesn't really limit itself to science fiction. As a matter of fact I attended a session of a World Science Fiction Convention (something which I rarely do) solely to appear on a panel discussion of this question, and to defend Clarion's approach.

Clarion's approach seems to be essentially the same as mine. Clarion is a writers' course and the emphasis is on writing. Good science fiction can't happen unless it's good fiction. Clarion had produced some astonishingly good fiction—and it is my conviction that this is because it is science-fiction-oriented. There is no hardlined, precise, nuts-and-bolts way of expressing this last. It's an air, an attitude, a posture, an approach to fiction and to thinking about fiction. Science fiction is (with poetry) the cutting edge of human ideation, the epiphysis (that's the bit of bone that can grow) of literature's body. One way of putting it would be that a student wishing to learn to write fiction—any kind of fiction—fast and in depth, would do well to try Clarion, purely because of its science-fictional quality.

Therefore to preclude any kind of fiction which did not conform to someone's sacred 1936 or 1952 concept of science fiction would be to preserve the field by embalming it. That's what you do with dead things.

I've been looking for a satisfactory description of "the Clarion quality" quite as hard, and with as little success, as I have been seeking a definition of science fiction which does not leak, but until a better one comes along, I should like to quote James Tiptree, Jr., in a recent splendid letter to the New York *Times*.

> ... There are reasonable grounds for believing that future critics will find SF valuable. Where so much of the mainstream is reshuffling the minutiae of suburban anguish, SF has been a fountain of imagination about the human condition. Like all true ghettoes, it has been *free*. Because no one watched us, we could put forth any idea, explore the consequences of any notion about humanity. Everyone is dimly aware that back before WW II, SF talked about atom bombs; but they don't realize that since then we've been conducting the social revolution a couple of decades in advance. Sexual mores, religions, war, drugs, ecology—name any of our current agonies and you'll find brilliant extrapolations on it years ago in SF. We were and are a chaotic fertile pocket of freedom. I'd hate to see it abandoned; to have the future find SF as extinct as the legendary Martian cities.

All Clarion sessions are not inspirational; some are sheer drudgery; but as there is conversation and Conversation, the big C slipping in and out of the room like a wasp when the window's wide, so at Clarion there are those vagrant moments when ideas and revelation explode and splatter the walls and the people, and leave and dry up, and give little hints that they are around somewhere, and come crackling in again. But it is the science-fictional nature of the course that permits this to happen with unexpected frequency, for there are no horizons, there is nothing banned, there is no forbidden direction, there is nothing unacceptable but dullness and ineptitude.

I am by no means content with my own performance at

Clarion, which is why I am so eager to go back and back again. I know I was able to convey to the kids some of the things which are important to me, and I know I failed totally to make contact on others. There is the matter of what one critic once called my "love affair with the English language." To describe this at all is to restate the fact that a writer is the strangest of lovers; for having installed writing as his mistress, he will then do his best to share her with all men. I have been to see a painter who kept me standing on his icy doorstep while we talked because he was mixing a certain flesh-tone he had developed, and would not let me watch—I who know nothing about painting or paints. I have known sculptors who kept special tools and cements under lock and key—not to protect them against theft, but to conceal their very existence, hence "How do you do that? How do you get that effect?" gets a knowing look and an armed silence. But I have never met a writer who was not willing to share his innermost technical secrets and discoveries. There is probably no single answer to this (there is, you know, no single answer to anything) but I suspect that the main reason lies in that fascinating concept *feedback*.

One of the facets of teacher-student feedback is that a man doesn't really know what he believes until he shares it, and to share it he must encode it in some way which can be read by others. Writing, of course, is made of this, but then the response is only the tiniest fraction of the output. Teaching, on the other hand—teaching right there in the room with the kids, watching their faces and their body-language, testing one's own ideas against their concepts, conditioning, convictions and (in the case of Clarion) vast eagerness, is hard on lazy thinking and prejudice, and the alterations and revisions and case-hardening that goes on inside the teacher's head have to be experienced to be appreciated. It is no more graciousness for me to say that I learn more than I teach: it's a hard fact. I learn not only what comes from fresh, talented and genuinely devoted minds (and yes, from the mistakes some of them make that even I hadn't managed!) but also the validity of what I think and believe in, and what I do and think I can do. Growth and change: if one does not grow and change, one has no genuine proof that one is alive.

I hope to teach again at Clarion, for all the above reasons, and most especially because next time there won't be the strangeness, the ice-to-break feeling; it will be an ongoing homecoming.

All of which, I hope, answers the implied question, Why teach at Clarions? Remember always, however, that there isn't one answer—not to anything.

Los Angeles
January 1973

The Teardrop

by Dvora Olmstead

Dvora Olmstead is twenty-six and has been a junior at Michigan State University for four years. She is an old-maid librarian in a medical library and—call me a male chauvinist—she has the most beautiful eyes and hair I have ever seen. She has worked as a cook for a kosher co-op and designed emblems for a pistol club, and was given to beating unruly customers with empty pizza pans when she was a waitress.

She writes, she says, about things that frighten her. "The Teardrop" is a tale of the end of innocence.

Sunlight poured into the library, releasing the warm, musty smells of inks, binding, wax and wood. The textures of old thoughts drifted from the shelves to float among the air currents, rich and almost tangible. Mythical beasts and heroic deeds had existed in such a light, in such an ambience.

The old lady stood, legs spread slightly for balance, solid in the midst of the rich buttery sunlight and the shimmering dust motes. Age dragged her flesh downward, filling her cracked old shoes, puckering the cloth over her hips, and leaving delicate little hollows around her collar bones, where the skin was smooth and slightly freckled. Her face had relaxed, except for her nose and chin, which were still firm and determined. She revolved a little in her place, hunting for her bearings. Finding the librarian in the group of middle-aged ladies by the fiction shelves, she advanced, keeping a handful of small books and boxes protectively in front of her.

The librarian listened politely but kept her eyes on the shielding handful when she noticed how the nervous headbobbing increased under the pressure of a direct gaze.

The old lady rushed her words a little, was a little strident, speaking but not listening any more. Once she tapped the books to make a point a few moments after the gesture was appropriate. She said something about some kind of horse, how it had died very badly, and how she had thought that someone might be interested in reading the story, which she had written from personal experience and couldn't get published, and so had printed herself and was selling. She recited two passages in a high-pitched, unnatural tone, and held her body rigid, though not quite straight.

> *"He was silken but not so gross as silk.*
> *He was cool and clean and yet He seared me where*
> *His breath touched.*
>
> *I am old before time exists;*
> *He . . . He was not . . ."*

And . . .

> *"Those eyes . . .*
> *Am I so pliant that even in those eyes I do not drown?*
> *Is there any way in which I could shrivel that*
> *I did not shrivel under the shadow of that horn?*
>
> *I answer the alchemist:*
> *Lead turns gold to lead and weeps for sorrow ever more."*

When she had finished, the only sound in the room was the faint, high drone of a distant fly. She looked at the women again, reluctantly. Their eyes were still, their hands were still, their lips were pressed tightly together and very still.

At the edge of the group a small figure in jeans and sweatshirt stirred and clasped her hands together.

The old lady understood this stillness too well. Her head ducked again in the hunting motion and in acquiescence. The coin of the spirit had been refused, but there was an alternate coin. Caesar's coin was in the form of little rosebuds fashioned of sandalwood dust, scented and strung as a necklace. They were khaki-colored and moist in the hand. They could encircle the neck or be left in the corner of a drawer to exude their odor.

The women moved closer then to look at the lifelike carving and agree on the practicality of the thing. One of the older women bought one, while the rest of the group melted away.

The girl who approached the old lady then moved eagerly. Her eyes flicked from the old woman's face to the books in her hands. One dimple showed when she smiled. She sketched delicate lines about herself when she walked, and yet she moved awkwardly. Her hands were raised a little, and half open, as if she were about to applaud. She didn't see the beads but reached immediately for the books. The old one didn't stop trying to show her the beads until several moments after she had begun to read.

"I write, too." She looked up, half defiantly, half questioningly. "No one believes me, but I'm going to be a writer. People poke fun at other people who are different, but I never would." Getting no response, she continued less certainly. "And I'll tell you another thing, I think people lie all the time. Do you believe in fairies and dragons, and things like that?"

"What, magic? Well, yes, I guess I do."

"So do I. Sometimes I think I'm the only one who does. I like horses. What kind was this one?"

The question was unexpected. It was the old lady's turn, now, to be awkward. "He was gentle. That's why it is such a shame, don't you see. He was just following his nature. He shone. And I thought people should know. We could help. We all could help. He looked at me before they touched him. I could have sat there forever. I wouldn't have moved."

"What happened then? Did you move, or what?"

"Some men came, and I . . . I don't know. It could have been anything, you know. A pebble could have fallen. They say they brought back his head. But he was all complete, don't you see, so they couldn't have. He wasn't made of parts like the rest of us. We change, you see. I have thought about it for a long time, and I'm sure that's it. They shine you see, long after the horn is just ground bone in some old man's cupboard." She stopped and fingered her books for a moment. Her eyes glistened.

"I've been writing these little pieces for years. I'm sure people care. We started a group once. We still correspond." Another hesitation, then she looked directly at the smiling girl for the first time. She wanted to give something more.

"I have a token, something special . . . look." She pressed one knotted finger against the corner of her eye. The lid trembled beneath the rough fingertip, and when she brought the hand away a drop of clear liquid rested there. Bending closer, the girl could just see a tiny, crystalline creature with a golden horn, shining in the teardrop.

They regarded the creature together, the woman as thrilled

as the child, until the image faded and the teardrop dried. A tear traced the young cheek, too.

"I knew it." She was close to laughter. "He's real and I'm going to find him, too. When I grow up I'm going to go everywhere and do everything, just like you. And everyone will know who I am because I'm going to write it all.

"Do you like it? Being a writer, I mean."

"I don't write much any more. I've been selling my booklet for a long time now. And of course the jewelry. Have you seen it? It helps me get along, and then there's Social Security and all. I had this book printed out of my own pocket, so people would understand." She rubbed her fingertips hard against the palm of her hand.

"Because they weren't bad men, you know. They weren't bad at all. I've never seen them again, of course. But someone should have told them . . . how such creatures are, and what it does to us, to look at them when they are immortal—and dying. I didn't know what I was doing, you see."

The young one, who had been leaning toward the voice, shifted uncomfortably. The air was suddenly too warm; her shirt was sticky. She scraped itchy skin from her neck. A sour cabbage smell came from the book she was holding and blended with the old lady's attar of roses. She was frightened. She tried to start at the beginning again.

"It was marvelous, wasn't it? You saw him, and it made you special. It must have been wonderful. I mean, I think it would be wonderful to have such an important thing . . ." She held her hand out to the old lady, pleading.

The old woman frowned and tapped her boxes of beads with a crooked forefinger. "Don't you worry about what anybody says. If you want to write you go ahead. You should do what's important to you now, when you're young. Everybody has to make their own mistakes, just so they'll know better. I know. They just have to get burned.

"When I was young I let people tell me what to do. It was the worst mistake of my life. I never wanted to go out to that hill, but they made me. I just did what I was told. . . ."

They had been standing free in the clear, timeless light. Suddenly, they were suspended in brittle amber, charged with electricity.

The girl had retreated somewhere within herself. She came back with a slight shake of her head. Her shoulders ached, now, and she hardly knew whether or not she was crying.

"You." She spoke softly. "I think it was *rotten* to betray him. Cruel and mean." Then she could turn away.

The old woman swayed slightly. She didn't seem to know what to do. Her eyes clouded and for a long moment only her eyelids moved, quick, furtive movements.

Bus Station

By William Earls

William Earls, who has an M.A. in English and once lived at the South Pole, is a free-lance writer living in Massachusetts, where people say to him, "You write, huh? Good thing your wife works."

She may be able to quit soon. Earl's work has appeared in Analog *and* Galaxy, *and if his contribution to this volume is any sign, he will not have to go back to bartending, reporting, teaching, postal-clerking, copywriting, or coaching football.*

"Bus Station" is the story of a blithe spirit who lives in a world by Kafka out of Spiro T. Agnew.

Hannibal rose and faced the jury. The bailiff rapped him on the knuckles.

"Face the judge," the bailiff said.

The judge folded his hands together, made a steeple of his index fingers. He looked very stern and pompous, as though he were sitting on something too hard and as though his shoes were too tight. He looked squarely at Hannibal.

"Young man," the judge said. "You are guilty, unquestionably guilty, of having far too much exuberance. This is, you know, a serious crime." He looked through the steeple with one eye.

"It is not good to be too joyful. Joy is the great destroyer. Yes. For with it, you become frivolous, empty, and shallow." He took a deep breath, broke the steeple, rubbed his palms together. Hannibal smiled at him.

The bailiff hit him on the knuckles.

"Obviously," the judge said after nodding approval to the bailiff, "you cannot be serious, young man. And that is a shame. Yes. A shame." He looked to the jury and watched the heads there nod in agreement. "We must then . . . make you be serious." He rubbed his pointed chin with his thumb and index finger. "It is not with malice that we do this, but for your own good.

"You are sentenced," the judge said slowly, "to six months

in the waiting room of the Ann Arbor, Michigan, bus station."

Hannibal was delivered to the station at eight the next morning. He was wearing dungaree trousers, a blue shirt, and white sneakers. The policeman who brought him was named Kelly.

"Six months," Kelly said. The stationmaster, who looked one hundred years old, nodded. He was wearing a blue suit that had been ironed years before and had a metal nameplate—Joseph—on his right pocket.

"Is that your first name?" Hannibal asked.

"None o' your business," the stationmaster said to him.

"Six months," Kelly said. He fastened the restrainers onto Hannibal's wrists.

"I got 'im," the stationmaster said. Kelly turned and walked out of the station to the street, not whistling, not swinging his club at the end of its rawhide thong, just walking.

"Well?" Hannibal said. He was standing in front of the stationmaster, looking down at him.

"You can't leave the building," the stationmaster said.

"I know. What do I do?"

"Whatever you wanna do."

"What's to do?"

"Look around. You get two dollars a day." The stationmaster walked into his office and closed the door.

It was a small bus station. One flight of steps led to the restrooms on the second floor. There was a soda fountain with seven stools, all of them ripped. Behind the counter, a high school girl chewed gum, looked blankly at the dish rag in her hand. She looked like she could use cheering up.

"Would you like a hickey?" he asked her.

"I *take* the orders," she said. "You want sumpin'?"

"Not now."

"Bug off."

There were eight shiny plastic benches with obscenities scrawled on them. He sat on the nearest one, slid along his fanny reading as he went, decided that Bobby and Jean, among others, had limited imaginations. He reached the end of the bench, decided not to try another.

It was just after eight. He took a seat against the wall and watched three men come into the station. Their faces were blank—any blanker and they wouldn't have needed noses, he thought. They stood in front of the ticket window, staring at the floor.

Hannibal rose from the seat, did a quick shuffle. He smiled at no one in particular and strolled over to the three-person line.

"Hi," he said. He was abreast of them. All they had to do was turn and they could see him. None turned.

"Hi," he said again. The first one in line asked the attendant for information on a bus to Cleveland. The second looked at the back of the first one's neck. The third ignored him. The first got his information, turned, bumped into Hannibal, mumbled something, and kept walking. The second asked for a ticket to Biloxi.

"Biloxi's nice this time of year," Hannibal said. The man looked as though he could use some cheering up—especially going to Biloxi. The man ignored him.

Hannibal walked into a corner and leaned against the wall. Above him the green paint was gray with smoke and dust, covered with fly specks. Spiders romped on webs in the steam pipes and flies buzzed them until they were caught and eaten. The floor was made of squares of pressed marble, each square surrounded with a thin brass ribbon. It was coffee-spotted and dirty.

Hannibal stayed against the wall most of the morning. It was a small station and he didn't want to explore more of it than he had to; if he was going to be here six months, he wanted to prolong every pleasure he could.

By noon he was hungry and had to go to the can. The toilet was cruddy, dirty, and old—three stalls, two urinals, and four sinks full of hair and spit. Bobby and Jean had their names on the walls here, too; the standard obscenities were alongside. There was nothing on the wall that wasn't on the benches below, Hannibal decided. He made plans to use a different stall every day, to read the right wall the first time, the left the second time, and hoped that, by the time he came round again, something new would be added.

For lunch he had a carton of milk from one vending machine and a small package of crackers from another. The second did not give him change for his quarter.

People came and went all day. He sat on the second bench, read all the obscenities he could, thought about adding some of his own, but couldn't. He hadn't been given a pencil.

There was a rush of activity around five. Four buses came

into the station within minutes and disgorged ten or twelve people apiece. Doors slammed open and Hannibal jumped to one bus to help unload packages—it was under the weather roof and could be considered inside. The engine kept running while he worked, sending raw gas and kerosene fumes into his nostrils. When he was finished, he coughed and looked for someone to thank him. No one did. People picked up their luggage and left. Five minutes later there was no one in the station except Hannibal and a sailor sleeping on one of the benches. The stationmaster had left his office. The girl at the counter had put everything away and had drawn the blind that sealed the counter.

Hannibal ate supper—another carton of warm milk and some more crackers. The sailor kept sleeping, his white hat over his eyes, one leg dangling off the edge of the bench. There was nothing to do.

Hannibal walked to the machine that said "Thrilling Views" and put in a dime. He watched slides of Mount Rushmore, the Lincoln Memorial, Niagara Falls, and seven other places.

The sailor woke up and looked around. Hannibal, busy reading the fine print on the shoeshine machine, saw him and walked over. The sailor was rubbing sleep from his eyes. Hannibal stood at the end of the bench.

"Hi," Hannibal said.

"Screw," the sailor said.

"Gee . . . I just said—"

"Beat it, faggot," the sailor said. He stood up—he was four inches taller than Hannibal. Hannibal backed away to the corner and sat down on a bench there. There was a hole in the seat and he was uncomfortable. The sailor was sitting on his own bench, feet flat on the floor, glaring at him. Hannibal looked at the floor. Each time he lifted his eyes, the sailor stared at him.

At seven-thirty, after two hours of staring silently, the sailor got onto a bus. Hannibal was so tired from the tension that he went to the bench the sailor had used and lay down.

He couldn't sleep. The bench was too hard and he was cold. Now that night had come it was cooler outside and there was a breeze blowing on him from a broken window in the skylight. He found a *Times*, pulled it over his chest for a cover and shut his eyes. The lights were not bright enough to read by. They were too bright to sleep under. He pulled part of the newspaper over his face and shut his eyes. Only one hundred and seventy-nine days, he thought.

He was stiff and sore in the morning. The janitor woke him at five-thirty, pulling the paper off his face. Hannibal blinked, looked up at the unsympathetic face above him.

"Hi," he said.

"Bum," the janitor said.

There was coffee in the vending machine, but the cup didn't drop; he watched the brown powder and hot water spiral down the drain.

He ran his tongue over the back and sides of his teeth, rubbed the dirt off, spat it out. The janitor hit him on the back of the legs with his broom.

"Don't spit on the floor," he said. "Bum." Hannibal wanted to say that he wasn't a bum, that he couldn't leave the station if he wanted to. Can't you see the wrist restrainers? he wanted to ask. Obviously the guy could—it was hard to hide a piece of copper and steel three inches wide.

"Pro'ly one of them laugher fellas," the janitor said. "Always running, singing, laughing. Don't want your kind." He pushed Hannibal with the broom. Hannibal got out of his way and watched him sweep the floor.

It took him sixty-two steps to cover the length of the station pushing the broom. At one end, he turned, swept the ashes, papers, butts, and gum wrappers into a pile, put it front of the broom, pushed it back down. As he went and the dust vanished under him, the first of the people into the station walked around him, dropping ashes and gum wrappers onto the floor.

The commuter buses came between seven and eight-thirty. Each of them parked outside and the exhaust smoke blew in through the open doors. Hannibal leaned with his back to the wall and watched the people push onto each of them, stare blankly out the windows before the buses pulled out.

The second day was even slower than the first. He tried the foot vibrator, then one of the three pinball machines. The foot vibrator cost a dime and shook him so badly that he stopped with twenty seconds left.

"Here," he said to a passing lady. "You can use this." She looked like she had tired feet.

"Pervert!" she screamed at him. "I'm happily married, you . . . pervert!" Hannibal hoped that the vibrator would shake itself to death. The pinball went "Tilt" on his first ball.

Around ten o'clock the street people strolled in. There

were eight of them, all teen-agers, and they played the pinball machines and talked to the waitress behind the counter. She wouldn't talk to Hannibal at all, just slapped his coffee in front of him when he asked for it and never offered him a glass of water. She talked about movies and football games with the teen-agers. None of them talked to Hannibal either. None of them laughed. Even when they were talking about football games and music they were serious.

The second night, Hannibal put one newspaper under himself. It was softer but he still slept badly. It had begun to rain around six and the commuters had tracked mud through the station. The bums on the street came in out of the rain, then the kids who would have been hanging around outside came in to play pinball. They made a lot of noise but none of them would talk to Hannibal.

On the next day he began to notice the people. There was a tired old lady with a long gray coat and rheumy eyes who came at eleven and walked from bench to bench reading the papers people had left. On the fourth day Hannibal found a *Times,* a *News,* a *Press,* a *Post,* a *Telegraph,* and a *Herald* and arranged them on the first bench for her. He knew she'd be surprised.

"You a wise guy?" she said to him when she saw him smiling. "I can't read all these." She threw all but the *Times* onto the floor. The janitor came over and growled at Hannibal for instigating trouble.

The weekend was boring. Even more boring than the weekdays. The commuter buses didn't run and there were no big crowds, merely isolated people walking into the station, buying tickets at the window, sitting down on the benches. Even the coffee counter was closed. The vending machine was still out of cups. On Sunday, the soda machine stopped working and the candy machine ran out.

The people came in one at a time. There were servicemen heading either home or back to a base; Hannibal couldn't tell. They all looked tired and dirty—even the ones whose uniforms were clean looked tired and dirty. They sat on the benches and sometimes talked to one another, but never to civilians. There were mothers whose young children kept crying or asking to go to the bathroom. Salesmen who looked like Willy Loman. College girls who looked with disdain on the rest of the crowd, kept their legs crossed as they read magazines or paperbacks by Camus and Kant. Most of them were tired and dirty, too.

In the second week he began to notice the cracks in the walls. He had exhausted the graffiti and nothing new was being added. Nothing was being removed either. The janitor came in, swept, put in fresh paper, went home. No one put cups in the coffee-vending machine. The peanuts he had liked in the candy machine were replaced with crackers that stuck to the roof of his mouth.

Each morning the stationmaster gave him two dollars in change. Each day Hannibal spent it all, always on food, trying to buy milk when the machine was working because he needed the protein.

The little old lady with the gray coat came every day to read the papers. She was growing older, or sicker, daily. He could watch the disintegration in her. She coughed all the time as she read the papers and he could hear her gagging and rasping behind them. In November she stopped coming and Hannibal guessed that she had died.

It grew colder. When the buses unloaded, people came in quickly and the cold wind swept through the station, forcing the heat to pump from the radiators. When no buses came for an hour or more, the people on the benches began to sweat and take their coats off. Once the doors opened, the coats went back on. Hannibal developed a cough. His teeth started to hurt, too. Probably all the candy, he thought.

On Mondays the stationmaster handed him a package with clean dungarees, shirt, and underwear. He changed in the men's room each time and brought the dirty clothes back.

"My shoes are falling apart," Hannibal said.

"What size?"

"Nines. I always wear nines. Did you know that when . . ." The stationmaster turned his back. Hannibal shrugged his shoulders.

The judge came by to see him once. It was late November and Hannibal had been in the station for almost three months.

"Smile for me?" the judge said. He was wearing black and looked even more somber than he had to, as though he had just sentenced his wife to death. Or hadn't been able to. Hannibal smiled. He'd almost forgotten how.

"Dance for me?" Hannibal gave a quick shuffle, stumbled.

"Shoes are wearing out," he said. Also his legs. Except for going up and down the stairs to the rest room—and he had the runs now so that he did a lot of it—he wasn't getting much exercise.

"Tell the stationmaster," the judge said.

"I did. No luck."

"Too bad," the judge said. "Smile at him." He hobbled out of the station into the sunset.

The snowflakes fell through the hole in the skylight. Hannibal moved his newspaper to the hall outside the men's room and was awakened about three times a night. Once someone threw up on him. One day a lady collapsed going up the stairs. Hannibal told the stationmaster, who didn't want to listen, about it but the lady was dead when the cops arrived. One girl—she looked about thirteen—had lost her ticket and walked around the station for hours crying until a businessman offered to help her and walked out of the station with her. The floor turned brown with mud and the janitor never cleaned it. Every time the door opened the cold air blew on him.

On Christmas Eve, two teen-agers beat up a little old lady and stole her packages. On New Year's Day, college students came into the station and threw bottles and cans around. Hannibal hid in a stall in the men's room. In the middle of January, the heating system failed. It took two days to repair; Hannibal slept under five copies of the *Times,* one of the *Tribune,* and still shivered. After the heat was fixed, it wouldn't shut off. He stood as close to the door as he could, not wanting to get too cold, trying to get away from the stifling heat.

He lost track of time. He read every word of every paper and magazine he could find, memorized the posters, the ads, and obscenities on the walls. One day he forgot to get his money from the stationmaster and couldn't figure out, next day, why he was given four dollars. His second pair of sneakers fell apart—with the constant mud he hadn't expected them to last long anyway but he forgot to tell the master. One of his teeth fell out. It was the one which always hurt anyway and he was glad to be rid of it.

It was over. Kelly, the cop, was there and he took the wrist bands off.

"All done," he said.

"Okay," Hannibal said. He tried to straighten up but his back hurt.

It was spring. The sun was warm and bright. It hurt his eyes. In the park across the street, the birds were singing. It bothered his ears. He walked under a tree and sneezed on the pollen. The grass was greener than he remembered, but it was full of bugs. He hadn't remembered that.

That was it. He hadn't known then. Of course, he had to learn a lesson. He stood up, walked off the grass to the concrete of the path where he felt comfortable. Up ahead he saw a newsstand—he'd grown used to the papers, reading about wars, murders, plagues, and crisis—and walked toward it. As he passed a bench, a lady sitting on it went into an epileptic fit. He stepped aside carefully to make sure she didn't kick him.

Say Goodbye to the World's Last Brothel

by Robert Wissner

Robert Wissner is a recent graduate of Tulane University who now teaches a course in science fiction there. His story "Frozen Assets" (Clarion II) *tied for first prize in the 1971 NAL contest for the Tulane and University of Washington workshops.*

Bob is a master of the absurd, as this story amply demonstrates.

Don carries a gun. He carries it in a crotch holster. He's always practicing his quick draw, unzipping his fly and whipping out the huge Smith & Wesson .38. Don's a bit strange. If he doesn't watch out he is going to be a lot stranger. If he doesn't watch out he is going to blow off his pecker. And who ever heard of a pimp without a pecker? Besides, a man has his dignity to consider. Can you imagine the massive indignity of being forced to begin a showdown by unzipping your fly and fishing around for your gun? Or your heater, as Don calls it. Personally, I'd rather be shot down in my tracks.

Marie agrees with me. Marie would rather I'd be shot down in my tracks, too. In fact, she'd like to do it herself. She doesn't like me. Marie gave the gun to Don in the first place and has been trying to get into his pants ever since. She wants to get into his pants for the usual reasons, as well as wanting to get that gun and blow my head down the middle for barging in on her and Don just about the time he stopped foaming at the mouth long enough to get it up and keep it there. Marie is Don's trainee hooker with a cold. She liberated the gun from the back pocket of someone who was dead at the time, and who probably still is.

But as the Lieutenant says: "You never can tell."

Don's trainee hooker without a cold is Marge. Marge is Marie's twin sister and the only way to tell them apart is that

Marie constantly sniffles and her eyes are watery and red. Marie always has a cold. They both have knockers out to there but Marge is the one who likes me. She likes me because I bring her bottles of wine and comic books I find in the city. *The Masked Marvel* is her favorite. In return for my gifts she lets me stretch my naked body over hers whenever I want. She says it is good practice for when she goes to work for Don. It's nice, but sometimes when I am engaged in the act of maneuvering my body on top of hers she pores over her comic books, reading aloud the passages she considers significant.

We all live together in a big house that we found. We did not find it together. We found it separately, but now we all live here together. No one has told us to leave and it does not look like anyone will. Ever.

"You never can tell," the Lieutenant said and bit into a lemon. The Lieutenant is an old coot. He must be at least sixty. None of us know in which branch of the military he served. We don't even know if he was ever a lieutenant at all. He simply told us that that was what we were to call him. The Lieutenant eats lemons. All the time. Constantly. He will sit for hours eating lemons, absolutely ruining everyone's day. We all walk around the house with our lips puckered and dry, barely able to speak; a bitter, psychosomatic acid constricting our mouths. Just watching the Lieutenant bite into a juice-gorged lemon is enough to make everyone uncomfortable.

"You never can tell," he said again. We were having our daily conversation about Don.

"Bullshit," I said. "Look, Lieutenant, we're the only ones left. Just us five and nobody else. All gone. Poof. So how the hell does Don expect to make anything out of being a pimp? For Pete's sake, there's nobody left to buy the service he wants to supply. No customers, no pimps, obviously."

The Lieutenant took another bite out of that damned lemon. My spine puckered. I did not say anything, though. One of the first things we all agreed on when we came here was that each of us was to mind his own business.

"Maybe he'll start charging you. After all, you ball Marge all the time."

"That's different. I'm not a customer. I live here. And anyway, Marge doesn't work for him."

"Not yet," he said. "She doesn't work for him yet."

"Well, she won't ever work for him. There's nothing on the radio, no smoke signals. Nothing. How the hell can she work for him if there aren't any customers, huh?"

"You never can tell."

Don and Marie walked into the living room. Marie blew her nose.

"Hello, Lieutenant," Marie said. The Lieutenant waved his lemon in greeting. "Hello, you bastard." That was for me.

Don swaggered over to the full-length mirror and went to work. He was practicing his domineering, woman-mastering gaze. Someone had once told him that the secret formula for being a successful pimp is the ability to curdle milk from a distance of thirty paces using only a steady, masterful gaze. He hooked one thumb over his belt buckle and held his other arm loosely behind his back. He squared his round shoulders and twisted his upper torso slightly so that his face was only inches from the mirror. Then he started practice in earnest. His lip curled up at the right corner, exposing a rather mossy green canine tooth. His eyes narrowed. His eyebrows arched and swooped to a point over the bridge of his nose. That was what got women, turned them into whores. That masterful look showed them where they stood, showed them their master. According to Don.

Don had not quite mastered the requisite stare. He looked like a weasel about to sneeze. Or a ferret with paresis. But he looked like nothing quite so much as what he really was: a skinny, homely guy with acne scars making faces at himself.

"Hey, Don," I said, momentarily wrenching him away from the power he thought he was generating. "Anything on the short-wave?"

"Huh? Oh. No, nothing as usual."

"No customers?"

"What?"

"Nobody wiring for reservations? Don, how do you expect to ever become a pimp if you don't have any customers?"

"Don't worry, I'll find a way." He returned to practice.

"Yeah, don't worry," Marie said. "Ya lousy bastard." She sniffled from where she sat on the couch across the room.

I told Marie that I thought her boobs were shrinking, even suggested that her cold had something to do with it. I explained that colds could do that sometimes, chest colds in particular. I knew that would rile her. She is very proud of her physical attributes, and for good reason.

"Go dry up," she said. "You don't know whatcha talking about."

"Gee, I don't know, Marie. I think maybe now you're a bit smaller than Marge." They may be identical twins, but Marie is proudly and fiercely aware that her bust is a full half-inch larger than Marge's. She sat up straighter, pushing her talent up and out.

"Ha! You won't live to see the day Marge is bigger than me." She sniffled. "Ya wouldn't live five minutes if Don would let me use his gun."

Marie's really a sweet kid. She is really a sweet kid who wants to splatter my brains all over the carpet. She's sublimating. She loves Don and he can never satisfy her.

Don wants nothing more in this world than to be a pimp. He's sublimating too. I do not think Don has ever been laid in his life. His problem is not that he does not like women. His problem is that he likes them too much. He's wild about them. He wants them with a passion that defies understanding. His every fiber craves women to such magnificent proportions that he can never control himself long enough to get inside one. He foams at the mouth.

That's it in a nutshell; a sloppy, wet nutshell. Don foams at the mouth. Whenever he gets close to the actual act of making love to a woman, whenever she begins to remove her clothes and Don sees all that smooth white creamy flesh, the long legs, the way the breasts loom out and shake when she bends over and slides out of her panties, Don is sabotaged by his own lust. Excitement is too tame a word to describe Don's condition. He enters a state of frenzy that would shame a whirling dervish. And he foams at the mouth. He gurgles and makes noises like a broken percolator. And then while he is foaming and slobbering all down his chest he realizes how ludicrous he must look and he loses his erection. Faster than a speeding dumdum.

So now Don wants nothing more than to be a pimp and play with his .38 revolver. Which he carries in a crotch holster. Marie loves Don and wants to get inside his pants. She wants Don to make love to her, but it is beyond him. But once, two months ago, Marie almost got what she wanted. They don't know how or why. They don't know if it was the mood, the atmosphere, Don's physical condition at the time (exhausted from foraging in the city), or the particular scent Marie was wearing (eau de fish and stewed carrots), or what. But for the first time Don actually seemed capable of making love. They stripped, hurriedly passed over the foreplay, and got down to business. Business was booming. It was going wonderfully.

At which point I stumbled in, looking for a cake of soap.

Don has not been able to repeat his almost-performance. Marie is frustrated as hell. She blames me, has sworn vengeance. Sleeping with Marge was always a pleasure. Now that I know Marie will not try to bump me off when there is a chance of hurting Marge it is even more pleasurable. Especially the parts when I can get some sleep.

"Don't worry, Jake," Don said to the mirror. "I won't let Marie get hold of the heater. I know you didn't do it on purpose. It was an accident."

"Ha! We'll see if I get that gun or not," Marie said and wiped her nose on her sleeve. The Lieutenant said something that nobody bothered to hear. He took another bite out of that lemon. I got up. When I reached the back door he was still gumming it. I could feel it.

I strolled out into the back yard. Marge was sunbathing there. The old house squats on the top of a hill overlooking the city. A pine forest covers the mountain except for the bald spot at the top. The front of the house is smack up against the forest, but in the rear is a large flat yard. Marge was lying in a lawn chair. She faced toward the west, toward the dead city, soaking up the last of the setting sun. She wore a bikini open to the sun and to any suggestion. As I approached her from behind I could see the tan line across her breasts and the lighter skin just beneath. Marie may be larger, but a half-inch is nothing. I'm not the sort to quibble over trifles. She looked up.

"Hiya, Jake. Feeling horny?"

"No. Not right now. Just wanted to get away from Don and your maniac sister. And old citrus mouth."

"Old who?"

"The Lieutenant."

"Oh."

She returned to her comic book. It was a *Masked Marvel* comic book.

"Interesting?" I said.

"Huh?"

"The book. Anything interesting in it?"

"Oh sure. I guess so. But I read this one already. Sometimes they just don't seem as good when you read them over again. I mean, I know what all is going to happen and all."

"Hmm," I said.

"It's funny, isn't it?"

"What's that?"

"It's funny like the way you can only read these things once and then they're not so good any more if you read them again."

"Hmm," I said. "I'll rummage through the stores next time I go down to the city and see if I can find some new ones for you." Some old ones, actually, but new to Marge. I did not feel up to correcting myself.

"Oh good, Jake. I'd like that. I'm getting kinda tired of all the others you found."

"Hmm," I said. I say "hmm" a lot when I talk with Marge. Our range of topics is somewhat limited. We all agreed not to speak of the past. The future is not worth the breath. There's just not much of anything to say. So Marge and I usually talk about her supply of comic books. Either she is enthralled with a new one or she is depressed and bored with their transient entertainment value. I once tried to get her to talk about something else. I wanted her to talk about herself. I asked how she felt about being one fifth of the world's population. She said: "Hmm."

That was my mistake, asking that question. Her answer did something to me. The utter simplicity with which she raised her hands in an open-palmed shrug, and then let them drop to her sides, sighing a simple "Hmm," did something to me. She had a beautifully childlike expression as she gave the only possible answer to my totally inane question. By the time her delicate hands had dropped back to her hips, I was in love with her.

So there I was, one fifth of the world's population in love with another fifth of the same, thinking all sorts of Adam and Eve nonsense. I still do in moments of weakness. But to start the whole mess over again seems several stages beyond futile. It seems downright asinine.

Marge looked up, smiling. She had found a part in the comic book she had forgotten. She pointed it out for me. The Masked Marvel was busy saving the world from destruction.

"I guess it's too bad it's only in a comic book, huh?" she said.

"Yeah, I guess so."

I started back to the house. There was nowhere else to go. Marge called to me and I stopped halfway across the yard and turned.

"I think I love you."

I thought that over for a little while.

"I think I love you, too," I said. "It's too bad, isn't it?"

"Hmm."

Marge turned a page and I walked up the back steps and into the house.

Where Marie stuck the gaping bore of an elephant gun in my face and ordered me to march into the living room. It was not actually an elephant gun. It was the .38 revolver. But things have a way of growing out of proportion when the bore of a .38 is staring up your nose with its one black eye. I marched.

Hup, two, three, four. Left face at the end of the dark paneled hall, right face through the dining room. Into the living room, hup ho halt. About face.

The gun, with Marie's hand attached to it, was still staring at me when I turned around. I realized I was doing my famous imitation of a goal post. It seemed silly for some reason and I let my arms drop. That seemed just as silly but more comfortable. I left my arms by my side. If I was going to get shot for a sudden movement I didn't want that movement to resemble the indecisive flapping of a ruptured duck.

I looked around the room, slowly. Don was snarling into the mirror. The Lieutenant was somewhere else. I told Don I thought he said he was going to keep that thing away from Marie.

"Sorry, man," he said. He grinned. "It's out of my hands."

I thanked him for his concern. Marie sneezed.

"All right, you stumblebum sonuvabitch," she said. "Now you're gonna get what's coming to you."

Marie began squeezing the trigger. I was sending postcards to my feet. Each card was marked Urgent and had one word in heavy black letters: Run. They all came back, marked Addressee Deceased. Marie was still squeezing. She closed her eyes and turned her head to one side, making faces that rivaled Don's. Don did not stir from his reflection. It was out of his hands. Marie and I were the only ones afraid of the noise that cannon was about to make.

It made that noise.

A bullet whistled past my head so close I swear the wax in

my left ear melted. I opened my eyes. Marie was staring horrified at the weapon. Don had turned to face me, the blood draining from his face. His knees started shaking and he crumpled to the couch.

"Oh Christ," he said. "Sweet Jesus Christ."

Marie sat beside Don. "Are you okay, Jake? Are you all right?"

"Yeah, I think so." I felt around. No blood. "Pardon a condemned man's confusion, but what the hell is going on? Don't you want to kill me?"

"Oh no, not now. Not any more. We were just kidding."

"Yeah. Honest, Jake," Don said. "It was supposed to be a joke. You know, just to scare you a little. We didn't really want to shoot you. Jesus, I thought the heater was empty."

"Empty!"

"Yeah, you know, unloaded. You don't think I'd carry a loaded heater that close to my pecker, do you? Jesus, when I think of all the times I've practiced my quick draw with a loaded gun . . ."

I sat down. We all thought about loaded guns. After a while I managed to ask what had changed Marie's mind about killing me.

"Well, we just figured out a way to make love," Marie said. "I guess we shoulda thought of it a long time ago, what with the Lieutenant around all the time."

"The Lieutenant? What's he got to do with it?"

Don spoke up. "What happens to you whenever he's around?"

"You have an uncontrollable urge to cram that lemon down his throat."

"Right. That's it exactly," he said. "Because watching someone eating a lemon makes you uncomfortable. And it makes you uncomfortable because there is nothing you can do to keep your damned mouth from puckering up at the sight of it. And if your mouth is all puckery and dry, you can't slobber all over yourself. I mean I can't slobber all over myself."

"You mean you're going to have the Lieutenant sit in your room and eat lemons every time you want to make it?"

"Yep."

"He'll have to wear a blindfold, of course," Marie added, smiling and blushing slightly.

I thought about it and said it might work. It might just work.

"Of course it will work," Don said. "It can't fail."

We all leaned back in our seats. We all smiled. Bygones were buried with the hatchet. We were one big happy family.

"Oh yeah, I forgot," Don said. "I've made a decision. From now on you'll have to pay for it every time you ball Marge."

"Pay for it! Pay! What do you mean, pay for it? With what, for chrissake?"

"Food, of course. Canned stuff you can dig up in the city. I figure ten cans a throw ought to cover it."

I told him he was out of his mind.

"Aw, come on, Jake. It doesn't look like I'm going to have any other customers dropping over.

I searched my mind for the worst insult I knew. I wanted to call him the lowest thing I could think of. I wanted venom to dribble from my mouth as I spoke.

I called him a pimp.

His face lit up in pleasure. He beamed self-congratulations.

"Yep. That's what I am. But look here, man, that's a nasty word. I like to think of myself as a businessman. You know, supply and demand. An entrepreneur."

I thought of getting up and beating the shit out of Mr. Entrepreneur, but Marie still held the revolver. She still held the unloaded revolver with five more bullets in the cylinder. Just then the Lieutenant walked in. He was chewing on another lemon.

"Well, well. Hello, Lieutenant," I said. "Don the pimp here has big plans for you."

"For me?" He pointed to his chest. He pointed with the lemon.

"That's right. He wants you to eat lemons in his room while he makes love to Marie."

"Lemons?"

"Lemons. You know, those juicy things you are always sticking in your face."

"Lemons?"

"Yes, lemons. Lots of juicy lemons just like that one you have in your hand."

"Lemons?"

It occurred to me that the Lieutenant was stuck like a broken record; that perhaps if I gave him a good shot on the side of the head it would start him up again. But then he looked down at the thing he held in his hand as if it were a plague-infested rat.

"Lemons?" he said. His mouth began to pucker. He had trouble working his lips. "Lemons? I hate lemons! These are lemons?"

I nodded.

"I thought they were oranges. Why didn't you tell me before?" He threw the yellow traitor across the room and collapsed into the leather armchair. He began to pucker. It was amazing. It started with his face. Then his whole body shivered and twisted into one tremendous, retrospective, monumental pucker. It was a full thirty seconds before he could push the desiccated words from his dry mouth: "I'll never eat another one of those things as long as I live."

Marge, still in her bikini, bounced into the room just as another bullet shot past my ear and shattered a vase behind me.

"Hey! What's going on?" she asked.

"I'm going to kill that bastard, that's what's going on! This time I'm gonna blow his fucking head right off his fucking shoulders!"

Marie sniffled. Marie sniffled again. Between those two concessions to her clogged nasal passages she fired another shot. She missed, but not by much. I jumped back, tripped over something or other, and tumbled head over heels into the fireplace. Marie was yelling for me to hold still so that she could get a bead on me. Marge still wanted to know what was going on. There were some hot coals in the fireplace and the coals, added to the adrenalin pumping in my veins, gave me the impetus I needed. Marie fired into the fireplace but I had already bolted. I did some broken-field running across the room, grabbed Marge's hand, comic book and all, and dragged her through the house, out the back door and down the mountainside.

That was four months ago. We must be in another state by now, if anybody cares about such artificial designations anymore. I don't. We have not seen Don or Marie or the Lieutenant since we left. We do not expect to see them ever again. We are very happy together. Marge and I are very happy.

Marge is not reading comic books any more. She is reading back issues of *Reader's Digest*. I admit to being unsure if this is a step up or a step down from comic books, but at least now she doesn't require pictures along with the words. In a little while I am going to hunt up a library and liberate a few books for her, a few books she can read and enjoy more than once.

As for all that Adam and Eve nonsense, I am still dead set against it.

But then, you never can tell.

Flat Hatter

by David Wise

David Wise is a seventeen-year old filmmaker who has recently moved from New York to California. At the age of seven, he made an animated short that won him both awards and notoriety. Some people, I guess, peak out early.

Of "Flat Hatter," Wise writes: "This story, which was written as an assignment for Avram Davidson, has been called "Burroughsian," "Joycean," "an obscure piece of fluff," and other things less polite, which just goes to show that nowadays people can't recognize a fast-action scientific romance when they see one. It is a portrait, drawn freehand, of what happens when a person sees the seriousness of his work as absurdity and vice-versa. It also has a certain baroque irony to it. You never do *know what people are laughing about, do you?"*

For the moment, there is a shuddery smarmy silence of night. Darkness rushes through the outer locks and everything stops telling us where it is. This will pass, and does. Dials cut through the night which enveils us, making paltry doe-daytime electronic truth-trust pseudomockery of sunlight seem obsolete. Muons sluice through the black sea, leaving ripply ectoplasmic trails which dance and dangle before our eyes wherever we look, outlines of the brain-trust of reality. There is nothing to see, nothing to hear. I want to be plugged in again. The circuits cut, dog-death night of eyes and ears would break my heart, but I can feel my fleshfound realhands, twitchy and tawdry-like, flexing to tell me that soon I will come to my psychosenses through them.

We will come back into real space. We will be twenty-nine lightminutes from Alpha Centauri.

My real ears, long out of practice and unamplified by crosscutting transistorized psychosensors, hear the familiar voice. Advolyn Geledaytivless, Captain of the crew (me),

Lord High Liege of the Putdown-Pickup Roundabout-the-Universe run Hypercruiser, speaks. "Fingers in."

The persistent presence of cool and cautious calm psychostrokes my mind and the tenuous tendigit probability gives me membranous reassurance. Nerve-end truthtellers lock into the console gloves, and the shuddery smarmy silence of night ends. The shining silver spaceship realworld flashes into retinal-dazzling existence around the muon dials. Spinebending slashcoms, cathode banks of show and tell, three outer sendoff diagdirectional coordinaputers and a wall of psychosensing cerebral hologrammatical synaptic linkups make themselves visible as we burst out of hyperspace. All is calm, all is bright. "Maintaining projected course," I tell. "Now twenty-eight lightminutes, forty-two lightseconds from lead star."

"Course and coordinates accepted," Advolyn tells. "Prepare to employ psychovisual receptors."

Soon we will see the silky star, eyes dead, minds enraptured, seeing all, though Advolyn Geledaytivless has not told me why we have come to this drape-distanced sector, so near the ashy-ancient homefront. There is usually a reason, and we must be crystal-calm, psychoserious, deadly dedicated. I am always all.

The sector signal is a microreceived message which always spins in on my psychovids. An inkish little moiré-voice it is and asks its upgrade graphic traffic questions. I answer with my mindvoice, coordinates and sector-signals in, assimilated, and responded to. Our course is accepted, it tells, and we are permitted to continue. It does not tell why we are being here, and I dare not ask Advolyn Geledaytivless, for full fear of disrupting his ramifications, which dodge and duck like viny synapse-chains. I will find out, I know. Five lightminutes have passed. We cannot come closer than two, or our ship would be as a puff of smoke in the hurricane—i.e., quickly dispersed: fried; burned; eliminated; done in. Two short and shooting lightminutes from the flamefurnace sunsurface and the hellheat could ash us as fast as a bulb burnout.

We are twenty-one lightminutes from Alpha Centauri. Advolyn Geledaytivless tells: "Prepare exterior psychovisual reception monitors."

I guide my milky mind with the help of resistorcondensor slap-on screen gages, underexposing the highbright light of the roundly sun—aiming, testing, irising, reaming brightness, glancing hither and thither through the nonsense night of space. Space is not a vacuum; space is not night. I peer through the paradoxical prism, the eternal tawny-dawny twilight, gathering together all the possible night sights, the starshine, the sunflare, burning bile gas, outside darkness and interior daydeath, pulling focus and pushing exposure, finally making a cohesive real-image, non-reversible, highplate-up to fullblown Advolyn Geledaytivless and I. I am psychoserious, steady as a rock, unrelenting and immovable. I must be.

I finish checking the muon showglow dials. We are thirteen dashing flowing lightminutes from Alpha Centauri, and I would prefer to be nervous and ask why, but I am not and do not. I am the rock.

"Connect visual function relators, and infuse all functions with the exterior image processation," Advolyn Geledaytivless tells, and I do. We are both crystal-calm, deadly-dedicated as the brimbashing mindfiller sun opens our heads and floods in like high tide at the fire-sea. All is scorched whiteness, whiting out, then whiting out again through crystal calm, but Advolyn and I are in reception of each other and—though I need not seek it—somewhere in the distant driving lessreal firmament is the ship's garbled interior, where the mu-mesons flash and retaliate, lost to us now, we who are mindfilling in deepspace darknight lightbright updown leftright. Alpha Centauri washes my mind. Images flip on and off in the sensory realrush. Alpha Centauri cleans out the sides of my skull and tingles wherever it can touch me, though I remain on top of it all, my calm a crystal which no realdeath fleshfear can scratch, shiny as the surface of this sun, hard and placid, its icy angles sending out cool white shards of light—

—The crystal begins to crack.

Advolyn Geledaytivless is doing something with his fleshfound realvoice that I cannot understand. It stirs a dusky dim memory which I cannot reach. I want to be nervous. I *want* to ask him what we are doing here, but I must repiece the cracked calm-crystal of my psychoserious deadly dedication. Reason demands that I do this. Logic demands that I ask him why and what for. I hear none of his mindvoice, and I am so unused to the real fleshvoice that I do not know how to comprehend his upthedown intheout manicsounding. The fleshsound could not be correlative communication, so I am deadly afraid I can find no reason for it.

It will help my icy cool, I tell myself, if I try to understand what he is doing. Silky sounds peal up and down throughout the audial spectrum as if he were running while he smashes the—

—The bottle is blown apart, slowly. Glass has white lines form in it; then the lines expand and split. The green glass is fragmented and flies out, turning end over end, each piece. The liquid within it appears to bubble, stretch, and is torn apart by the force of the explosion. The glass fragments become less and less together. Soon there is little left.

Alpha Centauri burns in my brain and we are four lightminutes, thirty-eight lightseconds away from it. In the chatter-clatter distances the inky moiré voice of the sector-signal screams microreceived whatfor questions of endangerment and whitedeath, all of which I already know, but I cannot answer the whatfors, and Advolyn Geledaytivless, his fleshvoice a torrent of shardy jagged larynxsounds, will not tell. My composure is gone altogether, forced out into the freenight settlement where I can never again reach it, burned out of my brain by the combusting power of solar spray, because I think we are going to die. We are close, too close. If I don't remember soon, I may never know what Geledaytivless is doing. I may never know why we have come here. I cannot move. He and I, we are going to die as if that star needed fuel and sent just for our ship. Advolyn Geledaytivless, tell me what sounds you make with your realvoice! Tell me why we're in this stronglit deathdealing heatsearing part of space! His sound spectrum fluctuates like jellyballs on the high seas and I know nothing, scared deathful. My hands wrench within the truthteller console gloves, the synapticonnections sparking and bashing on and off as the nerve ends flash with fear, telling me a truth I would give my all and everyone to prevent: my captain is going to get us killed. We are due to die and I can never know the reason now. All the wonderingly horrorscreeching wildness of the universe is down upon us.

We are two lightminutes, twenty-one lightseconds from the bileburning lightscream. Now, I remember the soupy, helpless word for what he is doing with his fleshvoice. He pauses long enough to tell: "All power back!" And then resumes.

We are two lightminutes, thirteen lightseconds away.

Advolyn Geledaytivless tells, "Look, there's Alpha Centauri, ha ha!"

He is laughing.

Baby Makes Two

by Gerald F. Conway

Gerry Conway, who just turned twenty, is a novelist, a short-story writer, and a senior editor for the Marvel Comics group, for whom he does about 20-000 words of continuity per month. His story "Silent Hands" in Clarion *has been anthologized in France. He has just been named editor of a new magazine devoted to tales of the supernatural. He is disgustingly prolific, frighteningly good at what he does.*

And what he does in this story is examine in deft detail a most sensitive matter of love, a triangle affair in which we have all participated in one role or another.

He woke a little after midnight and continued to lie quite still, listening to the electric hum whisper through the darkness of the bedroom. The window was open beside him, a soft autumn breeze passing through it, over him, touching his wife. She moved restlessly in her sleep, and he glanced at her, smiling as he watched her shift, her arm dropping from her hip onto the bed. Without the daytime layer of make-up her features seemed smooth, gentle. He liked the way she looked without the dabs of color on cheeks and chin, but it was a preference he could never make her understand. It didn't matter, not really. There were so many more important things that came between them. Vital things.

Like the baby.

He glanced across the room, wondering if something had happened to the baby—if that was the reason for his awakening. No . . . the equipment continued to hum, an undertone to the other sounds of the evening, the ceaseless murmurs of the apartment complex of which their studio was a small—though contributing—part. Carefully, trying not to disturb his wife, he slipped out of bed and moved through the shadows toward the glow of the baby's tank. Set in a corner of the one-room apartment, next to an inset shelf of books (a gift from his mother: family heirlooms), the rectangular unit pulsed with a milky light; he bent close and peered through the plexiglas surface at the dark form of the embryo within. Were there features, eyes, a nose? For a moment he thought he saw the curve of embryonic lips. But no . . . not yet. It was only the second month; the features wouldn't be visible for days yet.

He didn't understand the calm he felt as he stood watching the tiny shape turning beneath him. He didn't truly want to understand it: the feeling alone was enough, more than enough, and he remained, watching, for a quarter-hour. Then, still careful not to wake his wife, he returned to his bed and passed into a deep and grateful sleep.

The next morning, when he had finished with his duties in the 'fresher stall, he reentered the small apartment to find his wife preparing breakfast at the kitchen counter. He took a seat beside her and accepted the plate of food she offered him. "I was up last night," he said. "Looking at the baby."

She plucked a sliver of toast from the console and dropped it on her tray. "Is she all right?"

"Fine. I was just watching her. Everything seems so calm, in there. So peaceful."

His wife glanced at the tank. "I suppose it must be," she said.

"I see why everyone wants to go back."

"Do you?"

He nodded. "In a way," he said. "It must be pleasant."

"I suppose it must be," his wife answered.

Before leaving for the express tube into the central urban complex, he paused by the tank to re-examine the dials. The temperature was correct, the protein and calcium levels a little high—he keyed the computer manual control to compensate—and the general consistency of the fluid within the parameters noted in the handbook. He fiddled with the controls to adjust the pumps a trifle and then stepped away. His wife was watching him as she finished dressing, buckling on her shirt.

"You really didn't need to do that," she told him. "If the levels shift too far outside the limits, the computer is perfectly capable of making the proper adjustments."

"I understand that," he said, "but I like to help a little."

"It doesn't need any help."

"I know," he said. "I know that. I just like to help."

"Do what you want to," she sighed. She left without another word, and a moment later, he followed.

He arrived a few minutes before the rest of the men in his office. He had a console near one of the large window screens which lit the north wall, and he made a practice of getting to the office early so that he could choose the view for that day. It was something of a custom among the men: whoever got to the office first had the privilege of determining the day's diversion. He keyed the screen for a beach scene, centering the picture on a line of rocks leading from a shoreline of fine white sand. There were clouds in the distance, gray on the far horizon. Briefly, he wondered why the central programming agency would offer a view of storm clouds. It seemed wrong, somehow, as though the view was designed to foster disharmony—the direct antithesis of the window screens' purported purpose. Still, it *was* a beach scene, and he liked beach scenes. He relaxed before his console, absorbing the motion of the tide coming in, the sands appearing and vanishing, waters rolling, frothing, churning—and didn't hear the approaching footsteps until a voice startled him just inches from his right ear.

"Could I speak with you a moment?"

He swung around, reddening, wondering how long he'd sat staring at the ocean view. There were others in the room now, he saw, and they gazed at him with polite disinterest, at last returning to their consoles, making the necessary program notes for the day's business. Standing beside him, smiling with the pleasant pedantic sneer the clerks laughed about in private, was his supervisor, a tall man with large round eyes like the eyes of a startled bird. "Only for a moment," his supervisor said, widening his smile. "You can return to your work fairly quickly, I think."

"Of course, sir." He got to his feet and trailed after the tall man, down the corridor and into the cubicle set apart from the general offices. "Is there anything wrong, sir?"

"With your work? Oh no, no, there's nothing wrong there. You see, I wanted to speak to you about . . ." His supervisor frowned, apparently not sure how to proceed. ". . . about these views you choose for the screens. Not a thing wrong with them, of course, nothing like that. No. It's just . . . they possess a certain monotony . . ."

"Monotony, sir?"

"Yes." The man rushed forward, eager for the chance to explain. "The day before yesterday, a lake; yesterday, a mountain brook. Today, that seashore. You see the point?"

"I think so, sir."

"There seems to be some sort of . . . fixation . . . on water. If you understand what I mean. It's all well and good, but don't you think . . . ?"

"Of course, sir. I'm sorry if I offended anyone. I just like the water, sir."

"It's not a matter of offending anyone," his supervisor said quickly. "Nothing like that, no, nothing of the sort. People were just commenting on the fact, you see, and as supervisor, naturally it's my duty to see . . . that things are ironed out."

"I'm sorry, sir. I just liked the water. I'm sorry."

The other man nodded uneasily and smiled again, a worried smile, and nodded once more. "Yes. Yes, of course. Well. That's it, then. You can go back to work now, I think . . . unless there's anything on your mind . . . ?"

"Nothing, sir. But thank you."

"Yes. Of course." There was a tangible air of relief in the taller man's voice. "Well," he said, and held the door open.

Rather self-consciously he thanked his supervisor again, passed by him and into the corridor, and returned to his console and the view of the stormy sea.

Shortly before lunch he received a message requesting his presence at a counseling agency elsewhere in the building.

It was a two-room suite near the northern bank of lift tubes, set back from the main concourse in a tributary corridor. The walls of the office radiated a glow toward the ultraviolet end of the spectrum, a color he couldn't identify, but which he found oddly comforting as he entered and took a seat. The receptionist blinked a red eye at him from its niche in the wall opposite the waiting bench, and he leaned forward, belatedly announcing his name.

"The doctor will be with you in a moment, sir," the receptionist whispered, its voice silken, soothing. "Please make yourself comfortable. There are reading tapes in the table console."

He nodded, and waited with his hands on his knees, wondering why he'd been referred to a counseling service. Perhaps his supervisor had filed his name, or one of the other clerks; perhaps they were worried about him, worried about the views he'd been choosing lately. But that was silly; he couldn't understand that, really. He was grateful for their concern, but still . . .

The inside door slid open and a voice called from within.

"Would you step inside, please?"

He did so, and the doctor greeted him just inside the archway, gripping his hand warmly and then releasing it, sliding a paternal arm around his shoulders and guiding him to a form-mold chair near a plain wood-enamel desk. "I've heard quite a bit about you. You're good at your work, aren't you?"

"Did my supervisor say that?"

"He said you were a man of extraordinary diligence. But he's concerned for you."

"Is he?"

"Yes indeed. Indeed. Sit down, won't you? Do you smoke? No? I'm glad. I find it distracts me sometimes with a client." The doctor laughed, shaking his head at some private joke. "Is there some reason you don't smoke?" he asked finally. "Some physical effect you don't find pleasant?"

"No. I just have other things on my mind."

"Oh? Anything you'd care to talk about? I understand from your supervisor that you've a fascination for ocean views."

"Mostly just water. I like watching it. The water's . . . peaceful."

His doctor nodded, settling back behind his desk, resting his hands in his lap. "Go on, please. I gather you enjoy this sense of peacefulness."

"Oh yes. Very much."

"Well, there's nothing wrong in that, certainly nothing wrong in that. But your supervisor says this is a new preference. Something recent. Can you think of anything which might be connected with this sudden interest?"

"It's really not very sudden. I've always liked water."

"I see," his doctor said. Still smiling, he touched a button on the console near him. The small screen lit and flashed with words, then a series of briefly held pictures. The doctor studied these things and then flicked the screen off. He was nodding. "You and your wife are having a child soon, I see."

"In seven months."

"Home growth, by the report. May I ask whose idea that was, your wife's or your own?"

"Both of us. You see, we'd contracted for a six-year term marriage, and about two years ago we were told our genetic interface was very promising. We talked it over, at that time, and my wife agreed a child might be a good idea."

"Then you proposed the child, not your wife?"

"Well, I was the first to learn about our genetic interface."

"I understand the interface is a voluntary test."

"Yes, that's true. We thought it would be interesting to find out what our compared optimum would be. . . ."

"I see. Yes. And when you decided to have a child . . . ?"

"Naturally, we wanted to raise her ourselves. So we agreed to a ten-year infant-duration contract. That was a year ago. We had to wait for approval," he explained, and the doctor pursed his lips into a smile, inclining his head in the hint of a nod.

"I understand perfectly. Of course. Your wife, then, applied for the home-growth provision?"

"Yes. She did."

"Did you agree with this decision?"

"Naturally. I like to be a part of these things."

His doctor smiled. "I understand perfectly."

They sat in silence for several heartbeats, and he watched his doctor as the older man studied the darkened screen of the console, apparently waiting for something further.

"My wife . . ." he said finally, ". . . she isn't happy with the arrangement."

"Ah," his doctor said quietly.

"I don't understand it."

"I see."

"Before the child, we did everything together . . . everything."

"Of course, of course."

"But now . . . I don't think she cares about it."

"And you do."

"Very much."

"I would think so," his doctor said. "Yes. I would think so."

"Why is she acting like this?"

"Like what? What does she do that bothers you?"

"She . . . doesn't talk about the baby. She lets the machines handle everything. If I didn't . . ." He paused and pressed his lips together, closing his eyes.

"Yes?" his doctor prompted. "If you didn't . . . ?"

"If I didn't care for the baby, no one *would*," he blurted, and sank back, drained, not knowing why he'd spoken, not caring, simply satisfied that at last he'd finally explained, finally let it out.

"You think your wife doesn't love this child?"

"I know she doesn't."

"Why do you believe this?"

"Because she doesn't *understand*."

"In what way?"

"She doesn't . . . she just doesn't understand, that's all." He felt helpless, and knew suddenly that his doctor, too, was unsympathetic.

And overwhelmingly, it all became too much for him to bear, and he began, quietly at first, to cry.

Dimly, through the sounds of his own sobs, he could hear his doctor saying, over and over, soothingly, "There, there . . . there, there . . ."

And then he blacked out.

When he regained consciousness he found himself lying on his bed, naked, covered to his waist by a sweat-stained sheet. For several seconds he couldn't remember what had happened, and then he did, and felt his face warming with shame. He looked toward the window, saw that the glass had been opaqued and that the room was darkened. Gradually, he became aware of sounds in the kitchen nook, and he turned his head in that direction, curious. It must still be day, and so his wife would be at her office. Who . . . ?

Someone stepped away from the counter, leaning forward to peer past the 'fresher stall. His wife. She was dressed in her office clothes, her hair drawn back under the skullcap affected by business personnel that season. When she realized he was awake, she smiled.

"Do you want something to drink? You must be awfully dry; you've been sweating rather heavily, you know."

"I am" he said. He watched as she held a glass to the dispenser and pressed the tab for juice. "Shouldn't you be at work?"

"The doctor called me and told me you were ill. My supervisor let me leave early, and I brought you home. You were very weak. He gave you a tranc shot, I think."

She brought him the juice and sat beside him on the bed while he sipped it. His eyes followed her, watching her remove the cap and shake out her hair. It fell in waves to her shoulders, kinky from the pressure, yet still a rich black. She noticed his attention and laughed. "You're not *that* sick, are you?"

He smiled back at her. She turned away, abruptly; something in his smile made her turn away. "The doctor told me what happened," she said. "He told me how you felt."

He didn't say anything. Something was tightening in his stomach, and he set the glass of juice on the floor beside the bed. His hands were trembling, and he felt very warm.

"Do you really believe I don't care?" she asked him.

It was like a physical blow. "What am I supposed to think? You avoid everything that has to do with the baby. You don't help me with the controls. You don't look to see how she is. If I didn't do anything—"

"—absolutely nothing would go wrong. The machines are automatic. You *know* that. There's nothing for us to do. *Nothing.*" She was looking at him, her face open and concerned, but now he didn't face her; he didn't want to face her.

"That's not the point," he hissed. *"She's our baby!"* His voice broke and he paused, went on. "Our baby, don't you understand? She needs love, she needs our love, my love, your love—you can't just ignore her—you can't—"

He stopped and looked away.

She said nothing for several minutes, but her breathing was rapid and harsh. When she spoke her voice was ragged, as though she'd drawn something up from deep inside her, something he realized she hadn't known was there until that moment, and perhaps, not even now, not even as she said it—it was so much a part of her, it moved within her, independent of her, speaking *through* her.

"And what about me? Don't *I* need your love, too?"

He stared at her.

"I—" and he stopped.

Her voice was soft now, very low. A whisper. "Since *she* came along, you haven't touched me. Not really. Not one time, really."

"I didn't—"

"Not one single time."

It was true, he knew, and as he accepted the truth of it, he began to unravel the reasons why, the protective drives that had been frustrated, the paternal emotions that had been twisted, transformed . . . turned aside. He saw only a small part of the complex whole, but for the moment, it was enough, more than enough.

"I'm sorry," he said.

She came into his arms, and for a time, at least, the electric hum from the tank behind them went unheeded, their child, for a moment, unobserved.

Thrangs and Other Wonders

by Leonard Isaacs

"The Thrangs ate them, Thir."
"All of them?" re
-sponded/ -torted/ -plied/
SAID
the Director.
A tension precedes the Director's
ejaculation; alternate universes un-
zip for the reader: God
-like autochthones whose names
are Thir and Thor and Theseus.
Or perhaps our character only lisped
to show
(not tell) the reader
that the Galaxy's gone gay.

The Sun has gone nova
three times this week. I can stare
into that ghostglobe until I am Oedipus
Futurex
and still see those lines of force
-d-
enouement hang limply in the solar wind.
Inside jokes circle Sol
like inner planets, indistinguishable
from sunspots and other
blemishes.

A Star is risen in the East
Lansing area; it is off-
spring of Apollo and sets
the sci-fi world afire.
(Helioson has gone Casanova
three times this week.) The Star warms
and the Star burns, holds
satellites in synchronous
and sycophantous

oribts, draws a comet in and ends
by driving it away.

The Thrangs have got away;
the Moon has gone gibbous.
Nietzsche blocks Casanova's way;
and Apollo's mask is Dionysus.

Cantaloupes and Kangaroos

by Dennis R. Caro

Dennis Caro is a prolific ghost-writer who has been churning out fiction since 1964. This is his first appearance under his own name.

He also writes songs and sings them to his own guitar accompaniment. He sings well and his songs are pretty funny. So are his stories.

I think he decided to write under his own name one day when, as he reports, "Harlan sat at his typewriter and raved about the berserk turns his story was taking. His protagonist decided to have a metal pinkie that played classical music. Bob Thurston was up for a visit. The protagonist in his latest story had an orange pancreas illustrated with an obscenity about the AMA. The floor of my room was three inches deep in Polly seeds and Earls was only half through with the bag. So I said, 'What the hell, I'm just as crazy as any of you.' "

Harrison Williams awoke on the morning of December twenty-second with a lion on his chest. He opened one eye hesitantly against the sunlight coming through the venetian blinds, saw the lion, and closed his eyes again. I'm dreaming, he thought, considering the logical alternatives.

"Harry, if you don't get out of bed this instant you're going to be late for work."

"Yes, Martha." Harry opened both eyes; it was a lioness, it didn't have a mane. Its fur was golden, light and dark patterns, and the sun glowed through the tufts of hair around its ears. He could see through it into the kitchen. There was Martha in a forest of lion hair. Martha, he thought. I should have more sense than to dream about Martha.

"Harry, are you getting up?"

The lion yawned. Harry had never seen teeth that large. Its breath was sweet; he remembered reading once that carnivores had rancid breath from rotting meat and thought it interesting his dream had eliminated some of the more distasteful aspects of lionhood. There was no weight on his chest. Harry was slightly built; he knew a more realistic animal would have been painful. The lion yawned again, wider this time, and it licked his nose. Its tongue was soft and very wet. Lions had coarse tongues. Harry wiped his face with his pajama sleeve; it came away with a large wet spot. He reached out and touched soft fur. Logical alternatives or not, the lion was real.

"Martha? Martha, there's a lion on my chest."

"Harry, stop playing with that stupid lion and get out of bed."

Stop playing with that stupid lion? Harry sat up quickly and the lion rolled onto the floor. It looked up at him accusingly and he scratched behind its ears. Real or not, it was apparently a very nice lion.

The lion followed Harry as he walked around the edge of the bed into the bathroom. There was a parrot perched on top of the medicine cabinet, cleaning between its toes with its beak. Harry opened the cabinet and the parrot hopped on top of the light and began to sing "What Shall We Do with the Drunken Sailor," as he brushed his teeth. After two choruses it flew down, perched on the lion's back and squawked encouragement. Harry carefully screwed the cap on the toothpaste, returned the tube and brush to the medicine cabinet and removed his electric shaver.

Harry was an accountant. He'd kept the same job for twenty years and perhaps seven people in the entire company knew he worked there. The receptionist asked him who he wanted to see on the average of four times a week. He did his work in the same manner be brushed his teeth and shaved, meticulously. He unfailingly squeezed the toothpaste in the middle and he never remembered to clean the hair out of his shaver, but when he was through only a trained observer could have told he'd been there at all.

The parrot and the lion followed Harry back into the bedroom. He opened the closet door and a kangaroo handed him his brown suit. It was the suit he'd planned to wear; he took it and slid the door closed.

Breakfast was on the table when Harry walked into the kitchen. The eggs were cold; even the lion wouldn't eat them.

"Don't complain to me the eggs are cold." Martha hadn't turned around, she was still at the stove. "And stop feeding the lion at the table." He'd been married to her for twenty years too, Martha Braunschen Williams. She'd reminded him of his mother.

The parrot was on Martha's shoulder; it seemed to belong there and Harry had a sudden insight. The animals had something to do with personality. That parrot *was* Martha, which meant the lion . . . Harry decided he liked the idea of having a lion. But what the hell was the kangaroo doing in his closet?

The changes started on the subway. People took one look at Harry's lion and moved aside. He had no trouble getting a seat on the Lexington Avenue Express. Normally he would have been jammed against the door and perhaps even been pushed out and forced to take another train. He felt confident, and he liked that too.

The receptionist at Benton, Batten and Bloom was a redhead with a pudgy-cute figure. Her dresses came just to the rounded bottom of her buttocks and she never wore a bra. She was wearing a shirtwaist; Harry could see the edge of a very intriguing breast as she leaned over the desk and said, "Good morning sir, may I, Oh, what a marvelous lion." She looked up at Harry. "You're Mr. Williams, aren't you? Do you think I could, I mean would you mind if I petted your lion?"

"Sure. Go ahead. I don't mind if the lion doesn't." He was amazed at how offhandedly he'd spoken, how self-assured he felt. The girl stepped around the side of her desk and rubbed the lion's head. It nuzzled between her thighs and she looked at Harry and blushed. He'd never made a girl blush before.

Harry's office was an eight-foot windowless cube; he left the door open. It was another atypical action and he considered it as he pulled the cover from his adding machine. He wasn't the sort of person who deluded himself. Logical and practical were Harry's words; he was a very precise man whose innate shyness was a barrier only to those who didn't know him well. In comfortable company he was known for a sense of humor that extended heavily into bad puns.

He looked down at the lion; it had curled up under his desk and gone to sleep. He pushed off his shoe and scratched the lion on the back of the neck with his toes. It arched against the pressure and began to purr, a low rumbling sound that made Harry feel warm inside.

Harry settled into his normal routine. He was nearly finished with the Krepps file when his supervisor, Werner

Schranz, came into the room. Schranz had a cobra coiled around his shoulder and the two heads swayed in unison.

"Haven't you finished Krepps yet?"

The lion growled; its lips curled back. The cobra reared, tongue flicking swiftly in and out. Harry knew the cobra was afraid; he could see that fear echoed in Schranz's eyes. But he also knew it would strike if pressed. There was a matter of discretion here that had to be carefully considered.

"No, I haven't, Mr. Schranz," he said. "It should be ready in half an hour."

"Leave it on my desk before you go to lunch." Schranz spun on his heel and walked out.

"So Schranz has a cobra." Harry whispered the words in a heavy German accent. It was the first animal he'd seen since he left his apartment he could be sure was the same sort as his lion. There had been people with dogs, a cat or two and even a horse, but they were animals he was used to seeing every day. Harry wondered if there were mythical animals as well. How would dragons and unicorns stack up against his lion—and there was that man on the subway with a cantaloupe. Was there a limit?

He signed his name on the bottom of the cover sheet and flipped the Krepps account on Schranz's desk as he walked down the hall. The redheaded receptionist was getting ready to go to lunch too; she smiled when she saw him. What was her name? Janice.

"Do you know," he said, smiling back at her, "it strikes me that on a day like today a man should have lunch with a beautiful woman."

"Why Mr. Williams." Coy, yet. Harry couldn't remember a woman ever being coy with him.

"It's noon, Janice, a magic hour when business ceases to be business. My name is Harry." The lion rubbed against her leg and she blushed for the second time that day.

"Harry," she said. She looked up at him quizzically, with her head turned slightly to one side. The lion brushed her knee and she took Harry's hand as they walked into the elevator.

It was a warm day for Christmastime in New York. The temperature was close to sixty and there must have been a thousand people between 58th and 60th Streets: Christmas shoppers coming out of Bloomingdale's and Alexander's, businessmen, secretaries—and animals. There was a bear; over on

Third Avenue Harry could see a donkey following a fat man in a gray suit; there was even an elephant.

Harry guided Janice down Lexington Avenue toward a little Greek restaurant he'd always meant to try. The tables were small, designed for couples, and Harry had never gone in because he'd always been alone. She brushed against him as they walked, her hip against his thigh, and he released her hand to pull her closer. She put her head on his shoulder.

There was a green neon sign above a door near the restaurant. Hotel. Janice's arm was around Harry's back at the waist and she tightened her grip as they passed it. Harry was scarcely conscious of opening the door. The lion bounded up the stairs ahead of them, its tail straight out.

There was a desk in the alcove at the top of the stairs and the man behind it never raised his eyes from his newspaper. He didn't give Harry change from a twenty either, just a key. Room seven. The next flight of stairs curled around at the top; the lion was waiting for them. Room seven was at the end of the hall.

Janice leaned against him and Harry stopped on the landing and kissed her tenderly on the forehead. Her arms went around him and she arched her body. He could feel her nipples through his shirt; she was on tiptoe and their hips met. Harry kissed the top of her head and they moved down the hall toward room seven. The lion was waiting for them at the door.

Harry opened his eyes to the sound of running water; Janice was bent over the washbasin. He watched her dry her face and slip the dress down over her head. She came toward him and smiled when she saw he was awake.

"Hi."

"Hi yourself, Harry Williams." She knelt by the bed and kissed him. "Aren't you getting up? We have to get back to work."

"Work." The last thing Harry wanted to do was go back to Batten, Barton and Bloom and face Werner Schranz. "Not me," he said. "Not today. I feel like just lyin' around."

Janice giggled and hugged him. Harry tried to pull her onto the bed, but he couldn't move his arm. The lion was in bed with him. Janice saw the look on his face and reached over him to scratch the lion behind its ears. "Well, I've got to go back," she said, "even if you don't." She stood and walked toward the door.

"Janice?" Harry raised his head from the pillow and Janice turned. "I'll see you tomorrow," he said.

She blew him a kiss. "Tomorrow," she said, "and don't forget to bring your lion."

Janice was out the door before what she'd said registered. He pulled his arm from underneath the lion's stomach; it began to tingle as the circulation came back. He rubbed his elbow. He shouldn't have let the lion climb into bed with him; it was too heavy. Heavy? He hadn't even felt it when it was lying on his chest and now it was too heavy. The lion was gaining substance. Harry sat straight up in bed; for the first time he was afraid. Don't forget to bring your lion. The lion rolled over and looked at Harry upside down; he scratched under its chin. He knew it wasn't just a lion; it was a part of him, and he couldn't force himself to be afraid of it.

The temperature had dropped sharply; Harry raised his collar and pulled it tight as he stepped back onto Lexington Avenue. He was almost to 59th Street before he realized what he was doing. I don't want to go back there, he thought. He turned and started walking briskly toward Grand Central Station; sixteen blocks would give him time to decide. His mood had changed; he didn't feel like a man with a lion any more.

Harry tried to clear his mind by watching the people around him; perhaps he could get some clue from the other animals. All men are created equal, he thought, except some of us have lions. *Schranz had a cobra.* Was the man really that coldblooded? *Yes.* The snake didn't follow Schranz, he carried it. Harry held the image in his mind; there was something there he should have noticed. *The wall.* He'd been able to see the wall through the snake's body; was Schranz absorbing it, or was it just now emerging? Why did he carry it? There seemed to be a difference between the kind of animal that followed and the kind that had to be carried. Harry looked up. The lion was ahead of him and he reached out and grabbed its tail.

"I may not know what I'm doing," he said, "but you're the one that's following me." He pulled the lion backward; it seemed lighter than it had in the hotel room. He wondered if it were possible to control it, to make the lion work for him.

"Hey, man, you got some change?" There were four of them in front of the Graybar Building, three girls and a boy. One of the girls shook a paper cup with some coins in it.

Harry stopped and looked at them. This particular lifestyle was repulsive to him because in his own orderly scheme of things security was paramount. "You shouldn't be doing this," he said.

"Come on, man, we asked you for money, not a lecture." "Yeah, man, what's with you?" Harry knew all four of them were speaking, but the voices seemed to come from one point in the center of the group. "You don't like what we do, move on." "Yeah, what makes you so special?" He pointed to the lion; the tone of their voices changed.

"Oh wow, is that your lion?" "Hey, man, we didn't mean anything, you know." One of the girls, wearing a long blue print dress and a fur jacket that looked like it had been made in 1931, knelt and stroked the lion's head. She looked at Harry and he had the distinct impression she knew something he didn't. They all knew.

"That's a nice lion," the girl said. "Have you had her long?"

Harry shook his head. "Not very."

"Oh wow, she's big."

The four of them encircled Harry, each with a hand on his shoulder. "Come with us?" they said. Harry nodded.

With Harry in the center, they skipped down 45th Street, across Third Avenue and up two flights of stairs to a third-story loft furnished in Early American Head Shop. There were posters on the walls and multicolored drapes hanging from the ceiling. Harry could smell at least four different kinds of incense. He sat in an old red armchair; the lion curled up at his feet. There'd been a chair like that in the living room of his parents' home in Lynbrook and he felt very comfortable. He remembered the way his father had looked, sitting in that chair.

The four were rushing around the loft, looking for something; but they weren't an amorphous group to him now, they were individuals. Bas was the girl in the fur jacket; she had straight brown hair, a long open face and freckles. Aggie was wearing a woolen maxicoat with a large rip in the side; the lining was coming out. Ginger was adorably fat, and Ralph could have been a faun.

"Aha. I have it." Ginger stood on the couch holding a harmonica over her head. She looked vaguely like the Statue of Liberty. "We shall have music wherever we go," she said. They lined up facing Harry, as if for inspection. Bas and Ralph were at the ends, Ginger and Aggie in the middle.

Aggie grabbed one of Harry's hands and Bas took the other; they became the middle of a chain winding in and out through the Christmas crowds. They ran down 42nd Street, and Harry watched the people. Some stared openly; others turned their heads, remarking either to their companions or to anyone who cared to listen. Some smiled, and Harry smiled back.

They formed a circle around a gray-haired woman in a black coat and played ring-around-a-rosie. Her name *was* Rosie, and when they got up she kissed Harry on the cheek.

At the library, Harry climbed one of the stone lions. He waved his arms and tried to remember the signals he'd learned when he was a Boy Scout. *His* lion put its paws on the stone and looked at him. "Have you been lyin' to me," he said.

They sat in an empty fountain; Bas pretended she was the water and flowed over all of them. Aggie decided she was a boat lost in the fog and began to hoot. Ralph and Ginger were whales, mating; they leaped high in the air and held each other until they came down with a splash. Harry was an island. He lay on his back with his elbow in his navel to designate a palm tree and didn't know how cold he'd been until after he'd gotten up.

Harry was a traffic cop in the middle of Fifth Avenue. The girls said he looked like a Maypole and danced around him while Ralph played the harmonica.

Harry was explaining numbers to Bas when the man walked into him. He had a large cantaloupe in his right hand; his grip on it tightened and his eyes narrowed. Harry was almost six feet tall. The man dwarfed him.

"You dumb little . . ." The muscles between the man's neck and shoulder stood out; Harry stepped backward wtih his arms up protectively. The man saw the lion and froze. The tension in his face relaxed; the anger in his eyes was replaced by a look of pity—and fear.

"Oh jeez, guy," he said. "I didn't know. God, I'm sorry. Oh Lord, a lion." He shook his head; there were tears in the corners of his eyes. "A lion." He banged the cantaloupe against his thigh and grabbed Harry's shoulder with his left hand. "I wish I could tell you," he said. "I just wish I could let you know what it's like." He shook his head again and walked on down the street. When he reached the corner he tucked the cantaloupe under his arm.

"I had a job once, in a garage . . . selling tires." Ralph's voice drew Harry back into the group. They seemed to have ignored the entire incident.

"Tires have to be balanced, you know. Otherwise they wobble . . . wear out too quickly. Sometimes, when a tire's been on a car for a while, the balance changes—or maybe it wasn't right to begin with. You put it on a machine called a bubble balance to see which way it leans, and then you hammer a counterweight on the other side. Lots of different weights, all in a big pail. You don't always get the right one and then you have to spin the tire and put another weight somewhere else."

"That's one of the reasons I love numbers," Harry said. "They don't do that. You don't have to guess what's going to balance, you always know how it's going to turn out." He was part of the group again; the man with the cantaloupe didn't matter.

Bas walked over to Harry. She pressed her face against his chest and hugged him. "It's better not to guess," she said. "Sometimes it's better not to know at all."

Ginger hugged him too, and Aggie. "We love you, Harry Williams," Ginger said. "We love everybody, but we especially love you because you are Harry Williams."

It was after three a.m. when Harry said goodbye. He walked down 45th Street toward the subway, remembering. It wasn't just the lion. They liked him because he was Harry Williams. They wanted him to come back and see them again. He would.

"Well what do we have here?" A man stepped out of the subway entrance. He had a knife. "A little late to be out on the street, isn't it, man-in-the-suit?" The knife was shaking and Harry saw the man's knees were shaking too. He was wearing a ragged brown overcoat and baggy pants easily two sizes too big. He had no hat and his ears were red from the cold.

He moved toward Harry, backing him against the wall. "You're going to be very nice and give me your wallet, aren't you, man-in-the-suit?" He was talking too much, and there was something wrong with his eyes. He seemed to be having a hard time focusing them. He took another step toward

Harry and his knee buckled. Harry caught his arm and the knife dropped to the sidewalk.

There was sweat on the man's forehead. "You're sick, buddy," Harry said. "You're running a fever—hey, when was the last time you ate?" The man ran his hand along the sidewalk, feeling for the knife. Harry kicked it down the stairs. "You don't need that," he said. "I'm not going to hurt you."

His name was George and he said he'd been a dentist. A long time ago. Harry wanted to believe him, but he didn't. It didn't seem to matter. Harry helped him to the all-night restaurant on the corner. He was coughing, having a hard time standing up. Harry gave him twenty dollars because it would help—for a while.

"Why are you doing this?" George said. Harry didn't answer. He wasn't sure, he'd just done it. He turned away and started back for the subway. He wasn't sure about a lot of things. Bas, Ralph, Ginger, Aggie. The man with the cantaloupe. George-the-dentist. Janice. Nothing was the same any more. There were people in his life. He was a man with a lion.

The lion. He turned to look at it and at first he thought it wasn't there. The lion was almost transparent; he could see the light from the street lamp through it. Harry knelt and the lion laid its head on his thigh; he stroked where the top of its head should have been. His hand kept slipping through.

The lion licked Harry's face. Its tongue wasn't even wet. Its fur seemed to crackle, tiny blue flashes that lasted only fractions of seconds. The lion began to shimmer, like a reflection in a moonlit pool. Harry felt a strange sensation at the back of his neck; his shoulders hunched in reflex and the lion disappeared.

Harry started slowly down the stairs, but when he felt the urge to run he followed it without question. He was the lion now. He vaulted over the turnstile, not even glancing over his shoulder to see what the man in the token booth thought, and dashed down the stairs to the uptown platform. The Express was ready to pull out and he slipped through the doors just as they were closing.

Harry was the only person in the car, but he stood as the train rattled and shook through the tunnel and out into the winter night at Yankee Stadium. Each time it stopped he barely shifted his weight. Perfect balance, he thought. Like a cat. He was down the stairs at Burnside before the doors fully opened, on the street before the train started moving again.

Harry's apartment was dark, but he could see everything: the clock in the alcove, the pictures on the wall, the open bedroom door and Martha, a gray-white lump in the middle of the bed. He kicked the bed and watched her jiggle. Things were going to be different now.

He opened the closet door and reached for his pajamas. The kangaroo was wearing boxing gloves and it hit him in the mouth.

The Breath of Dragons

by J. Michael Reaves

J. Michael Reaves is a twenty-two-year-old Californian who alternates college study with a variety of what he describes as "meager jobs." He is unhappy in San Bernardino, a condition he says he shares with a good number of people.

Of "The Breath of Dragons," he says: ". . . most of what I write comes out nowhere near what I have in mind when I begin. This one was that way—it came from flying through storm clouds over O'Hare on my way to Michigan. The story damn near wrote itself. I sat back and watched, and every now and then walked out in the hall and joined in the watergun wars. I would come back drenched, and the story would still be going. I wish everything I wrote was this easy."

They flew over milky seas, pierced by an archipelago of mountain peaks, scudded into slow-motion waves by the wind. They were alone in the vast emptiness that lay between the clouds and the sky, hurtling silent miles over white quiet. Swerving to avoid the icy mountains that thrust from the hidden world below, dipping occasionally to scatter mile-wide crescents of vapor foam that gleamed in the sun. Searching, hunting. Dragon hunting.

"There's one," Cunningham said, pointing to the east. Perrin squinted into the early morning sun, saw a black silhouette with wings, rising. He swallowed nervously.

"Your first dragon, Perrin," Cunningham said, making a wide slow bank, coming in with the sun at their back. "I'll line it up for you. Remember, don't aim for the chest, or you'll hit the flame bladder. Try for a haunch shot."

Perrin could see it clearly now. It looked like a pterodactyl—ribbed, membranous wings, long pointed tail. Cunningham was throttling down, and Perrin lined the dragon up in the crosshairs of the scope. He took careful hold of the trigger. The feeling was at once more and less than he'd expected

—frightening, yes, the fear every Dragonhunter was supposed to feel before the harpoon snaked from its sheath, and yet—so distant, so antiseptic. So impersonal. He felt pity for the beast.

"It's not going to wait forever, Perrin," Cunningham said. "I'm surprised it hasn't flamed already. Shoot!"

Perrin set his teeth and pulled the trigger.

At that instant, he felt the huntship lurch violently, half heard Cunningham's startled yell, and then his head slammed against the headrest. He could smell the scorched asbestos padding. Through the bubble, against a world tilted sideways, he saw a second dragon, larger than the first, climbing in a steep loop. Bits of flame trailed from the center nostril. The gout of fire had struck full against the stern. The second dragon brought up sharply, catching air under furred wings, hanging motionless for a second before falling away. And for an instant's length of time that lasted forever, Perrin stared into the dragon's eyes.

He felt chilled, as if the icy rarefied air outside the bubble had blown over him.

Cunningham had grabbed the stabilizing sticks and pulled them together, leveling out. The ship was jerking in a peculiar, regular fashion. Perrin turned his head, and saw that the first dragon had been hit, more by luck than skill. Cunningham swore at the second dragon while he steered toward one of the peaks where he could drop the impaled one, instead of losing it beneath the cloud layer. Perrin, still dazed, saw the second dragon coming up fast, too fast, saw the gush of flaming ambergreen blossom almost lazily from the third nostril, and sear its way through the steel harpoon cable. The harpooned dragon fell away, and the ship, lightened, shot skyward.

"God damn," Cunningham was saying, over and over again. "God *damn.* That's never happened before. I've never seen two attack at once before . . ." He pulled the ship into a long turn, coming about until the peak was before them again.

The second dragon was gone. Cunningham approached cautiously—the hull wouldn't be able to stand another burst of ambergreen.

Then, suddenly jubilant, he elbowed Perrin. "Look!"

Below them, black against an ice cliff, hung the dead dragon. The harpoon cable had caught in a crevice, and the creature was dangling against the cliff, perhaps ten feet from the cloud layer.

"Pure luck," Cunningham said, gloating. "If the cable hadn't caught in that crack, we would have lost it for sure. Now, let's see you bring the ship in as close as you can. I'll have to take the sling-seat down, so you'd damned well better hold it steady."

"Cunningham . . ." Perrin said. He felt numbed, removed from what was happening. The memory of what he had seen in the dragon's yellow eyes filled his mind. He had killed his first and last dragon, he wanted to say. But the Dragonhunter was already preparing the sling-seat, and gathering the necessary tools. Perrin took the sticks and brought the hovering craft in closer.

Thirty feet above the body, he locked the controls and slipped on his oxygen mask. Cunningham popped the hatch, and the ship filled with sudden intense cold that Perrin could feel even through his insulated suit. "Lower away," Cunningham shouted.

Perrin pushed the button, watched through the transparent bubble as Cunningham swung down to the dragon. This close, he could see what he had known before—that the dragon was not reptilian. No reptile could survive at thirty thousand feet. The nightmare body was covered with thick brown fur. Cunningham drove spikes into the wings and neck, to hold it more securely. They went in easily; the bones were hollow, not filled with air cells, like birds' bones, but tubular, thin sheaths of calcium covered with the powerful muscles that drove the wings.

The Dragonhunter sliced away the skin, exposing the armored chest cavity. With a quick movement, he ripped off the carapace. Beneath was the flame bladder, a brown leather sac. Perrin exhaled. He had heard of episodes in which the harpoon had punctured the bladder, and the removal of the carapace had exposed the ambergreen to air. The resulting explosion could shatter a peak.

Cunningham tied off the sphincter and severed the cartilage that held the bladder in place. Perrin raised the sling-seat, leaving the dead dragon pinned against the ice wall.

Crucified, Perrin thought.

The yellow eyes were still open, staring. He wished he could somehow reach out his hand and close them.

"Full day's work, and it's not even noon yet," Cunningham said, as he settled down in his flightseat. "If you're lucky,

Perrin, you might get one of these in every three months. Usually it takes all day just to find one of the bastards. And then, likely as not, the bladder'll be empty, all flamed out. I'll let you take her back to Base." He settled down into his seat, and went to sleep.

Perrin stared at him, and thought about the flame bladder in the vacuum hold. Filled with ambergreen, a clear organic gel with a combustion ratio hundreds of times more intense than napalm. Ambergreen, a hypergolic secretion that, when ejected from the dragon's third nostril, exploded into a fireball capable of melting a steel cable. Ambergreen. The breath of dragons.

Look at him, Perrin thought, as he brought the ship away from the peak. A fat bull of a man, sleeping easily, with no conscience qualms. How could he be so blind?

How could they all be? How could the slaughter have gone on these past two years, without anyone seeing the truth, without anyone realizing the crime the Dragonhunters were guilty of?

The crime was murder. Perrin knew. He had looked into the dragon's eyes.

He tried to tell them. He went to Calbert, the on-planet director of Ambergreen Enterprises.

"Look, Perrin," Calbert said, "the scientists have been trying to decide whether or not dragons can think ever since we started hunting them. That's been almost two years. So far, they haven't come up with any real evidence that these things have minds. They've got brainpans that are large in proportion to their bodies, true. So do elephants, for that matter. One of the most common signs of intelligence or potential intelligence in aliens is the evolution of an opposable thumb. Dragons don't have thumbs, Perrin. They don't even have hands."

"Dolphins—"

"I was waiting for you to bring up dolphins," Calbert said wearily.

"They've been proved to be a sentient race," Perrin went on. "They don't have hands. Are you so blind to history that you can't admit the possibility of another civilization that doesn't build machines?"

"Sure, I'll admit the possibility. But only as a possibility. Anything's possible. The dragons may be intelligent. Elephants may be too. That didn't stop the market for ivory, and I can't let an unproved rumor concerning these *beasts* block us in obtaining ambergreen. I have orders to fill, Perrin. Ambergreen is used for everything from spot-welding to surgery. Until someone figures out how to synthesize it, the dragons are our only source."

"Today," Perrin said, "two dragons attacked the huntship I was taking my final training flight in. Two of them, simultaneously. Isn't it true that dragons have never before been known to operate in tandem, except during the mating process?"

"So you're saying that because two dragons performed the same action at the same time—"

"One was acting as bait, the other attacked from behind—"

"—that merely because two of the creatures happened to turn on you at once, you now have proof of intelligence?"

"If you had *seen*—"

"Cunningham was there," Calbert said. "He saw. He says that there's no reason to consider this as anything other than what it was—two dragons that happened to attack at the same time. It's unusual, no more.

"Do you have any more arguments, Perrin?"

The look in a dragon's eye, Perrin thought. That spine-chilling glare of hatred, of *understanding,* when the harpoon hit its mate. It was something no one, having seen, could fail to comprehend.

But how could he convince them?

"All right," he said. "You won't believe. Well, just wait. I'll be proved right eventually, you'll see. Until then, I refuse to hunt any more dragons."

Calbert stood up, his hands on the desk. "Perrin, I don't know why you signed on to be a Dragonhunter. But you did, and that means you *will* hunt dragons, and kill them too. You don't have an option to quit—you work until the next freighter puts in, or you'll go to jail for evasion of contract. And you won't get paid. Clear, Perrin?"

Perrin stood stiffly, a small muscle in his cheek jumping. Then, abruptly, he turned and left.

He ate by himself in the mess hall. The talk of the other Dragonhunters, their descriptions of the killing they had done that day, sickened him. He ate quickly, stopping once to move when someone sat down next to him. Calbert was right, damn him—the contract, once signed, indentured him for six months, until the freighter came. He had signed on a

TRUE

TRUE
20 CLASS A CIGARETTES
TRUE

month ago, knowing it was dangerous work. But he had been unable to hold other jobs, unable to work with people. The thought of flying alone in the cold air of another world had appealed to Perrin. Now there was no way out.

He had to kill dragons. He had no other choice.

His room was almost as small as his huntship. He lay in his bunk, able to touch both walls with his fingers. When he finally slept, he dreamed nightmares of huntships that chased him across the clouds.

On solo for the first time, Perrin rode the clear pure air above the mist. He gave reports and positions when the Base Monitor demanded them. The huntship soared in a straight line, except when Perrin found it necessary to avoid the mountain peaks, which gleamed like icebergs in the sun.

If they only *were* beasts, he hought. It was not a crime to kill animals. Why was he so sure that the dragons were sentient? The evidence of a single eye-to-eye encounter with an alien creature was not conclusive. He could not know for certain. He could not be sure.

And yet he was.

A black shape rose suddenly before him. Perrin grabbed the sticks, leveled off quickly. The flame crackled past him. He spun the ship as tightly as possible, and was face to face with the dragon.

A perfect shot . . . he grabbed the trigger, tensed for the movement that would send the harpoon plunging right between the dragon's eyes . . .

Perrin stared. He couldn't pull the trigger, shoved both sticks down instead, and felt the heat through the thermoplastic as the dragon's breath washed over the ship. Then he was plunging down; he leveled off only feet above the cloud layer, and opened the throttle. The ship hurtled away across the clouds like a stone skipping across a sea.

His hands were shivering. He gulped several times, tried to control his trembling.

He killed no dragons that day. He flew in great, looping paths until the sun was low in the afternoon. Then he headed back to Base.

He brought the huntship down slowly into the main hold. As he stepped off the rack, one of the ground men opened the vacuum compartment, and pulled out the empty plastic sack.

"Not much luck first time out, eh?" He grinned at Perrin. Behind him, Perrin could see other ships being unloaded, the men carting the flame bladders in airtight sacks to the processing labs. Someone put a hand on his shoulder, and he turned nervously.

It was Cunningham, with another hunter. He said, "Perrin, shake hands with Malquist. He just broke our quota record. Four dragons in one day."

Perrin looked at Malquist. The man was tall, and almost as thin as he was, but not nearly as pale. His hair was full, not balding at the temples. Looking at Malquist's grin, he was aware of his own pinched features. He disliked the man. "Congratulations," he said, and the tone of his voice made Malquist quit smiling. "Did you bring their heads back for trophies? How does it feel to be a murderer?"

"What's the matter with you, Perrin?" Cunningham asked, frowning.

Perrin folded his arms. "I'm curious, that's all." He began to rock back and forth, slightly, on the balls of his feet. "I'm wondering what kind of conscienceless bastard can murder four intelligent beings and then smile about it."

"Now, look . . ." Malquist started, surprised.

"I'm looking. I don't care much for what I see."

"Let's go," Cunningham said, to Malquist. He pulled the tall man away, talking in a low tone. Malquist glanced back once at Perrin, who stood staring after them, his hidden hands bunched into fists, and shrugged.

If there was a way to communicate, he thought, tightening his grip on the sticks, feeling the ship accelerate beneath him. If there were some way to show them that the Dragonhunters weren't aware of what they had been doing . . .

He saw the flash of another huntship, ahead and to his left, pursuing a dragon. The dragon was dropping toward the clouds, the ship attempting to line up a shot before it could vanish beneath the mist.

Perrin swiveled the scope around, and got a better look at the ship. He could read the insignia—it was Malquist's ship. He took a deep breath, and swerved toward it.

Murderer, he thought.

He came in low and fast, just skimming the clouds, coming up from below Malquist's ship. The man wouldn't rack up another four dragons today. He heard Malquist's voice over his radio. "Perrin, is that you coming up below me? What the hell—"

He pulled up sharply, flashing between the dragon and Malquist. The harpoon shot past him to the full extent of the cable, then dropped, to dangle from Malquist's ship like an absurd fishing line. "Perrin!" his radio screamed. He leveled off, twisted around in his flightseat, stared over his shoulder. His maneuver had startled Malquist—the crazy fool had veered, was coming too close to a peak—

"*No!*" Perrin screamed. The left wingtip brushed against a crag. Like a rock on the end of a string, the huntship swung around, angled up and then down, straight down, to disappear instantly into the cloud cover.

"Malquist!" Perrin shouted into the mike. "Malquist!" There was no reply. Then suddenly, the radio came on again. "Perrin, what's going on out there? What happened to Malquist?"

It was the Base Monitor's voice. Perrin was sobbing, the ship turning in endless, useless circles over the clouds. "Perrin! What—" He turned the receiver off.

He had to think, needed time to think. He brought the ship down on the peak, anchored it, then pulled an oxygen mask on. Without knowing quite why, he climbed out into the cold air, stood on a flat ice ledge, stared down into opaqueness. Malquist was probably still falling, maybe still alive. I didn't want this to happen, Perrin thought. I didn't want this to happen.

They'll accuse me of murder if I go back. But I have nowhere else to go. I didn't want this to happen. I couldn't let him kill the dragon. Perrin turned back toward the ship.

He froze, staring. Fifteen feet away, crouched gargoyle-like on a pinnacle next to the ship, the dragon watched him.

The twenty-five-foot wings were folded, batlike, against the body. The hammerhead was split with gleaming white teeth. It only looks evil, he thought. That leer is its natural expression.

For long minutes, the dragon watched Perrin. Perrin stood immobile, trying to forget his terror by concentrating his attention on the sheen that the sun brought to the dragon's fur, the way the membranous skin rippled in the slight wind. It's almost beautiful, he thought. Noble and powerful . . . he felt his fear lessening. Then suddenly the dragon opened its wings, loomed over him. He heard a loud hiss, but no flame belched from the center nostril. With a flap that sent Perrin sprawling, the dragon swooped gracefully from the crag, in a long low glide. Perrin watched it shrink to a black dot floating over white.

He stumbled back to the ship, pulled the thermoplastic dome into place over him. He had been right—they *knew*. They understood. The dragon had recognized him as the one who had saved him from Malquist's harpoon, and had spared his life in return. Perrin was sure of it.

But he had no proof. If he tried to tell the Dragonhunters, they would merely say that the dragon's bladder had been flamed out, empty. No. The only thing that Calbert and the rest of them would believe was that he was directly responsible for Malquist's death.

He had to prove to them that he was right, show them that Malquist had not died for nothing. Perrin could not bear the thought of Malquist's blood on his hands, in addition to the dragon he'd killed.

Something moving across the bright blue dome, shadows rippling across clouds . . . Perrin stared across the miles at the five black specks approaching. Dragons? One of them glimmered, an instant's reflection of the sun against plastic.

Huntships!

They couldn't be after him. Not yet. He had to think of a way to make them understand first.

The peak fell away from him; in a long wide glide, he shot toward the horizon, skimming over the paper-white ocean. He turned on the receiver.

"Perrin!" His name crackled. He did not answer. He fled from them over the cloud floor, toward the mountain range known as Planet's Teeth, a serrated line of icy mountaintops protruding from the clouds. Once lost among those sawtooth peaks, he would have time to think, to plan whatever it was he would have to do, to make Calbert and the others understand.

"Perrin!" The radio came to life again—it was Cunningham's voice. Perrin ignored him, teeth clenched, but did not turn it off. "Perrin, running isn't going to work. There's no place to go. You'll run out of food and air eventually. Come about; no one's going to hurt you."

They would take him and lock him up in another of their little cages at the Base. And the slaughter would go on. He was the only one who could stop it.

"Perrin! This is your last warning. If you continue holding to your present course, we're going to open fire."

He could see Planet's Teeth ahead, a line of glittering fangs jutting from the whiteness. He pushed the sticks forward as far as they would go.

There was a burst of smoke to his right, a muffled puff of sound that he left behind almost immediately. *It's not fair,* his mind screamed.

He felt a tremendous impact; the ship angled crazily. Perrin held onto the sticks. He was slowing, and he could smell the stench of the asbestos padding . . .

The first peak was coming up too fast. He pulled back, saw the ice and snow hurtling toward him, blotting out the sky. Then the screaming, scraping slide across the ice, the crumpling metallic noises that he never quite heard, until it was quiet, finally, except for the drifting of ice particles across his face.

He felt the blood freezing on his cheek. He felt it elsewhere, flowing too fast to freeze, warm down his side. It steamed when it touched the snow.

Through one eye uncovered by ice, he saw jagged clear plastic cutting into the sky, and beyond it, all around him, the concealing jumble of rock. He would not be found.

Then a dragon circled slowly overhead. Two. He watched them coming closer in slow lazy loops, saw the gleam of sunlight on their teeth. He stared up from where he lay, broken and bleeding, half buried in the snow and the fragments of the ship, into their eyes. And he knew he was right, had been right all along.

He began to feel the pain. The dragons dropped closer. Perrin watched them, dark and magnificent in the sky. Someone would prove him right. Someone else would try, and maybe succeed. I didn't want it to end this way, Perrin thought.

The pain was worse now. Much worse. The last color he saw was the yellow of the dragons' gaze, before he closed his one eye. Please, he thought.

And felt the breath of dragons.

The Source

by Kate Wilhelm

My father had many wonderful and strange friends. One of them was the captain of a steamboat on Lake Erie. One morning a puppy appeared on his boat, and since he couldn't keep a dog aboard with him, he gave him to my father. They promptly named the puppy Steamboat. He wasn't anything special, mixed breed, probably not very handsome, although I remember thinking he was beautiful, but my mother always said he could understand every word spoken to him, and he could all but speak in return. I can't remember getting the dog, only having it, just as I remember having my brothers and sister. They were there, part of the family from year one of my memory. The dog died when I was still quite young, six at the most. I experienced grief, bereavement, the guilt of not having been as good as I should have been to the dog. And I witnessed the grief of the others around me. There have been other bereavements since then, but none that has been more bitterly felt.

There was another friend, a circus clown, who used to perform his tightrope act for us. Even now I can see the setting: woods behind a clearing, a small house that was gray, a picnic table with many bowls of food all covered by a white-and-blue checked cloth to keep the flies off until after the show, and a dozen children sitting in the grass impatiently waiting. Then the magical clown in full costume appeared, as alien to me then as anything I have been able to imagine since. Awe, amazement, delight, joy, and strangely, a sense of something not unlike fear, because he was so different from the man I had seen drinking beer with my father only minutes before. Selves within selves, the other side of the personality, a hidden inner being, a strangeness not to be fathomed by the child, not yet to be quite understood by the adult, but a sense of the mystery of being.

That afternoon I felt all those things, and those things have been a continuing theme in my fiction from the beginning. Of course, I, the child, didn't say to myself: what is the reality behind the appearance? But that question was there in the non-verbalized wonderings, and it was there through the years when the memory returned again and again of that afternoon when the clown walked the tightrope. I think now that that afternoon may have ruined circuses for me for all time, however. The one small intimate glimpse of fantasy was much purer and much more direct than a circus could ever be.

How many kinds of fear and even terror does a child experience? Who knows? There was the fear of having to swim to shore from a sandbar in the lake. There was the terror of being on top of a ferris wheel. The fear was manageable, because I did swim back safely, but the terror was different. It was the terror of being in a situation where everything was out of my personal control, where the outside world had suddenly shown itself as not manipulable. There was still another kind of panic when I became separated from my mother in a very large library and wandered out a strange door into an even stranger world that I had never seen before. Too young to identify myself, to give my address, I was taken to a police station and cared for and fed candy and ice cream until I was claimed. Actually I could tell my name and address very well, but in a speech that no one could yet understand. Therapy when I was five corrected that, but the feeling of helplessness and panic that I experienced would be remembered, undimmed, unmodified through all the years. Today if I want a character to experience a situation where he is utterly helpless, where the world is suddenly too large and incomprehensible and uncomprehending, where panic comes in waves that bring nausea, I have exactly the right memory to create it.

There was an appendectomy before I was six, with the traumatic anesthesia-death, and separation from family, and pain. Times of loving, of being loved, of being held warm and safe on a lap, of being read to and touched and caressed. Feelings of being alone in a great city as I walked to and from school, or to the corner store. The amazement of seeing a small creature turn savage, when my father brought home an injured blue jay that immediately attacked everything in sight.

One last experience: a long sloping hill that led down to the lake, people everywhere on the grassy hillside, and a very dark sky with millions of stars steady and bright. Lying on my back I stared at the points in the sky until my eyes hurt, then erupted a sudden burst of fireworks, and the sky blazed, and the noise shook my bones and seemed to stay inside me even after my ears could hear it no more. Something that I couldn't identify until long afterward was awakened that night. Many times I came back to that Fourth of July display with a feeling of almost grasping something that was elusive, and that it was a powerful something was evident to me even then because of the way I could, and did, relive that night, down to the feel of the cool grass on my legs and arms, and the feel of the earth under my head. A child seldom explains his experiences to himself in words; he lives them, that's enough. But unless they are verbalized, they remain sensory, kinesthetic memories that must be relived if their true meaning is ever to be discovered, and it was in this way that I worried about that night, and wondered and tried to understand what it had meant to me. I remembered watching a blue starburst rise, rise, spreading as it went until it filled the sky, and the real stars vanished. Then the starburst was gone, and even though my eyes couldn't see them, I knew the other stars were there, that I would see them again. I think at that moment I came to some kind of awareness about scale, man's scale in the universe. It took me many years to realize, to verbalize this understanding.

Three decades passed and I stood on the Cape and watched a moon launch, and instantly there was a replay of that fireworks display: again I saw the blue starburst, and felt the noise inside me, and felt the grass under me, and all the while I watched the fiery white and yellow rocket trail and felt a vibration that continued long after audible sound was gone. With the two experiences merging into one, those nonverbalized feelings of the child seemed clearer somehow, and I began to understand why that scene had stayed so alive in my mind for so many years.

This seems perhaps material for an analyst's couch, or a book of memoirs: *How I Got To Where I Am Today,* subtitled, "But Where Is That?" I feel the search is continuing, the search for some kind of understanding of myself, or the world around me, the people in it, the mysterious inner selves that appear and vanish, the efforts of man that appear and vanish, the enduring stars.

Often a child will ask: Do you remember when . . . ? The question will be about an event that the adult has forgotten completely. To the child it was important, and it will endure as one of those primary emotional experiences; to the adult it was another of the endless happenings in the daily life of his child, who might even seem to be having a very dull life. But, in fact, he is filling a storehouse, his memory bank, with the happenings that record his emotional development.

I have never written one of those childhood experiences as it actually was lived; that is not where their usefulness lies, after all. My childhood was very little different from anyone else's. What child hasn't been certain that he was lost, abandoned? What child hasn't suffered from fever dreams, or unconsciousness, or anesthesia? What child hasn't suffered the irrevocable loss of a loved pet, or toy, or even a person who was very close to him? Nothing is unique about most childhood experiences. And in that lies the power. It is the commonplace that is communicable, that is universal, that is invaluable to the writer.

It isn't the objective fact of being lost that is the gain; it is the emotional impact. It was not the clown's face, or the act; it was the glimpse, my first glimpse, of one of the masks of man. And the wonder it aroused. And the first uncertain comprehension about scale can come about in many ways. I believe I watched it happen with my young son when he refused to acknowledge the ocean, turned his back on it and refused to see it for weeks. Scale, and man's place in the universe, and his mortality, all those concepts are signified in that one refusal to see the ocean. These are concepts only when they become verbalized; until then they are emotional experiences that arouse fear, awe, wonder, love, the many varied responses of children, never fully comprehended by the adult.

It is this primary childish emotion that is lived and felt without verbalization, without rationalization, without understanding that is the stuff of fiction. I know what it is to steal—didn't I swipe my brother's marbles? I know what it is to cheat and lie. I know what it is to love and hate and be abandoned and lost, and feel mystery and awe. We all know these things. I don't say that everything I write draws on these experiences consciously, but they have shaped my reactions to the world, and they are there to be drawn on, and when I don't use them, the work is flat and secondhand.

A writer may travel the world, may engage in myriad enterprises, jobs, adventures, may keep countless notebooks about places and people, but when it comes to writing people that live in fiction, he can only turn inward for the understanding that permits his characters to come to life. He can collect experiences as a child collects sea shells. He cannot change his childhood, and there is no need to. There is no emotional experience that he can suffer, or enjoy, in his adult life that can compare to the first, most immediate experience that he has in memory from his childhood.

Through the realization of one of these basic primary, childhood emotions he is able to give depth and meaning to his characters. Here is where he has at hand the gradations of all emotional states. The selfless love of child for pet, the egocentric love of parent, the ambivalent relationship of siblings where love becomes hate in the moment it takes to snatch away a toy. Even love carried to excess in orgies of play where hysteria finally overcomes the child and makes him collapse in tears. Here are the nuances of everything we call fear; defined: *A feeling of alarm or disquiet caused by the expectation of danger, pain, disaster, or the like; terror; dread; apprehension* . . . Words, words, words. But you know that the fear of a reprimand is not the panic of finding yourself lost and abandoned. The terror of the ferris wheel is not the alarm caused by a rising temperature in an ill child. Definitions can't be enough to write about emotional states of characters in fiction. Reading other works is not enough. No two people experience exactly the same emotions, just as no two people have the same brain waves, or the same fingerprints, or the same voice patterns. All we can hope for is enough insight to be able to describe honestly our own emotional states so that our readers can accept them as true of our characters.

If the writer can learn to use his own experiences, not directly, but through translation, he has gained a tool of inestimable value. A character must have an intuitive grasp of a situation? Haven't most of us had just such a quantum leap in knowledge? Perhaps the knowledge of a death, not because anyone spoke of it, but rather because of the quality of the silences, the vehemence of the evasions, the tensions in the family, until finally the hole is defined by what is around it. This intuitively gained knowledge can be translated into other places, other situations, other characters in fiction. The feelings of sudden awareness don't change, only the objective data that surround such feelings. A character is afraid? What kind of fear? It is there. The cause of the fear is unimportant now but the feelings of this kind of fear, or that kind, they are there, waiting to be translated into a new situation in fiction.

This vast fund of knowledge is available to all of us. Who hasn't felt the physical pain of injury? Or the emotional pain of loss? Or the fear of falling? Or the joy of love? By the time the writer is old enough to start to write, it is too late to add one smidgin of authentic experience to this source, which is, in truth, already inexhaustible.

Servants

by David Wise

David Wise again, this time with a story inspired by William Carlos Williams' "Tract."

"Williams' poem deals with a man who feels he knows how to handle a funeral, while his fellow mourners do not, which is largely the situation of the narrator of this story. The science-fictional transmutation of the poem's meaning, however, is this: The dimensions of what (or who) is actually being buried are expanded to take in not only the townspeople, but the town itself.

The major-domo scuffled across the floor on all sixes, glasses of djurie-frost glistening subtly, suspended on a tray which he clasped professionally with one of his intermediary sets of limbs. Parties are something plain and regular. Banquets are something annual and special, and though we had not had one for more than two years, I did not think it was because we are dying out, although we are.

Once, someone from a world distant, who came here and is now trapped by what he calls "outrageous fortune," said that the banquets were a "custom." Because of that, they are now. But until the faraway one said the word "custom," the banquets had simply been the way everything was. I remember myself as a young Saer, lying close with my father on the day the banquets stopped being the way everything was and became broken up, fragmented, annual affairs, compacted imitations of life. I was a young Saer then, and my father wept mannish tears which struck me as stupid until I later realized what he was really crying about. The rest of the time now, as in substitute for the banquet-life, is boredom hastily coated with a veneer of work-and-playisms. Life is a laughable scuffling for making the time go, just as the major-domo scuffled toward me at that banquet, his six legs pumping like some ancient fire-generator. I could tell by the way his triple-jointed elbows swung that the dark side of his mind had no jagged, barren areas. It was overgrown, and an overgrown dark-sided mind can prove useful on non-banquetal occasions, though in this case this proved not to be. I needed a confidant for my own simplistic aims—someone to tell why I wanted and someone to tell me what I wanted all at the same time. Sitting at the banquet was my ultimate disguise, and I wanted to show it. I wanted to prove that I could be not myself as well as all of myself and this is not what I succeeded in doing. I succeeded in getting trapped with the major-domo.

Doubtless, I thought, he will see me and pretend not to notice. If I move one of my left feet just off to the side of the terroxide metal table, he might think I meant him to take sexual liberties with me, or did someone make that up? Surely if I move my center-hind arm up to one of my sets of shoulders, he will notice me, crawl forward abjectly while the other servants look on in admiration (for is it not the major-domo's right to be admired?) and beg to display his sundry and diverse talents before me, like visions out of a wormwood desk, or am I dreaming, knowing as I do what happened between the two of us? I do not wish to be judged for it, though I most likely will be.

We are a race which will be studied. We are a race which will soon cause no more actions which might later be mulled over by some studious alien group. They will talk of our golden age in melancholy tones, even though they were the ones who caused our golden age to pass, unknowingly. Our artists are now growing old, and the avant-garde style which flourished only a few decades ago now lies crass and clichéd upon the scandoors and interiordecorations of the offices of high business officials. Only a few truly great Saer artists remain, and though their sculpture will never die, it pains me to think that the culture, race, and technology which surrounded the great masterpieces of our time will soon perish. So it was with the major-domo and I. We are a race thinning out, hanging off of a scrabbly ledge at a far corner of the universe. There are a few young Saer left, but only a few, for most of them have brought about their own deaths, and our once "avant-garde" now laughingly suggests that we kill the rest. To me, it merely proves how dependent age is on youth. But we hang on to our old customs (to use the alien phrase) because we know full well how sad it would make us to let them go. In spite of this, we are a people who continually let ourselves down.

I remember my experience in space. Certainly we have the necessary technology to propel ourselves to the stars and beyond, yet we have never done so. Our quadrant of our galaxy is encompassed by a decaying subspace structure, we are told, and we believe, for how can we know better, having never been out of our sector and being told we can never leave by the aliens who are themselves trapped here? So we shoot ourselves up and down for no reason except to enjoy the view. Mthardi's *Shuddering Void* is surely one of the most famous examples of the rendering of the subspace vision onto electronicanvas, yet I must readily confess that I saw nothing of what Mthardi saw when I was up. I was strapped into my multiple-limb contact chair (the Saer race, alas, being poorly designed for such forms of travel, which may perhaps explain our being situated in such an unreachable part of the universe) and was shot up rather like a bullet, guided on by smaller flames when freed from Saer's gravity. I'm told standard space is essentially boring, and our crumbling, subentropic sector is a glory to behold in its rapid decay, yet I can never really tell. I am unimpressed by such things. I sat contentedly enough, and viewed through the glass screen the washed-out colors of the void, changing from purple and yellow, now red and then green, with scattered suns dripping, blending, running in with one another, while around me the hue of space shifted subtly—red, green, yellow through the night. Our sun continually shifts form and mass, its shape never round as standard stars are supposed to be, we're told, but mawkish, a burning cell which bobs and bends on the verge of unrealized mitosis, no more round than it is square. I sat through all this contentedly enough, as I have said, though I might not put up with it now, knowing as I do that my people do not have much farther to go. But then, for the moment, I was content with the painted washout of space; and when it was over, they guided my craft back down electromagnetically. I have not gone up since then. Soon thereafter I met the major-domo.

Reality, I believe, is actually a series of images—pieces of our lives—which tend to move in an order which is associative rather than chronological. At least, this is the way it appears to be for the Saer people. When something good happens, good things follow, as if by association. Many things which are not at all good have been happening now, ever since the banquets ended. No longer do we parade up the streets at any and every cause. The days when the death of a great man was a cause for weeks of celebration are ended. I still love our parks, which remain beautiful and unspoiled, but soon I fear they will go the way of all else. Even the River K'rethnos, which divides virtually half the continent, is no longer used as a means of transport for everything from laundry to mail. Those days, what the aliens call our *belle époque*, are done with. It comes from associating with bad events, such as the aliens. My relationship with the major-domo was associative as well, but I tend to doubt it bore anything but a trifling resemblance to the chain of associations I tend to blame for our planet's downfall, because among other things our downfall will ultimately prove itself to be fated (because of the entropic destruction of the subspace foundation of our sector), which is fatalistic and is not in keeping with most occurrences which happen through association.

"What might I do to help you?" asked the major-domo.

I removed my center-hind arm from my upper set of shoulders and requested some of the djurie-frost he had perched on his back. I wanted the major-domo to go with me. I wanted to take him off and suffer in the happy pain of being alone with him. The way his joints moved, as if they might be chuckling at me, drove me insatiate with their power. Surely my wants were so intense that they expressed themselves physically, for he said:

"You look upset. Is there anything else I might do to help? You really do look upset."

All around us the banquet went on, the Saer laughing helplessly and carelessly, unaware (or seemingly so) that they were "an endangered species." Bright colors were placed everywhere, to keep people gay, although my gaiety was a dead, hopeless thing. It was well into the early-morning hours, when the sun would bubble up over the horizon, shapeless light spreading with the advancing minutes, and I was going to cry through this morning, I could tell, even though it was a banquet and no one else would cry. I would.

By my arrangement, the major-domo met me after the banquet, in the dawn hours, in one of the grand parks over by the Hreth district with its melancholy houses, graying and dilapidated, and its gigantic trees of green and purple hues, so near the mystic banks of the River K'rethnos. I arrived early, and had bought a newspaper which I read while waiting for him. The news was typical of our culture at the edge of its decline—women killing their own sons in heated frenzies, little Saer girls being gunned down in their front yards by men driving past in groundcars who had nothing better to do with their afternoon, and so on. . . . A culture is most violent during the pangs of its birth and death. We are not being born.

"Though you want to live in an environment which reminds you of the home you had as a child, you also suffer from a more serious problem—you are not satisfied anywhere," the major-domo later said. I thought about his relationship with the other servants of the house of the Great Mayor of Saer. Doubtless Zerimar lets his servants have a free reign over his house while he is gone, for servants such as the major-domo are expected to be trusted, they are so highly paid. Nonetheless, it is possible that the major-domo takes liberties with whomever he pleases in Zerimar's household, but I could, of course, be imagining this.

"I don't know where I want to live," I told him.

"You were born here. You can live here."

"No. Impossible."

"Then you could leave."

"No, no," I said. "I think I would rather live here, really. If I were to leave, I would rather leave this planet entirely, and that, of course . . ."

"Of course," the major-domo said, and scratched his nose with one of his hands. "Still, you could think of merely leaving the city. Surely there must be some part of Saer which would be enough like some far-off planet to satisfy you?"

I doubted him when he said that and doubt him still. Such talk was never the prelude to our making love, for we never did. I prefer to play the standard role, to live up to it, admonishing softly of my love, which never took any form other than verbal. Doubtless he received some pleasure from this as well, as his thirst was my drought. Perhaps he too played the standard role (and plays this role still?) and took pleasure from my pain. Could this be?— I would often ask myself in the early morning hours after our rapport was ended. I thought not. I thought that what we were doing, whatever game it was we were playing, was all a comfortable part of reality—something fitting on the chain of associations. I don't know what to think now.

"Surely you must think of art as more than mere trinkets to be dusted off in your master's house?" I asked him one morning.

"No," he said. "Nothing more, nothing less. That is all art is for. Something to be plugged in, turned on, dusted, kept clean, maintained, kept in good, working condition. . . . Why should I think more of it?"

He was bringing me close to the point of violence. "You—you don't think there's anything *more* to it?" I asked incredulously. "Don't you think there's a reason why your master buys those works of art? Do you think Zerimar collects art just to keep you busy?"

So close, so close this last rapport was to the present, to the Now, the This Time, so near the end, so distant from the beginning. Soon he will return, for he has paralyzed my soul, frozen my heart and made useless my mind. . . .

That is all, in our society, that the major-domo is good for. Leader of servants, he brings back memories of early and innocent days, when the smell of food was something taken for granted, when love was simply something everyone did with everyone else, when we were so youthful and thought we knew the meaning of that word, love. Perhaps when you grow older you lose your old conceptions, and words whose meanings you thought you knew turn out to be useless phrases, empty. Is this what was caused by the aliens? If so, why do we hang on so desperately to the likes of the major-domo? What smoldering force within us demands we clutch so childishly to the leader of servants? We realize we no longer understand simple words like love in the least, yet we demand that there exist a person of sufficient power to command the army of servants and domestic help. Why do we throw ourselves before the major-domo when we don't even know what love means? Because the major-domo knows, that is why. The major-domo knows our greatest strengths and weaknesses. The major-domo knows every one of our flaws. The major-domo knows our greatest pride and deepest fears. He knows what we only hope we know; he can tell what is deep in our hearts and high in our heads. The major-domo has been the single most important moving factor in the pattern of society in the past several hundred years. Doubtless when we die and turn to dust the major-domo will still be here. . . .

Are they waiting out there to study us? At least two thousand aliens now live on Saer, for they can get in but not back out again. However, there is talk that somewhere someone has perfected the means of getting out of an imperfect subspace warp. If so, then why do they not come? Are they waiting for us to die off? Are they being polite and not asking us questions in our death throes?

Soon this evening the major-domo will come again; no longer meeting me in the great parks, he comes to my mansion on the Great Hill of Firm Trees. He will come to talk; I will be the helpless rich one, and he the menace to my security. I fear I can never know just why or how I became involved with him. It may have been the motions I made that night at the banquet. Soon, though, there will be another banquet, and perhaps if I am shrewd, I can go through the motions which will get him off my back.

So, perhaps they will come for us only after we are gone. I have no opinion on the subject, although it makes me curious. Why do they want to go without speaking to us? Is it because of the slow entropy which is eating us away, molecule by molecule? I don't worry. I know they'll have no problems. I know that the two thousand of their kind will still be here after we've all gone. And when every last Saer is gone from this earth, they won't ever have to worry about the whys and wherefores, the hows and whens.

Don't worry at all. Just step this way, the major-domo will answer all your questions.

When Pappy Isn't There

by Lin Nielsen

Lin Nielsen ("In the Greenhouse"—Clarion II) *writes:*

"Chip Delany once asked me what I was doing living in Illinois. I told him it was a great place to be from.

"When the wind sweeps the dust along the snow crust and boots break through but paws do not, I am a shadow and run through the night hot-breathed. I can feel it when I crouch beneath a lilac bush in the muggy dark with a carpet of mosquitoes on my bare arms. I can feel it when I see the moon and suddenly want to run on and on until I fall down in the grass panting. Give me Illinois summers with the sweat running hot. Give me Midwest winters when the blood of the state flows thick and sluggish.

"Give me Illinois for a very simple story. The best thing of all is that Pappy does go away."

A sluggish ribbon of creek divided the summer burnt pasture from the pine forest. Its muddy banks were torn by cattle prints and the deep double gouge of a jeep's tire tracks. Pappy stood on his crutches within the veil of trees and watched the soldiers come over the brown hill quickly and cautiously. The first man reached the stream, paused, and waded across in four long strides, wet to the mid-thighs when he emerged.

Pappy knew the young man in the lead was about to die, and he felt the old bitter sadness as the gun in the woods sounded and the body tumbled backward to flush the stream pink with blood. Pappy saw himself at the crest of the hill, saw himself flatten on the grass and fire between the weeds. He leaned his shoulders back against the rough bark of the tree and settled to watch what he knew would happen. He had timed his arrival very well.

Sunlight came in dusty columns through the half-closed

Venetian blinds, but it did not brighten the front room. The glow of the television screen was as strong, and an afternoon game show spoke to itself in the silence of the old house. As she crossed the foyer, Kay glanced into the room. The recliner chair stood stiffly upright, its shiny leather back reflecting the television images. Pappy was not there. She switched off the set, reeled up the blinds, and opened the windows to chase the stale air out into the brick-hot sunshine of the day.

Pappy came into the kitchen as she stood at the sink trimming stalks and tails from radishes with a long knife. Kay turned as she heard his hesitant step and the soft sound of the plastic pads on the tips of his crutches.

"Welcome back," she said. "Lunch is almost ready."

"That's my girl." Pappy braced himself and reached with one hand to fill the brown coffee mug that had come home with him from the war. His face was preoccupied and sad.

"Where were you?" she asked, reaching back to wash another radish in the thin, cold stream of water from the faucet. "I can't keep track of you on those crutches." She smiled at him fondly.

"I was out on the porch for a while. Is there any mail?" He held the steaming cup with two fingers and rested most of his palm on the hand grip of the crutch.

"I put it by your chair. There's a government letter, so maybe your check came."

Pappy turned carefully in the tight space between the counters and moved slowly through the kitchen door. The crutch tops held up his shoulders the way a cross stick supports the frayed coat of a scarecrow. His head hung forward.

It would have been a terrible experience to see him shrink and fade overnight, but he had not failed so quickly. His decline was gradual over nine years. At the end he stood two inches shorter than before, and while some of that was from hunching, much was from the softening of muscles which had been hard since his youth. His eyes were clouded with cataracts, his arteries thickened with deposits, and his ball joints stiffened by calcium. He went on crutches, and he went slowly. The back porch was the horizon of his world.

Still she could not always find him. There were times she swore he must be hiding on the roof up by the chimney. He must have shinnied up the rope into the loft in the shed. He must have taken the pickup and driven off to Kankakee for a book sale. He must be over across the tracks shooting pheasants or maybe under the trestle fishing for bluegills.

He was always somewhere in the house. She would turn, and he would be coming out of his room or in from the front porch. Pappy would tease her with wild stories of where he had been, but of course he had never left.

The crutches lay like a patient dog alongside his chair. He lifted off his bifocals one stem at a time, folded them, and tucked them into the case clipped in his front shirt pocket.

"At least they're not all idiots," Pappy said, indicating the check on the small, cluttered table next to his elbow. "Right on time for a change."

Kay set up his lunch on an aluminum tray table and pulled it close. The television was on again.

"I'll go off to the bank this afternoon," she said.

"Good girl." He took a hesitant sip of coffee. His hand shook, and he put the mug quickly down. He looked at the sandwich.

"Pappy, is something wrong?" She saw the sad look on his face and thought of pain and of sickness.

He looked up at her and smiled. His eyes were milky blue. "No, girl, nothing's wrong. I'm just a little tired." The smile turned impish. "Do you want to know where I went today?"

"I wondered if you'd been off again. Let me guess." Kay settled cross-legged on the worn oriental carpet and reached behind her to turn down the television. "Have you been home to Rockford?"

"Nope." Pappy sat forward with his elbows on his knees. He enjoyed the game.

"Have you been to Rome for the chariot races?"

"No, I always go places I know. Never been to Rome."

"What about Joliet?"

"No, I spent enough time there before," he said.

Kay leaned back on her hands. "I can't think. Did you go during the war?"

Pappy rocked backward in the chair to make it recline a notch. She moved the lunch tray as the footrest came up. "Close enough, McKay. I went to see myself get shot that time in the Rhone valley."

"That's a strange thing to go back for," she said. "Were you hurt bad? Did you keep on fighting?"

"Well, I wasn't brave. I cried and I made the water in the stream dirty with my blood. And I was glad to not be dead like two of the other guys."

"But why did you want to see it?"

"I guess I forgot which parts really happened and which

ones my mind made up. I wasn't as calm as I remembered." He stared up at the pattern of sun reflections on the ceiling.

"You were hit in the shoulder, weren't you?"

"Yes," he said. "It wasn't all that bad. It wasn't bad at all."

Pappy's voice trickled off, and she saw his eyes blink and close. The game was ended. He was tired, and it was best for him to sleep. Kay wished he would not wear himself out with moving back and forth through the house, but she knew he chafed at his inactivity. These fantasies were part of that. She lifted the check quietly from the side table, smiled over him, and took the simple lunch away.

"Kay," Pappy bellowed. "Come and fix this damned set, McKay."

She came running. The television image was in convulsions. Diagonals of color danced across the screen, and at steady intervals the confusion flipped over.

"What did you do to it, Pappy? It's going crazy."

"I didn't do anything," he said. "It just died. It's the same on all the channels." He clicked the automatic channel selector. The colors changed, but the crazy patterns remained.

"Let me fiddle with it." Kay knelt before the set and played with the dials. The flipping steadied, but the colored lightning refused to focus back into a picture. She sat back on her heels. "It might be the aerial like before. I'll go up on the roof and see if I can fix it before I call the repair people."

"Be careful on that ladder." His face was suddenly anxious.

"I will, Pappy."

Slate shingles absorbed the sun and held the heat on their surface. The late-afternoon air was thickened by humidity which brought a glaze of sweat to covered skin. She planted the foot of the old house painter's ladder in the freshly spaded dirt of the flowerbed and climbed up toward the second story. The ladder's round rungs were splotched with paint from white-sided Illinois houses, and it tapered toward the top, reaching four feet above the gutter.

Kay held the ladder with one hand, braced the other against the brick chimney, and placed a tennis shoe onto the metal trough. The gutter held as she stood on it. The aerial was against the chimney and above her. It appeared to be all right. She raised her toes to the edge of the slates, put an arm against the ladder, and reached. Her foot slipped. The ladder slid away to the side. Her knee banged the gutter, but

Kay missed it with her hands. She screamed as she fell. The clods of dirt struck her hard.

Hands rough with calluses touched her neck. They grasped her shoulders and straightened her on the ground. Pain was sharp within her back as bones settled back into position. Arms slid under her ribs and her knees, and she felt herself lifted. Her breath shriveled in her throat from the sudden hurt. Tears poured into her eyes, and she tried to blink them away.

There was a man above her, beyond the tears. Oscar, their next door neighbor, must have heard her cry out. So dizzy that she barely understood what was happening, she squinted to squeeze teardrops from her lashes.

Not tired. Not worn. Not old. Pappy carried her in his arms up the steps of the porch. At least it seemed to be Pappy. She blacked out.

Kay had seen Noko, the brown tabby cat, out of the corner of her eye for weeks after he had disappeared. But every time she turned to look he would be transformed into an empty brown bag or a cardboard box or a sack of potatoes in the corner. Her mind had seen what she wished to see. Now she was confused, for her mind had played the same trick again.

"Pappy," she said as she lay on the couch with a wet cloth across her forehead. Her head felt buoyant. "I had a very strange idea after I fell off the roof. I thought that it was you who carried me into the house."

He stood over her on his crutches, his face wrinkled with concern. He did not speak.

She looked up at him. "Who found me and brought me inside?"

Pappy leaned forward, reaching out to brush her hair gently back from the damp cloth. Old, softened calluses still showed as thickened places on his hand. "Someone who loves you enough, Kay, to come a long way to help you."

"How long a way, Pappy?"

His voice was quiet as though he wanted to hide his answer. "Nine years," he said. "I always told you, but you never believed me."

She had seen her father young again. She had felt the strength in his arms and the lightness in his walk. She had seen his eyes a bright, unclouded blue. Looking at Pappy next to her now, she could make the comparison for the first time between what he had been and what age and sickness had caused him to become. Kay could see how much he had died. She did not want this for him. She wanted him strong and young and free to move within the world. She began to cry.

"What's wrong, girl? Does it hurt?"

She realized his concern must be greater because he could not clearly see her. He was trapped behind his eyes.

"It's all right, Pappy. I'll be okay." Cautiously she raised one hand to wipe her face, and she felt no pain.

"Sure you will, McKay."

Kay sat on the back steps in the darkness with her knees pulled up close to her chin. Her back was stiff and sore, but her luck had been to fall on the spaded flowerbed rather than the lawn. She was as healed as a week could make her. Pappy rested on his porch lounge chair as he often did from May until October, when the chill drove him indoors for the months of Illinois cold. The twilight was thick and warm, and they watched the deliberate sparkle of lightning bugs in the weeds along the railway embankment.

"Will you teach me how to travel in time?" she asked him.

"You're talking foolishness," Pappy said. "I don't know how to time-travel."

She turned toward him. "Of course you do. How else could you go away? How else could you have come to rescue me?"

"You can't call that time travel. I just went back, told myself what was wrong and how to get here, and sent him to help you." She could hear him fumble with a pillow in the darkness as he stuffed it behind his back. "It's funny. It's a circle. I went back and told myself to come forward. I don't know if I would ever have done it the first time if I hadn't been there to convince myself it was possible. I took a lot of convincing."

"If I hadn't fallen off the roof, you might never have learned."

Pappy shifted in his chair again. "I don't know, girl. I just know that you did fall, that I did come to find you, and that I already knew I would. There's nothing magical in that," he said. "I never thought about trying it again until it got so I couldn't move around like I used to. After a while I got bored. I got tired of waiting to die, so I started going places to watch myself."

"You make it sound like home movies," she said. "Did you

ever go to see things in history? Haven't you ever wondered what it was really like?"

He chuckled. "No, I never was any good at history, never thought to go any place I didn't know. I always figured if I couldn't fix the place clear in my mind I couldn't get there, so I've stuck to things I really remember."

The bells rang on the only crossing gate in town, their faint sound quickly drowned by the clatter of a freight train passing on the embankment.

She waited until it passed and asked again, "Do you think you can teach me how?"

"I don't know," Kay." Pappy's voice was soft and tired. "It's one of those feelings that you can't really put into words. It's like being blind and getting an extra something from your ears. It's like taking a taste and wanting a whole bite. It's wanting to be there."

"Wanting to be where, Pappy?"

"Anywhere but here. Really wanting to be in the past. Aching for the way things used to be," he said. "I don't think I ever missed the past until this old body of mine started reminding me that I had come a long way. I don't know, Kay. Can you feel that?"

She tried to pull a wanting out of her past. She tried to will nostalgia in a wave over her, but it was a hollow feeling. It was a general sadness, not a sharp, specific longing.

"Pappy, could I do it if you went along? Could we go together?"

"We can try." Pappy shifted on the lounge chair and sat up. He pulled himself up onto his crutches and shuffled toward her. She rose carefully, her back still sore, to stand next to him in the darkness. "Where shall we go, McKay?"

"I don't know, Pappy."

He was silent for a moment, and she wondered if he was reconsidering. She searched in her mind frantically for a place, for a time, for a feeling that she could anchor on.

He said, "Why don't we go see Mom?"

Her mother. Kay smiled, and she was sad. She remembered her Mom strong and healthy, hunching over as she picked strawberries. She saw her washing dishes with water-wrinkled hands. She saw her sick, pale against the blue bedspread. Kay wished to see her again.

"When?" she asked.

"Remember," Pappy said hesitantly. Then he laughed. "Remember how she used to go out in back to burn the trash? She always went by herself in all kinds of rotten weather, and I never thought anything about it until she got pneumonia that one winter and I had to burn it myself. Remember that? Remember the way there would be a single path through the snow leading out behind the shed? Remember the big box of matches and the way her nose would be all pink? Remember, McKay?"

A last flurry of snow drifted and settled past him. He stood behind the house up on the railway embankment, feet and crutches unsteady on the snow over the crushed rock. The wind bew bitter cold, but much of its force was blocked by the line of parked boxcars. He knew Kay was not with him.

Martha came from the house bundled in an old plaid coat and with a scarf wrapped around her ears and throat. She carried two sacks of trash to the wire basket behind the shed, dropped them in, and lit them with matches from the box in her pocket. Turned half toward him, she stood close to the warmth and watched the papers burn. The fire brightened her face.

It was a good face, a happy face. Nose and cheeks were reddened by the cold, and her frozen breath was thick before her face. She stood with bare hands tucked into her armpits, shifting from foot to foot in the snow. She was smiling at some private thought.

The urge to speak with her was strong, but he had neither the way to go down the slope on crutches nor the desire to let her see what he would become. He had protected her from many things; he would protect her from that. He was saddened not that Martha had grown old and died but that Kay could not come with him. She could not see her mother fine and strong and happy. They were caught in separate moments of time away from each other.

Pappy shuddered as the wind bit through his shirt. Gravel shifted beneath him, and a piece rattled down the slope. Martha turned her face from the warmth, glancing up toward the embankment. As he saw her turn, he went away.

Kay had not seen him vanish because her eyes had been closed with the effort of trying to remember. She opened them and found that he was gone. At first self-pity at being left behind touched her, and so did sadness at the loss of her mother. Both of those faded until she stood expectantly in the dark waiting for Pappy's return.

It was a long time since he had left. Kay began to wonder and then to worry. What if something happened to him in the past? He could fall so easily from unsteady crutches. If he hurt himself, would there be someone there to aid him? Kay wondered if her mother would recognize Pappy. He might have stopped to talk with her. Perhaps Mom would persuade him to stay with her. Perhaps he was not coming back at all.

Then Pappy was there, returning as simply as he had left.

Relief and happiness at his arrival flooded through her. Kay turned and put her arms around him in a tight hug, burying her face against his thin shoulder. He shivered once beneath her arms, his skin cold under his light shirt.

"I'm sorry, Kay," Pappy said. His voice was husky. "Maybe next time it'll work."

"It's all right, Pappy."

And suddenly she knew she just wanted this particular instant in time, no other, because if she could hold Pappy here she would always have him. He might be weak, he might be crippled, but he was here with her for this moment.

"Maybe someday, Kay," he said. "Maybe someday you'll want the past and need it enough to get there."

Kay held him tighter. "All I want, Pappy, is to have you here with me now."

"More I Cannot Wish You"

by Jean Sullivan

Jean Sullivan is a Friday-the-thirteenth Sagittarian raised in a Wessex-like atmosphere on a farm with a coal stove, kerosene lamps, and hand-pumped water. She attended Thiel College and the University of Buffalo and has worked as a waitress, welfare caseworker, university administrator, university teacher, and librarian. After a year at the Rochdale Experimental College in Toronto, she settled down to group living in New York.

She has, she says, "wanted to be a writer since the first time I read a book."

The material would make a beautiful dress. Even from the pattern Lucy had picked out. Damn her. Damn Lucy. Going for a ride with Dave. They could have gone some other time. Dave Dave Dave. That's all Lucy thought about.

But maybe she didn't need Lucy. Maybe she could do it herself.

Sandra picked up the pattern and removed the instructions. She had wanted the Vogue. But Lucy insisted. The Butterick would be easier to follow. Butterick 5647. Layout B. Fold the material with the bias edge on the long side, as in the illustration. This will allow with the bias edge on the long side, with the bias edge driving in a car with Dave. Not thinking about what she's doing. If she were going a little faster she'd lose control and crash into the concrete wall at the top of the hill. And die.

". . . I'll cut the dress out later, Sandy. Just as soon as Dave and I get back from our ride."

Drive faster Lucy. Just a little faster. That's right. Will crash into it now. Will crash into . . . another car! With that man and woman and their two kids. Where did they come from? Strange little kids.

Lucy doesn't know they're coming. That they're going to crash. They'll all be dead.

Lucy!

Slow down!

Stop looking at Dave. Stop laughing with him.

Listen!

Slow down before . . .

Lucy!

The instructions ripped apart as Sandra raised her hands to protect her face from the flying glass. The sound of the crash echoed through her mind. The car flying through the air and the broken bodies sprawled on the ground. The man who would cry no more silent tears, the woman who had nothing left to understand. Lucy lying on the road, and the blood. Sticky blood running down her mutilated face. Why had it been Lucy with Dave? Lucy shouldn't be dead.

Sandra didn't want Lucy really dead.

Sandra held the torn instructions in her hands. The paper was damp and swollen from her sweat. She sat shaking violently, her eyes staring blankly out the window across from her bed. With the bias edge . . . where is the bias edge . . . before the accident was the bias edge.

Disoriented, she staggered across the room to the desk in the corner. Frantically, she smoothed the torn paper. If only she could put the paper back together the accident wouldn't have happened. It had to fit back together because Lucy couldn't be dead. Harshly, Sandra pressed her fingers against the torn paper; desperately, digging into the desk, tearing the paper even more. Lucy couldn't be dead. Sandra didn't know how to live without her sister's help.

Still her fingers moved over the ragged edges.

She grabbed a roll of scotch tape and tried to tape the pieces together. But the tape wouldn't stick on the wet paper. She blew on the pieces. When they dried it would go together. She could see where it fit together. She could read it if she tried. Edge on the long side. This will allow place . . . nt of pieces j and f on the shorter side as shown in the illus . . . tion.

Go together damn you.

Sandra stood in a daze, clutching the desk to steady her gentle swaying motion. Closing her eyes, she tried to shut out the sight of the too familiar bedroom. The accident and the time since were a blur. Something terrible had happened. But what? What was it? Her tears left faint mascara smudges. Brushing away the tears, she opened her eyes and recoiled from the specter of a black glove on her hand.

No.

For some reason she couldn't go into the living room and ask her parents for comfort.

Not from Daddy, crying inside, unable to show how he really felt. Not from Mommy, who always tried but who never understood. Would Mommy know I tried to stop it—I really did try to stop it—would she know that I didn't want Lucy . . . to . . . Lucy.

Loved Lucy so.

Exhausted. Sandra sank down on her bed. Nothing had changed in the room. How could that be? When so much had changed how could the room remain untouched? She wasn't sure, though, just what she expected to be different. In her mind was a collage of grief and funeral homes and funerals and Lucy. Dead. Lucy haunting her, trying to remind her of something.

Lucy and Sandra. The leader and the follower. Always the follower. Always the strange one. No one loves strange ones. Daddy didn't love strange ones. But Lucy did. And she made me less strange. Taught me to concentrate to keep them out.

There is no one to do that now. Now I can be myself.

On the dresser was the picture of the two of them taken the night of the Junior-Senior prom. In its frame the faded blue ribbon—a remembrance of another dance, Sandra's first. Sandra hadn't wanted to go. She was afraid. Boys scared her, their minds were open to her. Like everyone else's but Lucy's.

But Lucy had laughed at Sandra; said she shouldn't be afraid. Lucy had known the secret of keeping out the thoughts that Sandra didn't want to share. The thoughts weren't real. It was only Sandra's imagination. The power to make people do what she wanted them to wasn't real. There was nothing to fear. If Sandra wanted to stop it, all she had to do was learn to be like Lucy. Then Daddy would love her the way he loved Lucy and the boys would stop thinking at her. And it worked.

She went to the dance with Jerry instead of David because Lucy told her that David would be harder to control. She did all the things that Lucy told her to. They had a good time—all she had to do was laugh real hard, concentrate on having a good time, dance a lot with Jerry while Lucy danced with David and think about happy thoughts.

And it kept working. The imaginings went away, most of the time. Didn't really control people. Could turn off their minds that weren't real. But where did it all come from? If it wasn't in them, then where did it all come from? If not in them then in . . . no . . . There's still so much I don't know. And now Lucy is dead.

Sandra searched frantically for something to do. Something to shut off the questions she couldn't answer, the fears she didn't want to face. But everywhere she turned she saw reminders of Lucy.

The expensive bikini they both wanted and neither could afford, so pooling their money they bought one and took turns wearing it. Not that Sandra had worn it much. Somehow, Lucy usually seemed to have made plans for using it first.

No.

She had to stop thinking.

Sandra moved to the dresser and laid her hands on the material. Such pretty material. The light-green background, the bright-yellow and purple and brown lines running through it. So smooth, such fine silk. Felt so good on her skin. Oh!

Sandra jerked her hands back as her fingers touched the rough edge of the cloth.

A shrill scream, like the impersonal shriek of a telephone, rang through the house. On and on. And the voice that couldn't be anyone she knew, although she wasn't sure why. "Sandra. There's been an accident. It was Lucy and Dave and . . . and they've all been taken to the hospital . . . and . . ." The scream shut out the horror. The recurring horror that would not go away. She cringed, her hands shaking, her body shriveling up, as a part of her was cut away leaving an empty void. A void which seemed to be bleeding. Hate blood, messy blood. But it was only her tears again.

What was it she wanted to do?

Sandra looked at the room that hadn't changed; searching. She found no answers in the picture, the bathing suit, the pennant from Southeastern University where she and Dave were going in the fall. The school Lucy had picked. Where Lucy would be coming next year.

Gradually she became aware that it was raining outside. She could feel the cold pouring in from the open window, leaving a chill in her bones. She felt an emptiness as the cold procession of time passed around her. The days of mourning existed as the unreality of a terrible nightmare. Why had it been Lucy? She would wake and find it wasn't real.

Lucy's body, lying in a casket, haunted her. Air. She needed some air. She was being smothered. Slowly, the casket was lowered into the grave. Smothering out Lucy's life. Sandra ran; trying to escape the dirt as it fell on the casket; trying to escape Lucy buried under the dirt. But Lucy followed her.

Lucy is dead. I saw her die. I tried to stop her but I couldn't. Really I couldn't. I learned not to so long ago. Lucy. Would save you if I could but I can't. It's smothering me. Run. Run. Must get some air.

Sandra crashed into the wall beside the window trying to escape to the air. The impact dislodged the Southeastern pennant which was hanging on the wall and it fell on her face.

"Sandy, are you all right? Wait. Let me help you up."

The sound of the voice, distorted by the pain and fear in Sandra's mind, filtered through to her consciousness. Lucy was talking to her. If she kept seeing and hearing Lucy she would lose her mind.

Sandra lay huddled in the corner by the window, shutting out the imaginations. Fuzz from the pennant stuck to her tongue and cloyed in her throat, making it difficult to breath.

"Sandy! Get up! What happened? We heard a crash that sounded like the house was being bombed."

Raising herself up by grasping the window ledge, Sandra stood with her face against the screen, gasping for air and trying to wipe away the fuzz from her tongue.

Lucy would go away.

Aloud, to give herself confidence, she said, "I'll get along just fine and won't disturb you any more. I'm going to go to the store and buy the Vogue pattern I wanted. Now you go away and leave me alone."

As she turned from the window, Sandra stared at the apparition which filled the doorway and concentrated very hard. Go to your grave. Don't come in here. Didn't mean to pull you from your grave. Had to get away. Before I was smothered. You must leave me now.

"I don't know, Sandy. Are you sure you're all right?"

Carefully ignoring the aberration of her mind, Sandra picked up her purse. She would concentrate extremely hard and Lucy would go away. Just like the other imaginations Lucy taught her to ignore. The Vogue pattern. What was its number?

"Honestly, Sandy, you're just being stubborn and throwing

a tantrum over nothing. You're getting yourself and everyone else upset just because you aren't getting your own way."

Moving resolutely toward the door, Sandra collided with Lucy.

"Sandy! For Christ's sake, what is wrong with you? Look, why don't you just lie down for a while?" Lucy helped her dazed sister to the bed. "Dad and Mom just called and they'll be home in a little while. Why don't you lie down and wait to go to the store till they get back?"

Sandra stared at her sister. Then she could feel her body shake and heard the sound of her own laughter as she remembered. The kids. Strange kids. The kids were imaginations. The kids were grown up and the man and woman would be by themselves.

Forcing herself to calm down, Sandra walked across the room and laid her purse on the dresser. Then she turned to Lucy and in a near whisper said, "Okay, Lucy. I'll lie down and wait for them to come home. I'll do that. Now you go on out and enjoy your drive."

Lucy stood hesitating for a moment. "You will wait for them?"

"Yes, damn it. Now just go and leave me alone."

As Lucy turned to leave she said, "Okay, I'm going. But I won't be long. And I'll cut the dress out later, Sandy. Just as soon as Dave and I get back from our drive."

Sandra listened to her sister leaving the house. For a moment she tried very hard. Tried to remember. But then she noticed the material in her hands. It would make such a beautiful dress.

The Deep Well of the Unconscious—Well, Well . . .

by Damon Knight

Unconscious? Nothing of the sort. Sleeping or waking, it goes right on, supremely *conscious*, aware of everything. You may doze, drop out, draw a blank—it doesn't. Forgive my saying "it"—it isn't it, it's you; but it's the part of you that we have agreed to consider "unconscious."

In fact, the truth is just the other way around. Everything that you experience goes through the surface awareness—call it the A mind (which forgets 90 percent of it instantly)—into the "unconscious"—call it the B mind* (which forgets nothing). The A mind is normally unaware of the B mind; the B mind monitors the A mind constantly. The A mind can manage linear reasoning up to a point of—if *x*, then *y*, and if *y*, then *z*. The B mind works in webs of association.

The A mind can think of poverty and legacies: the B mind gives you David Copperfield and Micawber.

B decides what you will do; A explains it afterward.

Communication from A to B is ample; what is lacking is communication from B to A, and there's the rub. The lines coming back from B are so few and so neglected that it often has to convey its imperatives and its conclusions in roundabout ways, in dreams and daydreams and "hunches" and "intuitions."

Freud did us a disservice when he labeled the B mind the "subconscious," and Jung an even greater one when he called it the "unconscious." Victorians could not help thinking of the B mind as the repository of all the filth rejected and suppressed by the A mind—desires for incest, murder wishes, fascination with excrement. And of course all that is there, because everything is there. Henry James called it "the deep well of unconscious cerebration"; C. S. Forester, in his posthumous autobiography, *Long Before Forty*, spoke of ideas

*These terms will never become popular, because they are not striking, not colorful, not emotionally loaded—not any of the things that they ought not to be.

dropping into the ooze of the sea bottom, to come up again covered with barnacles. All this is terribly misleading. The B mind is not a pit, a well, or a garbage heap. Ironically, if either mind deserves the label "unconscious," it is the A mind, which is unaware of 90 percent of the mental activity that goes on in its own skull.

If the B mind could communicate directly about all this, what would it say? Well, in hypnotic and other abnormal mental states, it can; its utterances are oracular, but often perfectly coherent, grammatical, etc. (For a provocative view of what the world might look like from the vantage point of the B mind, see Kate Wilhelm's novel *Margaret and I,* Little, Brown, 1971.)

Because of the emphasis on the "unconsciousness" of the B mind, it is easy to overlook the fact that nearly all our mental and physical activity is a collaboration between A and B. With suitable training, you can learn to use autosuggestion to tell yourself, for instance, that your right arm is going to rise: and presently, sure enough, up it will come as if it were being pulled by a string. (I don't recommend this, though—it's easier to start than to stop.) That is mysterious: but in what sense is it more mysterious than the way you ordinarily raise your arm? When you reach for a glass or take a step, the A mind is expressing an impulse or an intention, and the B mind does all the rest. If the A mind had to do all that by itself, you would be in deep and instant trouble.

Now then: where do ideas come from? They come from the A and B minds working in collaboration. This process is difficult—about as difficult as riding a bicycle—but it is not complicated. If you want ideas, all you have to do is follow these eight rules.

1. Decide what *kind* of ideas you want. Ideas for stories? How to get rich? To meet girls? Whatever it is, it must be something that you are sincerely interested in and willing to labor at over a long period—otherwise the B mind won't cooperate, and it won't work.

2. Determine to devote at least an hour every day to this project, preferably the same hour, until your immediate goal is reached.

3. Stick to it. If you don't, your B mind will be that much harder to convince that you mean it next time.

4. Analyze the problem logically as well as you can—break it down into categories, make lists of options. Write down any ideas that occur to you.

5. Put the whole thing out of your A mind—forget it; sleep on it. See what your B mind has come up with next morning.

6. *Use* the ideas you get. Look over what you have done and notice any shortcomings or errors. If you can repair these readily, do so—otherwise just notice them and forget them.

7. Repeat 4, 5, and 6 daily until you've reached your immediate goal. Then pick another goal and go on. The crucial parts of this system are commitment and regularity. Within your limitations, you can solve almost any creative problem this way, but you can't expect it to work on a frivolous or temporary basis. One more rule—

8. Never try to pump anything out of the idea tank until the B mind has had a chance to fill it. Nothing irritates it more.

When I was young I met a sports-fiction writer for whom a friend of mine was doing some typing. He handed her the rough draft of a story, then said casually, "I know what my next one's going to be about . . ." and proceeded to describe it. I was amazed that he could even think about the next one—to me, writing a story was a herculean effort from which I had to recover by resting my brain for a few weeks. But I now know that when you are writing stories regularly, the B mind comes up with all the ideas you can use. When the tank gets full, it stops—what would be the point of pouring in more? Except for that, I don't think there is any practical limit. When I was editing a magazine and needed ideas for cover paintings, I could and did think of half a dozen in five minutes. Once, in a period of emotional crisis, I composed and memorized six dirty limericks during the half-hour it took me to drive from my home in Milford, Pennsylvania, to Middletown, New York.

It may or may not be needless to say that you must know something about the area in which you are trying to get useful ideas. I could make up my mind to think of ideas for new household appliances, but they would be dumb ideas, unless I had first taken courses in mechanical and electrical engineering. If you try to get rich on the stock market or in business without knowing anything about either, you will lose your shirt. If you are planning to think of ideas for science fiction stories without having read a lot of science fiction, forget it—I can tell you in advance what they will be. (The young man and woman who find themselves the sole survivors of atomic holocaust, except for a Methodist minister; etc.) And incidentally, if you want to write science fiction, it doesn't hurt to know something about fiction and science.

Now you turn away. Your mouth pulls down at the corners. You say, "Oh, well, if you have to do all that *work*—"

And that's why I can tell you my secrets without the slightest fear that your competition will put me out of business.*

*My B mind dictated this—don't blame me.

Give My Regards to the Czar

by David N. Williams

David Williams is a twenty-five-year-old native of the Pacific Northwest, where—he says—it rains all the time except when Harlan Ellison is there.

"Give My Regards to the Czar" was written before the Munich Olympics but after the catastrophic Minnesota-Ohio State basketball game of the 1971–1972 season. Sports fans please copy.

Brass march music thumped above crowd noise.

Hanson strode the catwalk to the PA booth. Even the semi-dark seats back almost among the roof girders were occupied. From the benches dropping away beneath, faces turned upward to watch him. The glow started in his belly.

AUTHORIZED PERSONNEL ONLY. He palmed the IDeal; the thick door admitted him and closed behind him with a muted thud, silencing all but a murmur of people, a pulse-strong drumbeat. Air conditioning breathed.

Locked in. Looking down at the noon-bright court, he settled into the chair and let it mold to his back, buttocks, thighs. The teams, cloaked in baggy sweat suits, warmed up under the holo lights. Across the floor naked black cheerleaders cavorted to the pulsebeat; the bleachers in front of them were packed to capacity, yellow and black school colors, black faces. The balcony ringing the main floor was more ordinarily crowd-colored, more Caucasian. A full house. He smiled slowly, savoring his isolation. *Like children they come to me, craving amusement.* He laughed shortly. *Well, I'll give them a show*— His mind caught on the last word.

He relaxed and let the chair ease him forward between his up-angled boards: butterfly wings flaring around him, every button and control slide within easy reach. The stamp-sized central screens read seven-plus minutes to game time, luminous second-numbers obliterating one another in heartbeat sequence.

He touched the master slide, and the court monitors lit yellow; a wave of nervous anticipation/player thoughts swept over him: *jesus can't even dribble/those guys look awful tall/I'm* here *championship?/don't even look* scared *at the other end . . .* Hanson didn't allow the feelings to affect him.

He noticed a point of yellow-green on the McKinley side and nodded. Miller, probably. Throughout the tournament Miller had never hit more than yellow, even when his team was far behind. Hanson's gaze drifted to the McKinley players, who were standing in a circle batting a practice float around with their forearms. He could have— With a quick headshake he looked back to the boards, muting the court section.

He pushed the master slide all the way open. A tiny-squared mosaic lit his butterfly with varying shades of blue, green, yellow and orange. Emotion boiled over him, washing his own thoughts and feelings away: amusement, anger/*that's* my *seat get out!* lust/*look at those jelly pears bounce!* boredom, anticipation, impatience/*let's get this thing going . . .* Gradually he oriented himself *boards here, students there, bleachers there, chair under me* and sorted out one team's supporters from the other's. Woodlawn felt a bit more confident; but then, the suburban team was favored here. He considered cutting their confidence and rejected the idea; he could feel upset hope growing in the McKinleyites.

He muted the emotional monitors and fingered the familiar pregame-check sequence, touching the statistics buttons in quick succession, watching the columns of matchbook-sized screens to either side of the clock. Numbers flitted normally through them, glowing green against gray. Probably the only green the boards would register once the game began, he thought, wriggling against the chair in anticipation. He touched monitor slides without moving them; electricity in near-intelligent patterns flowed beneath his fingers *down to you, my children-for-a-night, through your seats and back to me*—. He pulled his hands back from the slides and completed the check sequence. The muted monitors rippled color changes, reaction to the flickering on the scoreboard hanging just below the booth.

The teams were leaving the court now for their benches, and the thumping had stopped. Hanson fastened the mike to his throat, touching the foot pedal to zero his stat boards. Five minutes. He touched the other foot pedal. "Ladies and gentlemen"—he heard his voice, faraway, echoing through the pavilion, and wriggled again—"welcome to the twentieth annual state high school foreball championship. Tonight's title encounter brings together two undefeated teams, the Woodlawn Wolverines, of Arcadia, and the McKinley Black Bears, of this city. On the scoreboard, the Black Bears will have the home side." The other side of the pavilion cheered, and tribal pride whispered from the monitors. *That's right, kiddies.*

"Now, let's meet the entire squad for the WOODLAWN WOLVERINES!" He touched a button, and WOODLAWN ROSTER glowed just beneath the clock screens. He read aloud, "Playing guard, a junior, number 12, Ted Adams!" A green-and-gold-sweatsuited boy trotted onto the court from the near side and turned to face his crowd. Five girls in green-and-gold-striped bikini bottoms did somersaults around him. A muted roar shook the booth: "Adams!"

"Playing forward, a senior, number 26, Rank Cragin!" The cheerleaders tumbled, and a shorts-and-jersey-clad boy walked confidently onto the floor. Iridescent green sheathed his arms from the elbows down and encased his hands in thumbless, fingerless gloves. He stopped beside Adams and turned, grinning. A twinge of apprehension ran through the McKinley monitors. Hanson smiled, touching the STARTER button beside Cragin's name. Cragin had been the star of the tourney so far, a spectacular shot and an aggressive defender; going into this game, he had the Most Valuable Player award virtually wrapped up. Hanson didn't let himself pause, reading the other Woodlawn names with enough intonation to keep McKinley apprehensive and Woodlawn cocky. Control slides were crutches this early.

" . . . And now for the McKINLEY BLACK BEARS!"

Names and color/emotions on his boards; he was beginning to get a feeling, a transmutation of glow into something precious that meant *superior*. He would pull a great performance from this crowd, and— A picture flashed through his mind, of his losing the crowd and the other announcers laughing at his ineptitude. He inhaled with a half-hiss, beginning to clench his fists. *Those shitheads! They've never seen me* really *work* . . . He pushed his attention outward, exhaling slowly.

"Playing forward, a senior, number 24, Miller DuBois!" Ah, Miller, his Miller, his guarantee: Mr. Cool, Mr. Playmaker, five feet ten inches of black spring with moves like a hunting barracuda's. He was the only one with a chance to take Cragin's MVP trophy; if Miller was on tonight—and Hanson *felt* him on, urged him—there would never be another game to rival this one, never. When Hanson had drawn the title game, he had started hoping, praying that Miller and Cragin would meet there. *Tonight, the clash of the century, and it's mine!*

"And now, ladies and gentlemen, our National Anthem." Hanson looked to his right, past the hanging inverted beehive of speakers that was his tonight's mouth, to the Stars and Stripes on the pavilion's rear wall. He let his hands run over both boards, caressing slides. Electricity flowed, *nerve to finger to board to you;* the two teams stood to attention; the cheerleaders stopped writhing; the crowd quieted, and the two bands played together. Hanson turned on his outside sound monitor, heart swelling; he folded his fingers together, letting the music spoon his soul.

Then the crowd was thundering, waving pennants of black and yellow, green and gold; he slapped at the sound switch and readjusted slides as the teams took position for the opening drop, Miller facing Cragin. The McKinley six's armsheaths were black. The ref android stood between the lines of players, holding the watermelon-like float above his head.

The crowd was comfortably anticipatory/yellow, only a few spots of green and orange left; the player monitors were shading toward orange, with the exception of Miller's, which was still yellow-green. Cragin's looked a bit more orange than the rest.

The ref left the float motionless nine feet off the floor. His form blurred; then he was standing at the sidelines, arms at sides, facing the teams.

The two centers, Grant Storen and Jerry Siller, leaped simultaneously toward the float. Woodlawn's Storen, taller, got the tip of his sheath on it and sent it wobbling back to his teammates. Hanson started the clock. McKinley fell back to its end of the rectangular court.

The goal was a four-foot-square hoop hanging unsupported ten feet above the back out-of-bounds line; the McKinley players formed a loose circle around it. Woodlawn brought the float toward them, batting it from man to man in easy straight lines. McKinley moved out to meet the other team, maintaining the circle, and the float's speed from hand to hand, player to player, increased.

Warner, a Woodlawn guard, got the float and slowed, batting it from hand to hand, shifting first left, then right. Abruptly he jumped, juggled it up to eye level and swatted it end over end toward the goal. It went to the left of the hoop, bounding upward off the boundary clearfield. Fifteen feet above the floor it hit the ceiling field and angled downward, spinning slowly. Cragin leaped as it came down, his green-covered arm reaching above Miller's black sheath to bat the float into the goal. It stayed there momentarily; the ref signaled, and it floated downward. Owens and Mann, the McKinley guards, went toward it as the rest of the players ran toward the other end of the court.

Hanson chorded on Woodlawn statistic buttons—attempted-goal twice, once holding the Warner button, once the Cragin; goal once, holding Cragin; Woodlawn score—at the same time stepping on the floor pedal to say, "Woodlawn goal by Rank Cragin." The crowd below him was on its feet cheering, monitors cresting toward orange, sending the thrill of first blood through him. McKinley balanced him with disappointment-young-game/yellow.

Batting the float back and forth, Owens and Mann trotted across the center line. Their teammates started from the sidelines and crisscrossed toward the goal, Woodlawn players matching them step for step. Miller stopped and started, and Owens batted the float to him past Cragin's flailing sheath.

Miller looked toward the goal, juggling the float upward; Cragin came around, hands up, ready to block a shot. Miller tensed and Cragin jumped too soon. Miller ducked under him and started to shoot. Another Woodlawn player left Mann to guard Miller, who batted the float under the other's outstretched arms to his open teammate for an easy five-foot goal. McKinley cheers and orange monitors; Hanson touched buttons. *Nice move, Miller.*

"McKinley goal by Henry Mann, on a pass from Miller DuBois." He felt a flash of Woodlawn admiration/yellow, reached for slides, and checked himself. *Let the first quarter run itself.* But that trend needed watching.

Each team gave the float away once: Storen touched it with both hands simultaneously, and Mann hit it with bare skin. But Hanson felt their nervousness draining to game calm as they realized each other's fallibility. He felt the crowd beginning to settle into balance, too, each school up when its team scored, down when the other did. *Yes. They're good kiddies. They wouldn't spoil their own show, would they, now?*

"Goal for the Black Bears by Miller DuBois."

Yellow-green Miller and up-and-down yellow-to-orange Cragin: Hanson could almost feel their moves and their sweat. He reached for slides, stopped. The show—but it was running smoothly. He pushed the controls, damping every monitor except Miller's and Cragin's, letting the two stars' emotion/thoughts fill his head, running and dribbling the float with them. They were easy to separate:

Miller: *they run sloppy patterns these guys aren't so good.* Cragin: *he's fast like they said but I'll handle him taller/score more.* Miller: *as they're supposed to be PASS.* Cragin: *seen tougher guys before he won't take MVP away GOT THE FLOAT GOT TO GET AROUND.* Miller: *he's got it he's taller timing's the key OWENS DON'T let that.* Cragin: *SCORE GET OUT OF MY WAY BLACK BASTARD.* Miller: *guy open like that take it easy Miller nobody's perfect he didn't see it anyway what happens if we push him a little easy to rattle?* Cragin: *moves too FAST GET TO THE GOAL SHOOT SHOOT POINTS! he stopped me that time but I'M BETTER I'LL FIND A WAY AROUND ENOUGH TIMES—*

A real fighter thought Hanson. *He'll make it, the bastard.* He slapped the rest of the monitors open again. *No, Paul, it was only because you were too small—*

The clock zeroed and the horn sounded, startling him. *Got sidetracked. Careful, Paul.* He looked at the statistics: Woodlawn led by three; Cragin had six points, Miller two and several assists.

Hanson leaned forward, and apprehension and anger dissolved before the renewing glow: second quarter! *Now, my littles, we begin. Come along, and let Papa Paul help you . . .* He partially undamped the crowd section to put delicate boosts into the two-minute exchange of cheers. When the ref held the float up for the resumption of play, the two crowds were between yellow and orange, balanced on the fulcrum of the teams.

Woodlawn controlled the drop again, this time getting the float to the goal before McKinley could set up a defense. Hanson, touching buttons, pedaled and said deliberately, "Woodlawn goal by Rank Cragin. Woodlawn by five, their biggest lead of the night." He shivered as the hint of depression from the McKinley side pulled down at him.

And so went the quarter:

McKinley running tight patterns and not hitting the resulting easy shot; Woodlawn playing more chaotically but working the float in to Cragin and Storen enough to pull away, away . . .

Cragin shooting and finding a perfectly timed Miller sheath knocking the float away; Miller dribbling along the clearfield and Cragin guarding, using his height to prevent the easy goal . . .

Hanson's hands unconscious on buttons and slides; crowd monitors almost of their own accord spreading yellow to orange across his living butterfly; McKinley hurting, even Miller climbing away from green as his patterns produced more rebounds than points.

"Touching foul on Miller DuBois; Rank Cragin shooting free for the Wolverines." The teams stood, McKinley and Woodlawn players alternating, in parallel lines extending away from the clearfield on either side of the McKinley goal, two McKinley forwards closest to it. Cragin stood unguarded between the lines, juggling the float and batting it through the hoop.

Miller . . . are we going to have a hot night after all? Hanson damped the crowd monitors and the rest of the players, letting the McKinley forward into his head.

"Goal by Rank Cragin . . ."

Miller: *what's the matter with us anyway? We must be shooting less than twenty percent.* (Hanson touched buttons and saw the McKinley second-quarter field goal percentage so far: nineteen-eight. He whistled softly. Nice guess.) *Patterns work all right, defense super when you think about the height they have on us. Call time out.*

The teams huddled.

Something in Miller's mindset resonated poignantly in Hanson. He wanted to know more; he reached for Miller's control slide, but jerked back as his fingers touched it. *Don't mess with him!* The teams' emotions were inviolate; he really had no right to be eavesdropping. He started to mute Miller's monitor and stopped. *Right? Bullshit! It's my show, isn't it? Why* can't *I listen to him?*

Now the game was resuming. Hanson pushed at McKinley slides, trickling hope into the crowd. Miller: *our float now c'mon guys move the patterns try seven-A here's the sign make it tight!*

"Tight!" whispered Hanson. *No, Miller, that was my word and you can't make it that way, hide yourself in the patterns because you're scared.* Hanson jerked in the chair, making arrested imitations of Miller's motions down on the court. *You've got to come out and fight, and your size won't make any difference and you won't end up here . . .* He blinked, nodding.

Miller passed, and Cragin deflected the float. The whisper of crowd regret reinforced Hanson's pouring back into the wiring. Miller was playing too well not to be rewarded.

What? He damped Miller's monitor, opening the crowd's. The Woodlawn board was a deteriorating pattern of orange, yellow and green, overblown confidence and *Hanson's simpering* letting them admire an enemy player's efforts in a losing cause. *You're going to blow it, again.* For an instant he heard the other PA men's laughter—

Miller prevented a Cragin shot, and Hanson stopped the Woodlawn response before it started, feeding the green and gold crowd disappointment and the tiniest increment of hate *for you, Miller!* Too bad to distort things, but it was what he deserved for fantasizing.

"Woodlawn goal by Rank Cragin." Now, triumph. The boards began to show unity on the Woodlawn side again. But not enough . . .

Halftime.

Hanson arched his back; the chair arched with him. Ordinarily, halftime was delicate, with little to help maintain the crowd's excitement. Now, however, he would be able to take advantage of Miller's absence to rebuilt the earlier balance. *You're lucky, Paul. You could have—* He touched McKinley slides, letting that crowd hope as he pedaled and said, "Halftime score, Woodlawn 43, McKinley 27."

He saw the Woodlawn band preparing to play and quickly stifled their desire, simultaneously boosting the McKinley musicians'.

The naked McKinley cheerleaders took the floor, and Hanson fed envy and desire to the Woodlawn crowd. *C'mon babes, make 'em lust.*

"WE like our team!"

The crowd responded slowly. *C'mon!* He worked slides, watching the bouncing breasts and gleaming hips without really seeing them. *No, no, you couldn't have— it's only halftime, a whole two quarters to go and they're getting away—*

"We LIKE our team!"

There, the Woodlawn side was coming around, smug superiority melting, restless desire to see *their* cheerleaders replacing it . . . *Why? I like these better.*

"We like OUR team!"

. . . hating a little now . . .

"We like our TEAM!" He gave the McKinley monitors a boost on the team, and the other side of the pavilion roared like a territorial lion, obscene gestures and thumbed noses flashing. *Good, good.* The Woodlawn side responded without prompting, and he backed down the controls slightly. *Don't use it all at once.* He began to relax and eye the cheerleaders. Nice bodies. The one in the center especially slim with those small breasts. He was disappointed when they left the floor.

The Woodlawn band took up almost before McKinley's stopped; he watched the cheerleaders begin their routine. These weren't bad, either— *But what difference does that make? They wouldn't want you—* He stopped the thought, giving McKinley a little shot of contempt for the conservative bikini bottoms. The crowd responded with a trained seal flash of orange.

He slipped back into his boards, letting the last unpleasantness from the cheerleaders fade away. The clock measured out the seconds and minutes of the allotted halftime fifteen, and he adjusted slides. The glow came over him again; he had them back. The show would run!

Now the teams were on the floor, running through their abbreviated second-half warmup. Last cheers shook his booth. He made final adjustments to Woodlawn's now fully competitive mood, McKinley's come-from-behind expectations. The court monitors showed both teams yellow-orange; McKinley felt more determined.

And now the players were arranging themselves around the ref. Hanson's nerves were electric, internal precious merging with magnetic butterfly. The pavilion's energy was *his. Now, kiddies, the real show begins.*

"Goal by Rank Cragin for the Wolverines."

"Henry Mann gets two for McKinley, on a pass from DuBois."

"Foul is on Rank Cragin. Miller DuBois at the line, shooting two . . ."

The teams were playing even. Hanson felt McKinley: *come on, just a little more and we'll catch 'em!* and Woodlawn: *just keep on and it's ours!* He juggled the teams' support, running the big balance, accentuating the ups and downs when a good play came along. Green Miller and orange Cragin virtually neutralized each other. Hanson found himself opening their monitors wide, letting them into his head again. *I'll do them and the crowd at the same time tonight.*

Miller: *shooting better now we'd be creaming 'em if it weren't for that second quarter see if we can rattle 'em a little superior teamwork has the edge . . .*

Think you're calm you're fooling yourself, thought Hanson, damping Miller slightly for:

Cragin: *he only had four first half I thirteen all I have to do GOT THE FLOAT SHOOT OPENING DRIVE* SCORE! *TWO MORE FOR ME WE'RE EIGHTEEN UP NOW stop his assists he helped make sixteen others Christy cheerleader make her tonight she'll love me and how do you like that, father? Get a scholarship* without *your well-placed friends . . .*

Bastard. Hanson remembered the Cragins of his school days, looking down at him, parents living off the fat of the computers pushing pushing pushing the little Ranks—even naming them snobbishly! But he sure could play foreball—*your boards, Paul!*

"Goal by Rank Cragin . . ." He flowed over slides, extending sparking fingers into the seats and minds of the crowd. He touched buttons smoothly. Full orange, full balanced orange by the end of the quarter would do it.

Miller: *dribble so wide apart I'll take it away . . .*

Hanson's hand flickered with Miller's as the McKinley boy stole the float and raced unopposed to the Woodlawn goal. Miller: *no one to stop me easy now one step jump IN!*

"Goal by Miller DuBois for the Black Bears." Hanson actually had to reduce the McKinley monitors to keep them out of the red.

Although, who knows, maybe we'll have a controlled *red going by the end.*

He snorted. "Easy, Paul, easy." It was good, but it couldn't be that good. The only other announcer to attempt a controlled red had been killed before the sleepgas quenched the riot.

Still, this was a better booth, with sleepgas controls built right in.

Woodlawn brought the float back upcourt after Miller's solo goal—and McKinley's Owens stole a pass. He and Miller and Mann raced toward the Woodlawn goal, only Cragin and a Woodlawn guard to stop them. Cragin: *stupid shits getting careless GO GET THE OTHER GUY WARNER CAN'T YOU SEE HE'S WIDE OPEN black bastard's got it thinks he's fast I'll be right with him when he jumps OH YOU BASTARD!*

At the last instant, Miller, jumping for the goal, underhanded the float to Mann for two uncontested points.

"McKinley goal by Henry Mann." The entire crowd went wild, admiration sending monitors to red-orange.

Hanson tensed. *Oh, now, isn't that cute? Little devils playing.* He worked with Woodlawn slides, beginning to sweat. *Lost them in second quarter really?* They—no, it was impossible, but—were fighting—no, abrupt changes always took a little time to take hold. There, they were coming around: Woodlawn apprehension grabbed his viscera; sudden fierce McKinley hope set his heart pounding.

Woodlawn brought the float upcourt, worked it around, and Cragin hit a twenty-footer. *Like it, shitheads!* Hanson shot electric adrenalin into the Woodlawn crowd and it responded with a fountain of plastic cups, some of which hit the court. A roll of electric-green toilet paper arched high over the bleachers and streamed to the court at centerline. Before the ref saw it, a boy darted from the stands, tore off the unrolled portion and leaped back into the crowd with the rest.

Hanson pedaled, apprehension burning in his gut again. "Ladies and gentlemen, please refrain from littering the playing surface."

McKinley came upcourt; Miller keyed a four-man pattern, and the Woodlawn section approved. Hanson set shame knifing through the wires; red-orange hate glared at him, pulled his lips back from clenched teeth. He hissed.

A shower of plastic cups hit the court. Electric-green paper arched again, and Hanson spied the boy who'd picked up the first roll jumping and waving his arms. "All *right!*" He swelled with a sudden cold determination, straightening and leaning forward. Just because he— *they* couldn't take it away from him! He flipped the Security Intercom switch and snapped, "Section G, row six, a boy with long blond hair throwing shit on the court."

The ref had called time out to clear the floor; Hanson pedaled. "Ladies and gentlemen, it is a standard rule of this establishment that any person causing a game-delaying disturbance be ejected from the premises, and the game stopped until such person has left." He looked down, hands hovering ready over slides.

Two cop androids walked onto the court between the

clearfield and the Woodlawn crowd, then up into the bleachers. The people shifted away from them, and Hanson smiled at the loathing and fear in the monitors. As the cops picked up the boy and carried him away, he waved a green and yellow pennant and jabbed his thumb at one of their buttocks. The Woodlawn monitors flashed relief and orange derision.

Little bastards! Hanson fingered slides, wringing a raucous cheer from the McKinley section, augmenting the Woodlawn derision with a bit of hate; green and gold screamed across at yellow and black. Miller was looking from side to side, his monitor radiating wonder; Cragin was glorying in the noise.

The ref gave a Woodlawn player the float at the clearfield, and he batted it to Cragin. Miller's sheaths flickered between Cragin's, and the float wobbled upward. They jumped after it, and Miller managed to push it toward the Woodlawn goal. The crowd started to approve.

The quarter horn sounded.

"At the end of the third quarter, the score is Woodlawn 60, McKinley 45." Quickly, Hanson prodded the section where the McKinley cheerleaders sat, and the five girls bounded out onto the court; he fed envy and desire to the Woodlawn side, cut it off for inaccessibility. Admiration subsided. *That's right.*

The security intercom buzzed, and he slapped at the switch. "What?"

The worried voice of the android controller came from the speaker overhead. "Hey, Paul, they're gettin' awful excited. You sure you know what you're doin'?"

Everybody trying to stop him! "Certainly. Mind your androids and leave the humans to me." He broke the circuit.

Once again Woodlawn controlled the drop; McKinley set up its defense, and the green-and-gold team began working for an opening. Hanson fed both sides of the pavilion expectation and tension/orange. The fire seized him, and he increased intensity to red-orange. *This is it, bastard-littles.*

"McKinley goal by Miller DuBois."

Woodlawn had two second-team players in the game. One of them took an off-balance shot and Siller caught the wobbling float in midflight. Miller was racing downcourt ahead of everyone. Miller: *got them beat now the pass off the ceiling A LITTLE FASTER nice pass!*

He put on a burst of speed, barely touching the float, using its momentum to push it ahead of him and up to the goal.

Cheers and marvel/orange from the pavilion as a unit. Hanson pushed slides *no, no you can't I've lost them—*

Miller was cool green coming back upcourt. Cragin: *bastard think you're HE LEFT ME OPEN IRWINS* PASS! *YOU SHIT-FOR-BRAINS tired can't just a little longer OH NO YOU LET HIM* STEAL *IT! NOW THEY'RE UPCOURT TWO ON TWO Irwins never oughta get off the bench THEY MISSED!*

Miller caught the missed shot off the clearfield and the rest of the teams arrived downcourt.

Woodlawn's crowd was settling into admiration/hope, and Hanson shifted electric color, trying to swallow the lump in his throat. Cragin was near-red as he guarded—. Miller: *got 'em going now pattern six c'mon Foss and Henry not tired are you?* Cragin: *black bastard think you've got something special I'VE GOT YOU OUTSCORED EIGHTEEN TO EIGHT AND OUTREBOUNDED EAT THAT SHITHEAD!*

Hanson seized the hate and threw it into the Woodlawn monitors. *See, your big daddy knows!* The crowd responded and he added red-orange. *More like red,* a part of his mind warned but he ignored it. *They're coming around! That's it, do it, do it!*

"Foul on Grant Storen. Gary Siller shooting free for the Black Bears."

The McKinley team monitors shifted as a unit, drawing strength and direction from Miller. The team ran patterns, defended, passed as though the game were only starting. Miller's monitor edged up to yellow and settled back to green. Miller: *don't get excited now's the time to be cool they're tired we're clicking THERE IS JUSTICE in foreball twelve points three minutes we can do it.*

Justice? Hanson laughed, and his voice cracked. *Justice? My boy, you have a lot to learn.* His hands were electric flame in the wiring, feeding and eating the crowd's excitement. He turned up the amplification on Miller and Cragin, running and panting with them. *A show, a show's all there is, Miller!*

Miller: *really sloppy Rank GOT THE FLOAT DOWNCOURT HENRY hit it now up and BOUNCE got it two more!*

The Woodlawn crowd was forgetting the game again, watching Miller. *Behave yourselves, stinkheads! He's not that good.* But he kept the player monitors open.

Cragin: *he can't do this he can't HE CAN'T IT'S MY*

GAME BASTARD. Miller: *we're outplaying 'em now enough time PASS.*

Eight points, seven, six. A minute and half to go. The pavilion crested to a solid unity behind the McKinley team.

Hanson kept statistics only through fifteen years of habit. His body was aflame, his mind a racing network of batting floats and monitor slides and *little shithead devil bastards why don't you this is my show yours stupid idiots*— He fed hatred, contempt, envy to the Woodlawn crowd; he pushed their monitors all the way into the red zone. His arms were superconductors, his fingers guiding smooth slipping power, and still they resisted.

His speaker mouth said, "Goal by Miller DuBois, foul on Rank Cragin. DuBois at the free-throw line."

A minute to go, four points down. Both crowds were on their feet screaming. Hanson's singing nerves urged the Woodlawn people on. *You're going to lose!* Buttons and slides, *I'll red you, you*—

Miller: *they're stalling foul.* Cragin: *KEEP THE FLOAT KEEP THE FLOAT DON'T SHOOT DON'T SHOOT.*

"Foul on Foss Owens. Grant Storen at the line."

Miller: *rebound we've got the position he MISSED got the float OWENS DOWNCOURT HIT!*

"Goal by Foss Owens for the Black Bears."

Cragin: *black bastards full court us will they where they get all the energy?* Miller: *thirty seconds we can do it.*

Hanson pushed all the slides against the stops, pounding at them, barely holding himself back from the player controls.

"Foul is on Rank Cragin. Miller DuBois at the line, one and one."

Hanson was with—. Miller: *take it easy plenty of time deep breath relax juggle up and PERFECT.* Cragin: *I'LL REBOUND* MISS *BLACK BASTARD GOT TO STOP HIM HE CAN'T TAKE IT AWAY NO POINTS THIS QUARTER FUCKER MADE IT!*

Tie game.

Miller: *full court 'em I'll play safety Cragin's down here nice pass Warner don't let him lay it up he's too rattled to make foul shots. Ten seconds we'll rebound . . .*

"Foul on Miller DuBois; Rank Cragin at the line . . ."

Cragin: *NOW I'LL SHOW HIM SHOOT GOOD! GIVE ME THE BALL STUPID REF SHOOT IT UP i missed.* Miller: *one point ten seconds.*

Hanson was color *controlled red! controlled red!* and running with Cragin and Miller and buttons and slides. He opened the outside sound channel and swam in the screaming and sweat *controlled red controlled!*

Miller: *get the ball upcourt.* Cragin: *stop you now bastard!*

Hanson wavered over his boards; the crowd surged, great tides of emotion sweeping whole sections back, away, forward . . .

Five seconds, four, three, two. Miller: *got the float one shot has to be good they're double-teaming move shift trapped rat in the basement.* Cragin: *black bastard's not BLUFFING AROUND ME THIS TIME.* Miller: *open SHOOT THE HORN'S made it! PATTERNS WIN! PATTERNS WIN!*

McKinley monitors flared, then plunged as the ref android signaled *too late.*

"Woodlawn wins, 69-68," said Hanson's speakers.

Cragin: *I'M KING I'M KING I'M KING WE WIN WIN WIN!*

Miller: *too late patterns win but I was too late . . .*

The crowd was berserking onto the court, Woodlawn for McKinley; KILL screamed Hanson's every copper nerve. His hand found the sleepgas button and light switch; thuds sounded against the door behind him as darkness and white fog descended outside his booth. The monitors faded to maroon, to pink and gray flickers, to darkness, leaving only the glow of the statistics and the zeroed clock. *Your show kiddies i did it.* Hanson fell forward onto the boards, exhausted.

He became aware of the security intercom's buzz. He flicked the switch and sat up. "Hanson."

"That was beautiful, Paul! We haven't had a championship game like that for fifteen years! The holo'll have that final scene on for a week!"

"Huh?" Oh; the android controller must think Hanson had been manipulating the teams to get that finish.

"Christ, you even made the MVP award. Miller DuBois, unan. You know he shot eighty percent for the game, and he held Cragin to eighteen total, just one free shot in the last quarter? Great show, Paul, great."

"Yeah." Hanson smiled slightly. Poor Cragin; Miller probably wouldn't even care. He looked down into the darkness. Light from the booth dimly outlined seats and bodies. *Well, I did it.*

He slid the master slide shut. *Good night, kiddies.*

Molten Core

by Donnel Stern

Donnel Stern is a doctoral student in psychology at Michigan State University. His very real talent as a writer threatens to seduce him from the comfort and security of an academic career. As an academic administrator, I can assure Don that he is needed in the university. As an editor, I can assure Don that he is needed in the world of letters.

I wonder how good he is at conflict resolution?

The Core. Relic buildings, deadwood, history in the flesh, urban renewal's embarrassments. Enclosed (encased) in a shiny, ten-mile wall of twenty-foot black plastic. Populated by the old who would or could not change—time's laggards. Deserted by the young, the children, who, when they understood it, had moved outside to the glass and the concrete and the steel, bought the little cars that skimmed above the ground, joined the Core Preservation League, and now came back to visit on dainty-clean tiptoe feet.

John Tallow knew all that. And yet, every morning, before the sun came over the Wall, he enjoyed sitting in front of his bookshop in an old folding lawn chair on the sidewalk and looking out across the four lanes of broken pavement. Across the street, the sign above the cafe blinked on and off in blue and yellow neon. *Marge's . . . Marge's . . . Marge's . . .* The tourists liked the old lights. Marge turned them on early so the first group of the day might prevail on their tour guide to let them stop at the quaint little place for coffee and a roll.

Tallow was an old man. His gray hair curled long over the gold earpieces of his glasses. He wore a blue-and-white-checked shirt, and inside the collar his neck was ringed with deep creases. His gray workpants were stained and wrinkled, and he wore a fraying herringbone coat over the shirt.

The Wall stood only a few yards behind Tallow's building. The gate, two massive sections of wall that opened inward at the touch of a lever in the gatehouse outside, was closed now, and it blended into the rest of the Wall at the end of the street. Tallow looked around as the familiar groan of its hundred-pound hinges rumbled echoes down the empty streets. The first crowd of the day laughed and mumbled and ran inside. Tallow watched them jostle past. He saw the collectors head toward the garbage piles that the city would not haul away for another hour. He saw the first-timers bend down and touch the wondrous hard surface of the street, then follow their guides through gas stations and dirty alleys. And he saw the pickets from the Core Protection League, their hair perfectly coiffed and luminescent fingernails shining in the sunlight that now came like a wide, white road from the open gate.

Tallow stood up, folded his chair, and walked downstairs into the shop. He clambered onto the stool in the front of the store and sat there like a gargoyle, fingers hooked under the edge of the seat, waiting for the tourists to come and buy his books and take them home and put them on their coffee tables. He pulled a handkerchief from his back pocket and spread it in his hand. He covered his face with it, grasped his red-veined nose between thumb and forefinger, and blew, shaking his head back and forth so that the muffled bubbling noise alternated rapidly from one nostril to the other.

The shop was a musty grotto of second-hand pulp adventure and used belles-lettres, an underground cavern of books. Inside their faded and warping covers, the millions of words lined the shelves and lay in piles on the damp concrete floor. Heavy, plastered columns stood close together in two rows down the length of the small room, and block-and-board bookshelves leaned against each one. Cracked under the four-story weight of the empty flophouse above, the columns were stained with sienna streams of rust that grew down like stalactites from the leaking pipes somewhere in the ceiling. Muddy sun slithered through the gum wrappers and cigarette butts banked against the outsides of the street-level windows. Tallow's bed, dresser, sink, and stove occupied a corner in the rear of the store.

Brass bells hung by red yarn from the back of the door, and they bang-jangled against the wall as the door opened. Tallow looked up and saw Henry Porter, administrator of the Core's third district. He was a small man, young, dressed in a pair of bright-green laythelene slacks that made a swishing noise as he walked. Porter stopped at the threshold, fingered the peeling decals on the doorglass, smiled. But the smile was a forced turning-up of the corners of the mouth, and Tallow prepared himself.

"Good morning, John." Porter walked across the room and faced Tallow over the counter.

Tallow nodded.

Porter made rotating motions with his hands, as if he didn't know how to express himself. "Uh . . . I suspect you have some idea why I'm here?"

"Some idea, yes. But you tell me." Tallow folded his arms over his chest and sighed. So it was time.

"Well, you know the compromise the city made with the CPL . . . moving the Wall in a little at a time, modernizing, spreading it over the years?" Porter looked down and rolled his lips inward, pressed them together.

Tallow slumped, looked between his legs at the seat of the stool. "I guess you don't have to tell me the whole thing. I know."

Porter brightened. He smiled and took a deep breath. "Thanks, John . . . I didn't know how I'd say the rest . . . Actually, you're lucky, in a way. After all, the city owns the Core. Would've torn down the whole thing twenty years ago if it hadn't been for the CPL."

"I know, I know." Tallow's head did not move, but he looked up at Porter over his glasses. "That doesn't help too much now, though, does it?"

Porter was silent.

"So how long do I have?"

"Three weeks."

Tallow nodded.

"Is there anything I can do for you, John? Help you move or something?"

Tallow ignored him. He stared at the ceiling. "Have you ever been to a slaughterhouse, Porter?"

Porter shook his head.

Tallow spoke softly. "Well, you look at the animals milling around in the pens, you look at the way they move and the way they smell the blood in the air, and you can tell they know they're going to die." He glanced at Porter. "If I knew I had to die, if I knew there was nothing I could do about it, I'd want to do it myself. It's sitting around and waiting for somebody else to do it that's so bad."

"But you're not going to die. You can just move into another building."

"No, I'm not going to die. But I've lived here forty years . . ." He gazed into the air.

"Are you sure there's nothing I can do for you?"

"Just go away, Porter. Leave me alone."

Porter turned and walked to the door. He hesitated, then opened the door and climbed the stairs to the street. The bells clanked against the wall.

Marge's restaurant had white walls, and the floor was tiled in red and white squares of linoleum. The place was clean, but there were scrape marks on the paint behind the aluminum-tube chairs and the linoleum was laced with a network of deep, black grooves.

Tallow sat at the counter with Edgar Shiele. Edgar was thin and bald. He held his bony hands in his lap, clasping and unclasping them. He massaged the back of one with the other, covering the blue veins that pushed up against his dry skin. Marge leaned against the counter from the other side. Her gray hair was pinned in a neat bun and she wore an apron tied across the bulk of her abdomen.

They were silent. The only sound in the small room was the slurping at the edges of cups of hot coffee. The streets and the stores were empty; the outsiders had gone home for the night and the gate was closed.

Finally it was Edgar who spoke. His voice was quiet and his face was turned down, watching his hands comfort each other in his lap. "I'm doing OK, you know . . . You could come in with me for a while, maybe help me find stuff for the store . . ." There was no response, and Edgar continued softly, almost apologetically. "Well, hubcaps going good. You could help me find hubcaps."

Marge glowered at him. Edgar leaned back on the stool with his skinny shoulders pulled in around his neck. Tallow shook his head. He could see that Marge was about ready to blow up. "Calm down, Marge. It's not him you're mad at, anyway. There just isn't anything to say."

"Well, that's all right for you. You can move your books. Where am I going to find another usable restaurant? I can't move my whole kitchen in three weeks, not without a lot more help than a bunch of old rattlebones like us can give me."

There was silence again.

Tallow made the decision to tell them. Core people leaned on one another; he knew they would not report him. He took a deep breath. "I'm not going to move the books." They jerked their heads toward him. Tallow put his hands palms down on the counter and sat straight up. "I'm going to burn it down."

Edgar's mouth fell open and he stared. Marge's eyebrows jumped to her forehead. She covered her mouth with her hand, sucked in her breath.

Tallow went on slowly. "I've planned it for months. Went all over and found plenty of cans with gas and oil left in them. They're all hidden in the hotel. Up there." He pointed across the street. "Nobody ever goes there."

He stopped and looked at them. "I wanted to tell you. It means more if someone else knows. And what does it hurt, anyway? The fire department will be here before anything else catches. I just want to do it myself if it's got to be done."

"But they'll arrest you." Edgar's voice trembled.

"I know. I'm going to set the fire and let it get going. Then I'll call the fire department and wait for them outside. I won't resist if they figure it's arson. I'm just going to let them pick me up. It's all planned."

"Why are you doing this?" said Marge. "Why don't you just move and let them tear it down?"

He explained, and they challenged him, and he explained again. The black sky outside turned gray, and then pink. They were still sitting in the cafe when they heard the gate opening. They drank the dregs of their coffee, and Edgar and Tallow started out the door. Marge called after Tallow, and he turned back toward her.

"I think I understand it, now, John. I really do. But still . . ."

Edgar turned to Tallow and nodded curtly. "Feel the same way myself."

Tallow walked across the street and opened his shop for business. He made a cardboard sign with an old felt pen and taped it to the iron railing of the stairs on street level. "Closing Sale—All Books ½ off."

The alarm clock broke his sleep. He opened his eyes, looked around the basement. The silent shadows of the bookstacks lay in skewed squares and rectangles on the far wall. He went to the window and looked up. The streetlights threw rows of soft, cold circles down each side of the pavement. The sky was blue-black, like a bad bruise, and the moon was orange behind the smoke of the city. There was a tall ribbon or darkness on the horizon that he knew was the Wall.

He had explained when someone had told him it was foolish or too dangerous, and when they were still not satisfied, he had shrugged his shoulders. He had talked about it more than he had thought he would, and more of them had wanted to hear about it than he had expected. But now it was time, and he was afraid.

He looked down at his hands. They were trembling. He knew that if he tried to eat he would throw up. He tried to brush his teeth in the sink at the back of the shop, but he gagged before he could get the brush halfway into his mouth, and he spit the paste and saliva into the brown-circled drain.

He turned on the small stove beside the sink and stood with his back to it, warming his hands behind him. He could still back out. He could still just do nothing and wait until the big crane and the swinging iron ball arrived at nine o'clock. He could start moving the books right now. He could move into the center of the Core. There would be time to live out his years in the center. He could live in an old house and never hear the grinding of the hinges on the black gates. He could take walks in the evening and come back to Marge's and drink coffee.

But he could not really do these things any more, and he knew it. He had invested too much of himself to stop now. It was all planned. He could not let them tear it down. He had a horrible image of bricks flying in slow motion through the air and of four-story walls crumpling like cardboard under bombs. Books soared over the Core on the gently flapping wings of their covers, and everyone knew they were his. Somehow they had voices, and they cried out his name. Their pain was his pain, and he was with them as they struggled like moths toward the mammoth flame that rose from the earth to consume them. And then he *was* the books and the leaning buildings and the lightposts and the pavement and . . .

He shook his head, picked up his flashlight, and started up the inside stairs to the hotel. Each stair answered his step with a creak, and he climbed lightly, carefully, keeping his weight on the warped outside edges so he would not fall through if one of the treads caved in.

He opened the door at the top and leaned on the check-in desk. The pigeon-hole mailboxes were choked with cobwebs, and the veneer on the surface of the desk had cracked in thin strips and curled up like springs. He shuffled to the next flight of steps, staying on the path he had already cleared through the thick dust on the floor. He climbed to the fourth floor and went into the room where he kept the gasoline and oil. The cans were neatly stacked against the wall by the window; the room was otherwise empty. He went to the window, lifted the yellow shade and looked out over the Wall. All around, the city, sticking its long fingers into the sky. Red and green and blue and yellow and all colors blending and streaming upward, blotting out the stars. Smaller fingers and lights right up to the Wall. Then darkness except for the streetlights.

And directly below him in the street, a small crowd, a kinetic collage of white- and grey-haired heads, silvered and metallic in the cold glare of the streetlights. It only made sense that everyone would want to come and see, but he had not thought of it before. He liked it that they were here; he had made an impact. He laughed. He started to lower the shade, then stopped himself. Nobody had any use for it now, anyway. He wanted to tear it off the wall and throw it on the floor. But no, he thought, don't give in to it. Stay rational.

He picked up an armful of the cans and carried them out into the hallway. He started at the far end, just as he had planned. He dragged his foot to clear away the dust and then poured the gas and oil on the bare floor. Its wet gleam reflected the beam of his flashlight and there was mud where it splashed into the dust at the edge of the path. He went back and got more cans when the first ones were empty, and he slopped gasoline down the stairs to the third-floor hallway.

He was not afraid any more. He poured the liquid and ran to get more and poured and ran. He was out of breath, but he was laughing. It felt good. The tearing in his lungs hurt, but it was good, too. It had been years since there had been something worth being out of breath for. He felt the pounding of his heart in his chest. He opened cans of motor oil and spread the oil on the second-story hall floor. He was impatient; it ran too slowly. He hesitated, then threw the can down the hall and went back upstairs for gasoline. He came to the first story, the lobby, then the stairs to the basement, and then he was pouring gas and oil on the books, on the cement floor, on his mattress. He flung the empty can through the window. (No. Don't.) Glass shattered loudly onto the sidewalk, and there were cheers. He was surprised—they liked it.

He walked to the door of the bookshop and took out his

old Zippo. He stopped in the middle of the act of lighting it and unhooked the bells from the back of the door, slung the red yarn over his shoulder, heard the tink-tink sound of the clappers hitting the insides of the bells that were dead because they were resting against the muscle of his back. He bent down, lit the Zippo, and set fire to the oil. It burned slowly at first, billowing black smoke. He picked up a book and threw it through a window. More cheers from outside as the smoke escaped through the jagged hole. Now the flames jumped, flared red and orange and blue, began to feed on the books. Scorch marks appeared on the walls, and the air was hot. He turned and slammed the door, ran up the stairs to the street. Again the crowd shouted, louder this time, and people he had never met slapped him on the back. They filled the street now; their numbers had grown while he had worked his way down the stairs. And they were not just watching. They were laughing, milling and laughing and pointing at the flames that flicked like snake tongues from the basement windows. Tallow moved through the crowd. He felt it.

He stood in the middle of the throng, trying to keep his balance in the pushing and shoving around him. He laughed with the crowd. He saw Marge. Wisps of hair had fallen over her eyes and she laughed, too, clapping her hands in front of her face. Edgar—it made Tallow laugh even harder—picked up a brick and threw it at the wall. And then the windows in the higher stories began to explode, one after another, and the sky rained shards of glass. Coats were raised over heads, but Tallow saw that two or three people were down, pools of blood spreading over the pavement and spilling into the cracks. The laughing stopped. He remembered that he was to call the fire department.

Then, over the fire's roar and the crash of windows, came the rumble of the gate. The crowd quieted and turned toward it. Five of the bill-caps' black-and-white cushion cars burst through and rushed to the edge of the crowd. The people were silent, waiting. The roof of the building behind them thundered as it fell in, and the shell erupted flames like a volcano. The crowd turned back to it at the sound and the yells began again. The bill-caps got out of their cars and waded into the crush. No, thought Tallow, but his hand picked up a chunk of pavement and heaved it through the windshield of one of the black-and-whites. The shouting became a bellow, and pieces of pavement flew toward the cars from all around him.

He found himself running beside Marge. She was puffing, she had lost her shoes, and her dress was soaked with sweat. The bells on his back clanged and thudded against him, but he did not feel them. The air ripped ragged bits of phlegm from his lungs, but the flame was inside him now, fanned by every spurt of adrenalin, and nothing hurt. Far away, muted by the buildings in between, there was a resonant boom, and he knew the gates had closed. From close behind came the slaps and patters of sixty-year-old feet fleeing with him into the alleys and deserted buildings of the Core's heart.

Science Fiction, Archetypes, and the Future

by R. Glenn Wright

What you are about to read is a speculative exercise, one that I have been thinking about for a number of months, and, to date, it remains at best a hypothesis.

For many years I have been intrigued with Carl G. Jung's theory of archetypal patterns of the personality. I am not a psychologist; I teach literary criticism, and my interest in Jung and his work has been in the general area of psychological criticism, namely, that (1) virtually all imaginative literature contains central archetypal patterns; (2) as readers we are seldom consciously aware of these patterns; but that (3) the writers' adeptness (conscious or unconscious) at portraying and projecting archetypal designs is intimately involved with our judgment of the merits of a literary work. In short, I believe that one of the reasons why we like or dislike a particular work of literature is grounded in an author's ability to make us positively respond to an archetypal situation.

Let me back up a little. Jung distinguishes between the personal unconscious and the transpersonal unconscious, and in the process defines the concept of archetype: " . . . when fantasies are produced which no longer rest on personal memories, we have to do with manifestations of a deeper layer of the unconscious where the primordial images common to humanity lie sleeping. I have called these images or motifs 'archetypes' . . ."*

Jung died in 1961 at the age of eighty-six. His collected works run to nineteen volumes. Unlike Freud, who scrupulously organized and revised his written work every ten years or so, Jung resisted such endeavors, and, while he was concerned with delineating the concept of the archetype throughout his life, he never systematically made a complete list of the principal archetypes in man. A friend of mine who teaches psychology and I have made a tentative beginning

*C. G. Jung, "On the Psychology of the Unconscious," in *Two Essays on Analytical Psychology*, Meridian books, p. 76.

list. Some representative Jungian archetypes are the Persona (the social masks we wear—e.g., as son, father, student, lover, etc.); the Shadow (all the things we are afraid of or dislike in ourselves); the Wise Old Man; the Great Mother (from which comes the imagery of mother earth—the Great Mother has two aspects, the comforting, warm, all knowing "virgin," and the "terrible mother," the witch, the temptress, the female figure of death). Other archetypes are the Father, the Hero, Time, the Animal, Paradise Won and Paradise Lost, Mana (spirit or power), and Freedom.

Now, what has all this to do with science fiction and the future? In my reading of fiction I have been struck with the fact that the two genres in which archetypal patterns are presented most starkly and unambiguously are the fairy tale and science fiction. Why is this the case? I am not really sure, but these are my speculations: The fairy tales of Andersen and the Brothers Grimm (which represent one major source of modern fantasy literature) present the eternal verities and vanities of man. They do so didactically, simply, and often cruelly. Their content tells us how to behave and how to dare; the form of the presentation is fantasy, wish-fulfillment, and make-believe; both, I believe, come directly from the transpersonal unconscious. Because of the content, which is often almost surreal in its power and severity, and because the transpersonal unconscious, the home of archetypal demands, is full of pure, amoral power untouched by civilizing influence, the ego (all the conscious contents of the images of self) and superego (the part of the self conditioned by society's rules of conduct) dictate some sort of mediation, a tempering of what is said. The representation in action of archetypal drives can be frightening, because in some important senses we literally don't know what we are doing, or why. We can seldom openly confront archetypal imperatives without a screen, a metaphorical persona that euphemistically masks what is being said or asked of us. In the case of the fairy tale it is the form of fantasy, of "once upon a time . . ." That is the screen.

At least a part of the reason for the demands of the superego and ego is the contradictory nature of the content of so many fairy tales. They do tell us how to behave. (If we did have three wishes we would almost surely use them foolishly; ergo it is better that we cannot have just anything we might happen to wish for. We should think, plan, or work for what we want.) But they also tell us to dare, to question and challenge accepted modes of conduct. (If Simpleton had been "wise" in the ways of the world he would never have gotten the golden goose. It was an innocent child who pointed out that the Emperor had on no clothes.) Personified innocence and archetype often go hand in hand. If Jung is correct, archetypes represent the elemental in man. Our civilized personas often obscure our nature, demean the unconscious because we are afraid of its contents. But the transpersonal unconscious will be heard. It protects us, through our imagination and fantasy, from ourselves.

Herein, I think, is the relevance to contemporary science fiction. At least since the end of World War II, science fiction has been very much concerned with man's future, the role of the hard sciences in our lives, and increasingly with principles expounded by the social sciences as they affect our individual and collective behavior. The men and women who write science fiction extrapolate from the now into tomorrow and the far tomorrow. Their abilities as soothsayers are often staggering. Among other things they have demanded that their audience face up to the fact that we are an endangered species on an endangered planet, and that we as a species have brought this unhappy state upon ourselves. It is a cliché that Western civilization has become increasingly more complex over the past two hundred years and that one of the primary sources of this complexity has been our technology, a technology that has transformed the principles and discoveries of the pure sciences into the tangible realities of machines, rockets, methods of modifying our physical world and gaining increased control over it.

We have increasingly relied upon the technicians of our society to translate and transform the findings of science into aids for us all. The technicians have often been brilliant; they have also made a lot of mistakes. Often their little learning has indeed been a dangerous thing, and it has only recently come to us just how fallible this group might be. Very few individuals in our society even begin really to understand Newton's laws, let alone Einstein's or Max Planck's. Yet we live in a world in which the natural laws expounded by these men play an intimate role in our destiny. It is clearly unwise for the mass of men to be controlled by something that only a handful of them understand. It is doubly dangerous when, because of the political and economic systems predominant in the West, the men who wield political power are not among the few who understand the developments of contemporary physics, neurophysiology, or molecular biology.

Periodically, I suppose, most of us worry about some of these things. The trouble is that not very many people apparently worry constructively about them for very long. How do we learn about Einstein and Planck? Theoretically the answer to that is easy. We pick up a textbook or go to lectures and laboratories and learn. A scientific colleague of mine assures me that many more than 12 living individuals really understand the theory of relativity—perhaps from 1,200 to 12,000 do. This somehow is not as comforting as it might be. Einstein, I gather, is hard, very hard, to understand. The background of learning one must have to begin with is monumental, and even then, according to my friend, it's just plain true that most people, even most educated and intelligent people, are not smart enough to understand what $E=mc^2$ *really* means.

Then what? Isn't there some way to "translate" Einstein and all that he represents, to put him in another language so that by means of analogy or metaphor we can cope with what he is saying to us? I think that the answer is a limited yes. The social sciences and their practitioners are the priests of the hard sciences. Like any priests they seek to interpret the difficult sayings of the fundamental abstracts in our lives. They attempt to use the scientific method and explain the effects of men in masses in general, in political masses in particular, in primitive states, and as individuals full of fears, drives, and complexes. The social scientist seeks to do all of this on a number of levels; chiefly he seeks to explain facets of ourselves to ourselves within the context of the most explicit power in our lives—science. To date it seems that the social sciences have not done very well, but they are very young.

There is another way into the problem of "scientific translation": through art, specifically, arguing in the present context, through that sub-genre of literary art, science fiction, for it is science fiction that has met the power, glory and horror of science, scientists, technology, and technocrats head on. In the early days of E. E. Smith and his compatriots, before the full bloom of technology and its attendants, science and the scientist were treated as a panacea, as a manifestation of the Holy Grail archetype found. Science was Mana. The scientist was the Hero, full of ascension fantasies. After Hiroshima fell the Shadow. The Hero took on shadings of the

Demon. Now even the Earth Mother herself is in danger because of her children.

I stated earlier that science fiction since World War II has dealt more and more boldly and openly with the effects of scientific power. A number of writers of the genre are trained scientists; many others have made themselves expert in specific areas of the sciences soft and hard. As their writing has become more demanding upon the reader, both in content and in form, the central images of the writers have become more and more heavily archetypal. Take Frank Herbert's *Dune* as an example. Paul is the perfect Hero, presented complete with the various trials he must overcome in order to gain Mana. The Spice is a medium to Mana. The Bene Gesserit is Mana combined with the Great Mother, both good and evil. Water is the most sacred thing on Arrakis; it is the water of life, the Holy Grail. Eventually it is through water that Paradise Lost will be Paradise Regained. The worms are symbolic Animal archetypes. Virtually all of the major characters exhibit various personas, none more explicitly than Paul with his many names and faces.

This is not the place further to explicate this excellent novel in these terms, nor would there be much point in giving other illustrations, though they abound. Any reader who cares to can note the heavy archetypal symbolism in science fiction, and numerous critics have commented on the phenomenon. The question is, what is the significance of the fact that there are lots of archetypes that many authors may or may not be aware of placing in their works?

I think that modern science fiction is functioning in much the same way as the fairy tale does. It is telling us how to behave—what to do and what not to do—and, as importantly, it is telling us to calculatedly dare, to crack apart the nut of conditioned behavior, to question the basis of political, sociological, and technological assumptions that we have assumed as givens in our lives.

Here is the core of my hypothesis: When a culture is truly *in extremis*—in very dire trouble—and must either make a kind of inductive leap into its next phase of development or die, I believe that manifest archetypal drives are extremely important in determining whether that culture will make its leap or not: I would argue that in medieval Europe during the thirteenth century men and women were able to make a transition to what we call the Renaissance partially because the representative modes of expressing archetypal demands significantly altered in such a way that society could change with relative ease and with relative swiftness. By the same token I would argue that Greek society after the Peloponnesian War in 404 B.C. was so prostrate and so rigid in its thought that Greece could not make another transition in its development that would historically be evaluated as continuing its tradition of greatness. If I read Jung correctly, the primordial images common to humanity were every bit as potent in ancient Athens four hundred years before the birth of Christ as they were two hundred years previously, and as they are today. The difference in how they function lies in three areas: (1) what the powers of society are willing to allow in the way of pre-codified imaginative thoughts; (2) the quality and quantity of that imaginative thought, and (3) the ability of later social and political leadership to translate the new imaginative archetypal responses into forms of social and political action that can and will become standardized assumptions upon which thought and action can be based.

In speaking of the fairy tale I postulated that the screen of "once upon a time" functioned in Freudian terms to defend the reader (read "society") against some of what was being presented by archetypes of the transpersonal unconscious. In similar manner it appears that science fiction, particularly since World War II, has offered problems present and future, and suggested solutions so radical that the guise of fiction has been a necessary protection. Pohl and Kornbluth's *The Space Merchants*, for example, is not just a savage satire on Senator Joe McCarthy and his tactics; the novel predicts the ecological havoc that has come upon us, the dire threats of the population explosion, and the growth of megalopolis. It was first published in 1952 without a ripple of general response. Had the authors been famous in mainstream literature (like Arthur Miller, who created a tempest when he attacked McCarthy's methods in *The Crucible,* presented on Broadway in January 1953) or somehow managed to make their views known in essay form in *The Atlantic* or *Harper's,* it is, I think, safe to say that there would have been all hell to pay.

The example illustrates a larger point. Science fiction is radically free to speculate, propose and dispose of all sorts of issues, precisely because, relatively speaking, no one cares. The only wide audience that really discusses science fiction, even today, is that incredibly complex network of the young (in high school or college) who pass the "word" among themselves in mysterious ways of which fanzines are only a part. The "word" says what is good—what is exciting, and what has kindled their imaginations; and if by chance a parent tunes in on a Jefferson Airplane song that talks about Water Brothers, said parent would not only not know what the phrase meant, but would almost surely be amazed to learn that it represented the Holy Grail and a new way of life divined by a man named Robert Heinlein in a mammoth paperback novel called *Stranger in a Strange Land*.

The point that I want to stress, however, is that it is primarily college and high school age youth who respond most positively to SF. They are coming to the problem of the world fresh as a part of their rite of passage into adulthood. Their innocence (only in the sense of fully realizing that as adults they are going to have to cope with overpopulation, the state of nature and the machine, gigantic power shortages, etc.) combines with their daring, and they are more than willing to question the assumptions upon which political, social, and technological decisions are based. Science fiction is not only one means of explicating and expediting the movement from adolescence to adulthood; it, like the fairy tale, suggests what can be done, how, and what some of the dangers are. Above all, the genre calls to the hero archetype: "Come, innocent, before you are wise in men's ways, use your imagination and dare for the good of you and your kind."

If our present culture is indeed *in extremis* (and proof seems everywhere), then the inductive leap of new and vital approaches to our problems is mandatory. Somehow we must be able to understand the scientific wonders that geniuses of our kind have put in our grasp. The pragmatic technocrats are not enough; nor are the fledgling social sciences. Nor, apparently, do the two of them together suffice to save us from a very real sense of existential powerlessness, from a paralysis born out of not knowing what forces move us and how they work.

In no way do I propose science fiction as any kind of panacea for the present ills of the world. What I do propose is a closer look at the psychological concept of archetypes in a social rather than an individual context. Specifically, I think that man's imagination and fantasy, springing from both his personal unconscious and from the archetypes of the transpersonal unconscious as expressed in the creative arts in general, provide a very important indicator of how we are going to respond to our future.

Science fiction represents one of probably many manifestations of a fusion of Jungian ideas with our present fears of science and technology. In much of the science fiction being written today the authors have limned the future in heavy archetypal design. Since many of the men and women who write science fiction understand much more than most laymen about science itself and the nature of scientific inquiry, and combine that knowledge with what wells up from their imaginations—from their personal and transpersonal unconsciousnesses—their speculations are, I feel, much more important than we have hitherto given them credit for being in pointing out directions for future thought and action.

The Diggers

by Donnel Stern

Readers of previous Clarion *volumes are aware of my weakness for the fey. Here, Don Stern makes a delicate assessment of one of the true universals of life.*

Ilsa had looked for a sign of the diggers all the years of her life. There were dewy mornings outside the back door when she searched every inch of ground for proof that the bedtime story of the night before had not lied. And when she found none of the telltale holes in the grass, she cried and explained to herself that the diggers were hiding. There were long walks home from the marketplace when she smelled the dying scents of autumn and told the others that, no, she was not looking for anything in the fallow fields, that she just liked to see the richness of the bare ground. And there were the journeys in the thickest part of the woods when she held aside the fronds of a delicate fern to look underneath, when she muddied her clothing in the dank marshes as she tried to reach the islands of solid ground where there might be a hole.

And never a single support for her faith. Never the smallest disturbance of the soil that her long-trained eye could not identify as the scratch of fox feet or the half-built home of a mole.

Trudging home after another day, she gazed at the crescent of red sun resting on the roundness of the foothills and felt certain that the stars were the only magic she would ever see. And seeing magic was not enough. She wanted to touch magic, to talk to it. Sadly she walked into her thatched cottage, and it was with limp and disappointed hands that she put the pot over the fire. But as she sat at the heavy table, head in hands, watching the flames dance shadows on the walls and listening for the bubbling of the stew, the desire flared in her again. Then she could see the diggers in the flickering on the wall, and she imagined how one day she would ask them why they dug their holes.

Ilsa was breaking the ground, making it ready to nurture the seeds she would buy at the market. She hit the hoe against a rock when the moist clods that clung to the blade made the tool too heavy to wield. Spring had been long coming this year, and the fields were still muddy. The crops would be healthy and large.

The snow on the peaks saw the summits of the foothills, and the foothills looked down on the fertile valleys. Ilsa wiped her forehead with the back of her hand and gazed at the crags on the top of the world. There was magic in the sight, and it made the work more pleasant. It was still a magic she could only look at, though. It was nearer than the stars, but no more tangible. The mountains could never understand that she loved them.

When her work was finished for the day, she leaned the hoe against the logs of the cottage. There were still three hours of daylight, so she took the path to the woods.

The path was the same as it had been last year, the same as the year before that. It was narrow and hard-packed, and it curved around obstacles that had never been there. Ilsa followed every twist and walked toe-to-heel when normal strides would have left footprints in the earth outside the path's boundaries. She had made the path her tightrope to the woods.

The trees' shade fell on her, and her excitement grew. The rotting vegetation and pine needles were springs under her feet, lifting her from one step to the next. She brushed against reeds by the stream and they sprinkled her with drops of water. She walked until the trees were close to one another and the ground cover was as thick as a hedge. And then she pulled herself further. There was a dale in the center of the forest, and whenever she had enough daylight to get there, it was the first place she visited. The spot felt like magic.

She burst through the dull-blue spruce trees that ringed the small valley. There was a hole.

The light was dim, and she had to bend down to see the hole clearly. Her heart pounded in her throat, and the weakness in her knees made it hard to kneel without falling down. She brought her face close to the hole and looked into it.

In the soft earth at the bottom were the impressions of tiny boots. And around the sides were the hard, smooth marks that she knew could have been made only by the bites of a tiny spade.

The hole was fresh; the rain had not yet blurred its edges. The digger must still be near.

She looked up, searched with her eyes the area near her. There was slight movement in a bush ten feet to her right. Slowly, she crawled to it and moved aside the leaves.

He was less than a foot tall, and he was dressed in a pair of faded blue coveralls. In his hand he held a small shovel, and she could see dirt on his palms. He was trembling.

A digger should not tremble.

Ilsa reached out very slowly. Closer and closer her hand came to the creature, and still he did not try to escape. His trembling shook him more violently as the hand approached, but he did not move.

She held her breath as she circled his waist with her fingers. She picked him up gently and brought him near her face. She whispered to him so his ears would not hurt with the sound.

"Digger, why do you make holes?"

The digger shook so hard that his words were unclear. "P-Please, let me go. I have d-done nothing to you. You are so l-large." And he started to cry.

Ilsa was stunned, then shocked.

He does not understand, she thought. Magic hides, but should not fear. Magic is frail and gentle, but it is noble and should not weep.

And when the digger squirmed in her hand, she was not ready for it. When he bit her thumb, she opened her hand in reflex. And when he scampered into the bushes, she did not follow. She sat on the ground, her hands resting palms down on the earth behind her.

She did not want to know what she had learned: Diggers dig holes because that is what they do. There is nothing more to it. They dig as I hoe.

The undersides of the clouds blazed with the last of the sun's gold as Ilsa walked slowly home.

She stopped outside the cottage and looked at the hoe leaning against the logs. There were nicks on the dull edge of the blade. I must sharpen it soon, she thought, maybe even tonight. There is work to do tomorrow.

She opened the door, closed it behind her, put the pot on the fire, and sat down at the table. She watched the firelight on the walls and imagined how someday she would ask a digger why he made holes.

Play It Again, Sam

by F. M. Busby

F. M. Busby, who is introduced elsewhere in this volume, writes of "Play It Again Sam": "This story grew out of a class assignment: complete the sentence beginning "What this world needs is . . ." When the sentence was completed, the story took off and wrote itself, except for the ending, which I had to do twice."

Can the reader imagine any alternative ending? I cannot.

"What this world needs," said my friend Sam, "is an instant-replay with some good editing." He sprinkled a suspicious-looking powder into his Martini and stirred it with a ball-point pen. The sun was copper through the smog drifting from the west, but still popped sweat from our skins in large beads and dried it in place.

Sam is my schizoid friend. He has brains he hasn't even used yet, because the line is always busy. The problem doesn't seem to slow him down much.

"You feel like an editor today, Sam?" He nodded. He kept nodding. I nudged him loose from the beginning fugue. "What would you like to edit out? Or in, for that matter?"

"Just out, Pedro. I am not of a creative bent today; only critical."

"OK." I'd play along; I like Sam's games. "What do you want to cut from today's scene, besides the smog and that red ant crawling up your shin?"

Sam lowered the glowing tip of his cigar until the ant fled and dropped away. "Today, Petrov? I don't mess with today. It's too soon to know what to cut. I might blow it. Today's mistake might be tomorrow's salvation. No, I go back to where causes become obvious. That's where I edit." He sipped the Martini, made a sour face. "I always put in too much." I never ask him what; he might tell me.

"OK; where do you want to start? With the war?" He

shook his head. I waved my hand before his eyes until the motion died away. You have to watch Sam.

"The war? No, Peterkin. I know many answers, true. Some of which have not yet the questions. The times are out of joint, as Willie used to say—and so am I; my stash is bereft. But it's only some of my radical chums who know all about the war, Pyotr; not me. Today's war stems from yesterday's kitchen-midden."

I sipped the last of my warm beer and pulled a cold one from the ice chest. "You mean to say you're not a radical any more, Sam?"

"Not I, Petrovich. Not me; nicht mich." He took another sip of the Martini, regarded it with extreme distaste and gulped the rest. "In these decadent times I am reduced to being a free radical, in the chemical sense. I am quite highly ionized."

I'd noticed. "Try a beer, Sam. Great reducing agent." He reduced it a bit, then more. I handed him another, which he set down without spilling.

"The war, you say," he said. "I do not edit the war. I do not edit claptrap. I go before, and edit causes. And probably I blow it, but no worse than now." He frowned, and moodily sipped the beer. "I am chicken, Peter-san; I start late with small causes and work back slowly, carefully. Chickenly." He nodded. I stole his beer.

"Peter the Great, first I would delete a few assassinations." I ignored the compliment. "Such as that you are killing my beer." I gave him another, not wishing to be deleted so early in the day. "I would erase some murders.

"Helter-skelter I would resurrect some Kennedys and a King, such folks as the victims of Speck and the Texas sniper, not to mention the I.R.A. That's just for starters. Then I would—"

The cigar stump was about to burn his fingers; I rescued it or maybe him. "How, Sam? Delete the assassins themselves? Whole armies? I mean, what are you going to do about, say, the six million Jews?"

Sam lit another cigar and pondered. When I returned from visiting the bathroom indoors, I jiggled his chair.

"You're right, Pierre," he said. I resolved to mark the date on the calendar, for seldom more than once a year does Sam admit such a thing.

"About what, Sam?"

"It's risky to edit out people. So I don't erase Lee Harvey

Oswald; I only make him a lousy shot. A touch of astigmatism should suffice; not so?

"As for your six million Jews," as if I'd ever owned six million of anything, let alone people, "most simple is to give the young Adolf Schickelgruber a happy childhood. Or a very bad case of asthma, so he can't make speeches."

"You're deleting World War Two entirely?" Sam always did think big.

"Oh, that." He shrugged immoderately, knocking the ashtray off one arm of his chair and his freshly opened beer off the other. I retrieved both; he didn't notice. "War Two is unnecessary if Woodrow Wilson stays out of the European war of 1914. As president, you understand; I don't mind if he enlists."

"How do you keep him out of it?" I was between beers for a while.

"What if Teddy Roosevelt stays buddies with Taft and doesn't split the Republican vote in 1912? Do you suppose that is sufficient?" I supposed so. "Then there is no unconditional surrender in Europe, no punitive Versailles Treaty, no niche for Schickelgruber or alternate demagogues. Just the normal territorial adjustments following another European squabble. Nicht wahr, Per?"

The sun was lower. The light diminished as the sine of the angle but the heat did not. The smog grew worse. Dimly I could see my wife puttering about the terrace above; she was getting restless. All to the good; the more restless now, the better later. It was an effort to bring my attention back to Sam, wherever he was.

"No World War One, either, Sam?"

"A trifle, Petersen. A nothing; don't thank me." I didn't. "This latest war, now; I have thought on it. The answer may seem obscure but is still of simplicity. Nikolai Lenin must only miss his train. Permanently."

It needed a twist of thought. But yes, if Lenin hadn't returned from exile, the Menshevik revolutionists wouldn't have been eaten alive by the Bolsheviki. No later power struggle between Trotsky and the paranoid Stalin. No Iron Curtain, no Cold War.

A whole new world. That deserved a drink. Beer would do.

"You have anything else in mind, Sam? While you're hot?" Hot. The parching breeze, the smogbound heat fixed in place like armor. Blessed be cold beer.

"A lot of things, Pietro. Some too big, maybe; I knew I put too much funny-powder in that Martini. It tilts my head, counterclockwise. Figure Mohammed with no sense of direction and too stubborn to ask the way to the mountain. Henry the Eighth with sons by Catherine of Aragon, just one more one-wife Catholic king. Maybe England goes Protestant later on, maybe not. Fret on the Bishop of Carthage, Pope Whoever of around the First Millennium. Suppose he did not lose his own potency and thus come to visit celibacy upon the functionaries of his church in perpetuum?"

"You're freaking, Sam." I wasn't sure, but he sounded like it.

"Not so, Peder. Napoleon decreased the average height of Frenchmen simply by killing off the taller men of one generation in his wars. What do you think it did to the average intelligence in, say, Italy—the centuries of railroading most of the brighter kids into a celibate life?"

"Take it easy, Sam. I'm half-wop myself, you know."

"Kind of you to prove my point, Pieter. Kinder of you to hand me a full can. Thank you. The visible sun sinks soon; when does the invisible furnace turn off? I am thinking into the void, but none of you think back at me."

"What else, Sam? While you're editing?"

"What? Oh yes, Piterluk. A less bloody relationship between Neanderthal and Cro-Magnon. Neanderthal was of a gentle and reverent nature for all his primitive appearance. His genes are too much missing in our heritage."

We sat, we smoked, we drank—but Sam spoke no more. He was wherever he goes when he gets tired of things. After a long silent time the sun was gone; so was the beer. Sam moved, stretched, shrugged. I knew he was back.

"Hey, Pete! Great bit of non compos, wasn't it? We miss any bases?"

"Not that I can think of." From the west the breeze increased, harsh with irritants. "Unless you'd like to edit out this goddam smog?"

"Too late for that. We would, you understand, have to start from the grassy African plains and breed for an entirely different strain of man. Eliminate the gene for pollution. And what might we get in its place?"

"There speaks the cosmic editor." He had a point, at that.

Sam rose, stretching again as he stood. "Locally, of course, the solution would be simpler . . ." His voice trailed off.

"You want to drive home," I asked, "take a cab, or flop out in the beach house?"

"Yes, I think so." Sam always knows what he wants. I left him to it.

I dozed. And woke chilled, smelling the clean scent of pines from the eastern foothills. How long had I slept?

Upstairs a light still shone. My wife's shadow moved back and forth across the curtain. She looked to be about the right grade of restless.

As I climbed the steps to the terrace, to the house, I wondered what might happen if Sam ever got restless.

But to the west, over the ocean, rose the familiar comforting glow of dawn.

Till Human Voices Wake Us...

by Lisa Tuttle

*Lisa Tuttle ("Stranger in the House"—*Clarion II*) has made four professional sales since her stay at the Tulane-Clarion workshop in 1971. She was the subject of a feature article in* Seventeen *magazine, "Face to Face with the Uncanny World of Lisa Tuttle." She is a junior at Syracuse University.*

"Till Human Voices Wake Us . . ." is a love story.

The sun shone directly into Albert Hartwell's eyes when he tried to look at his editor, so Hartwell kept his head turned slightly, looking at the bulletin board over Warren's shoulder.

"There's no rush on this," Warren said. "We won't be able to use it before December. You seen any recent pictures of her?"

Hartwell shook his head. "She hasn't been in the news much lately. That's why I think she'll make good copy." A big pink-and-yellow construction-paper daisy hung from the bulletin board wearing a smile and the words "I love YOU!" in its yellow center. Probably a gift from Warren's latest girl friend, Hartwell thought. He'd met her once when he unintentionally interrupted them—Hartwell had been embarrassed, Warren and the girl had not been—and although Warren said she was in high school, Hartwell didn't think she looked any older than twelve.

"Sure, sure, she'll be good copy," Warren said, shrugging. "I was just wondering if she'd be any good for the center fold-out. Better not plan on it, I guess. But get some good, arty shots of her, just in case."

"What if she won't let me?" He wished Warren would shade the window. That damn sun . . .

"Hell, of course she'll let you. Don't you remember? She'd do anything—she was the dream of every PR man." Warren looked thoughtful. "I had a chance to work with her once, but . . . I guess that was before your time."

"I was sixteen when they found her." Hartwell stood abruptly.

"A mermaid. Jeez. I didn't believe it—for two years I didn't believe it. I kept expecting the hoax to come out." Warren shook his head thoughtfully. "One thing I never could figure out was her attraction—some jacko actually married her. I mean, sure, she looked great on top, but who wants to make it with a fish?"

"I'll have the story and photos for you by the end of the month," Hartwell said, moving toward the door.

"No hurry, no hurry . . . and you know the series format."

"Sure."

Hartwell walked down the cool white corridor, pushed open the heavy glass door, and stepped into California sunshine. The cars winked blindingly at him from the parking lot, and he slipped on his sunglasses. Sure, sure, he knew the series format. And he thought the series sucked. "Where are they now?" was such an incredibly old idea, crumbling at the edges with age. But still it sold magazines to all the millions nervously enmeshed in nostalgia: remembrance was better than reality, and everybody's past was better than anybody's present.

He drove in a web of nervous tension, trying to calm himself; it would be a long drive and he might as well relax. What would she be like? He had requested this assignment, had suggested to Warren that "Whatever Happened to Mara the Mermaid?" might make a good feature. And now he was going to meet her. Hartwell gripped the wheel tightly. His dream of ten years was finally to be realized.

She'd been everybody's idea of a mermaid when they found her in '74—and nobody could believe it. Found on a rock off the Florida coast, combing her long green-gold hair, she was frightened by the grabbing and prodding and poking but pathetically eager for friendship. She couldn't speak—at least no human language—but soon picked up English and did her best to answer the questions she was bombarded with.

Scientific tests—they were many and often painful—finally established her authenticity in the minds of all but the most determinedly skeptical. Press coverage ranged from the sleazy sideshow of the *Enquirer* to a cover story in *Time*. She was a natural: a big-time news story people could smile at rather than cry over.

Just as her popularity in the pages of the press was beginning to show signs of waning, and as the question of what was to be done with her arose (that she should be returned to her solitary rock was apparently an idea that did not arise—nor, strangely, did she seem to mind; she'd been lonely in the ocean, although, as she said, the porpoises *were* perfect dears), Romance raised its photogenic head.

A wealthy young man—not a millionarie, but close enough—came along and swept her off her . . . well, her tail. He promised to keep her comfortable and happy, to cherish and love her always. And she did as she had been taught by the magazines and television and promised to be a good wife.

Their marriage provided fuel for the press for the next five years. They were always good for a filler or feature or photo on page six. But despite the hopes and speculations of the public, no issue was forthcoming to the fairy-tale couple, and after the wars and starlets and assassinations in ten years' worth of periodicals, they were effectively forgotten.

Hartwell stopped once along the way for a cup of coffee, but when he stepped into the roadhouse he realized that it was empty of customers except for three women seated at the counter. As one, they swiveled to look at him. He saw they went topless, their breasts decorated by painted or tattooed mouths filled with pointed teeth. Whatever the women were, he knew he didn't want to get involved, and he hastily turned and went back to his car. One of the women said something in a low voice; the other two exploded into laughter.

Hartwell drove, thinking of his boyhood home in Arkansas. He'd like to move back there, he thought—California really wasn't for him—but there was no money in Arkansas. He thought of his room as it had been then, pictures of Mara on all the walls, stacks of magazines under the bed. And over his bed he had had a poster: a long, empty white beach washed by a blue, clean sea. He'd never seen the ocean until he had grown up and moved to California: and then, somehow, it was different. All those people, and all the garbage deposited on cluttered beaches by the murky seawater.

He still had the poster, and the pictures of Mara, but he kept them in a bottom drawer, and until he got the assignment he hadn't taken them out in years.

He turned down the long, pebbled drive winding through trees which let the sunlight through to hit his car in choreographed beats. The house at the end of the road was just another big house, one that would have awed the Arkansas Hartwell, but by now he'd seen too many. A snotty-kid butler let him in and led him through a long narrow hallway, the walls of which were covered with blown-up photographs of men and women indulging in various activities, portrayed so graphically that all possible erotic appeal was submerged. Hartwell kept his eyes on the red pile carpeting.

She was old: that struck him first. She lay in a shallow pool of tepid water—the room had been composed around that pool—and she looked like hell. Her breasts hung, sagging, the dugs of a sea-cow. The legendary loveliness was almost gone—or masked so well by makeup and sorrow that it might as well have been. The weariness and hurt in her eyes signaled that if she were not near death, then she wished that she might be.

They spoke. Her voice was cracked and tired. Hartwell tried to put her at ease, not realizing he was the one uneasy.

"Um . . ." Hartwell glanced at the sheet of standard questions Warren had given him. "Do you—" No, beauty secrets were out. It would be a mockery. "What do you, uh, do? That is, what are your main interests?"

"Making people happy." There was a note almost of questioning at the end. He waited and she amended, "Being a good wife . . . when he wants me. He's not here a lot of the time."

Hartwell felt embarrassed for her, as if she were failing miserably a test he wanted her to do well on. He laid his camera down. He would take no pictures. He wanted to protect her. He glanced at the mimeoed sheet again.

"Do you make love often?"

She shook her head. He noticed that her hair had green roots.

"He's come to me twice in the past year—both times stoned—and then he wanted me pretending to be a shark attacking his genitals—and after that he nearly drowned because he insisted love was only beautiful on the bottom of the big pool."

"Why do you stay with him? Or—why are you telling me this? Why did you permit an interview?"

She moved and her tail made gentle ripples in the water. She smiled at him sadly.

"I must give you what you want—I've always done so. And I stay with him because he has not asked me to leave, and because no one has asked me to come. Why does it matter to you?"

"Because . . ."

How to tell her of all the time he had spent thinking of her, dreaming of her—that whole year of a room filled with her pictures and her voice. How to tell her of his dreams. How to tell her of passing out several times holding his breath, and of the long afternoons swimming relentlessly from one end of the YMCA pool to the other. How to tell her she had broken his heart by marrying someone else, by not waiting for him to grow up and take her away with him to a faraway island. And how to tell her that it had all come rushing back to him, stronger than ever, the moment he saw her. She was older—hell, so was he. He knew that if she was happy again she would be beautiful again.

She looked at him as if she understood him. Maybe she did. What in God's name was a mermaid?

"Why are you the only mermaid?" he asked, although he did not need to, for he could still hear in his mind her televised voice from the first time she had been asked that question.

"I don't know. I wasn't terribly aware of anything—at least, not to the extent of wondering who or what I was—when I was found. I played with the porpoises, and sometimes sat alone, and sometimes I got lonely. But I don't know how long I've been alive, nor where I came from—and I don't remember anyone else like me."

"Maybe you're just a hoax, a gag, a publicity stunt."

"Yeah. Maybe." She caught his tone perfectly. Startled, he caught her eye and saw that she was smiling. He smiled back.

"Hey," he said suddenly. "Where's your old man?"

Her smile faded. "He's been gone a week."

And suddenly he threw it all away, everything he'd had before. Why should he follow the rules? In a world where there could be a mermaid, why couldn't there also be a happily-ever-after for him—and for her? The words came tumbling out, somersaulting over one another: "Will you run away with me? I mean—" And she understood, and nodded, and wrapped her arms around his neck.

She was astonishingly heavy, and very wet, and the feel of her lower half was very strange. Yet he felt himself aroused, and he wanted to tumble into the pool with her. She would not object, he knew; he was beginning to realize that she never said no to anything—she wasn't human, of course.

He thought of the human girl who worked on the magazine with him, and about the day she'd followed him into the supply room, had pressed her body against his, slipped her tongue into his mouth, fumbled with his belt buckle and—and how terrified he had been, and the excuses he had made.

She, at least, had not laughed at him. He thought about the girls he had dated and, in the midst of so much willing, eager flesh, how few times he'd actually gotten laid.

He looked into the mermaid's eyes and knew that she knew his thoughts, and then she pressed her face to his, gave him a soft kiss. Her lips were closed and cold. He thought of warming them, and she shivered in his arms.

He kissed her again and kicked his camera into the pool and broke the kiss when his arms ached from her weight, and carried her out to his car. If he could find a mermaid, he could find an island.

When Dreams Become Nightmares: Some Cautionary Notes on the Clarion Experience

by Harlan Ellison

The first indication I had that the gargoyles might be taking over control of the cathedral came at the 27th World Science Fiction Convention in St. Louis, 1969. It was a personally horrifying experience, and one that showed the first hairline cracks in the beautiful vessel Clarion had become.

It began on the evening of the fancy-dress masquerade held by the St. Louiscon. In company with Robert and Barbara Silverberg and several others, I returned from dinner and entered the ballroom where the masquerade had been in progress for some time, to find the convention committee chairman, Ray Fisher, wearing the expression of a man who has just been advised that the short-circuit in the electric chair has been located and the ceremony can proceed as scheduled.

"What's the matter?" I asked.

"We're five hundred dollars in the red," he replied, his face going a shade grayer, his head sinking just a little deeper into his shoulders.

As I had done some auctioneering that very afternoon, and as the auction had brought in close to a thousand dollars, I could not understand how such a condition could exist; and I said so. Fisher nodded his head toward the stage on which the costumed sf fans were trekking back and forth, displaying their multifarious weirdnesses. "Look up there."

I looked, and saw that the lower left side of the huge motion picture screen, on which fantasy films had been shown through the night, was badly ripped. "That's going to cost us five hundred bucks; the hotel is raising hell; we haven't got five hundred bucks overage when we've paid all the bills."

He looked as though he would have killed himself and only the thought that his chemical components were marketable for less than a dollar was stopping him. "Listen," I said, "if you want, Ray, I'll make an appeal for contributions. If everybody here"—and there were hundreds in the room—"just gives a dollar, you'll be in good shape."

At that moment, I was popular with the fans. I'd given a speech earlier that day—in which I'd prominently mentioned the Clarion Workshops, then in their second year, and had even introduced many of the Clarion students who had come almost directly from the Workshop in Pennsylvania to the Worldcon—and the speech had been greeted with a standing ovation. Additionally, my stock as a writer was high that year: I was up for a Hugo Award. It seemed reasonable that such a beloved figure could raise money for a worthy cause.

Ray Fisher thanked me and went to speak to Elliot Shorter, who was emceeing the masquerade competition. It was agreed that when they took a break, before announcing the winners of the competition, I would be given the hand mike and would do my number.

When the moment arrived, I stepped into the huge circle of fans that jammed the ballroom, many of them sitting on the floor, and I proceeded to do an Elmer Gantry. I made a strong appeal, based on the fact that the young fan who had slipped while parading across the stage and had plunged through the screen was innocent of malice, that the convention committee was going to be hundreds out of pocket if we loving, family-like sf *aficionados* didn't blow the cavalry charge and come to the rescue, that it was us against the hotel . . . the usual charity-drive appeals to emotion.

Almost before I'd finished asking for a dollar each, people began leaping to their feet, began rushing at me, began thrusting dollar bills into my hands. For the next five wild minutes I was smothered by fans caught up in the camaraderie of the moment, and when the circle cleared again, there I stood with great bouquets of money clutched in my arms. More than a little nonplussed, I carted the money over to a big table at one side of the ballroom, in plain sight of everyone, and dumped it all out, to be counted by members of the committee.

I thanked them profusely, blessed them for their love and cooperation, and beat an exit through the adoring throng. (If you begin to get a whiff of what's coming, I only wish you had been there to hip me at the time, because from that point forward to the hideous conclusion of the affair, I was in a mental state commonly known as *non compos mentis,* as blissfully unaware of what was happening as a retarded rabbinical student warming himself at one of Eichmann's ovens.) (And, incidentally, it occurs to me I may disremember the exact amount Ray Fisher first told me was needed to get straight with the hotel for the replacement of the movie screen. It may have been only three hundred, not five, but that's a minor point and doesn't really confuse the basic issues raised and yet to be raised.)

A few minutes later, when the money had been counted, Ray Fisher asked me to announce that everyone had been so generous, that there was an overage . . . how much I wasn't told. He asked me to announce that the overage would be used—since it was clearly impossible to attempt a rebate for those present—to throw a big beer bust the next night. I took the mike and announced it. Great huzzahs from the crowd.

Again I did a fast exit offstage right. Then it was pointed out to Fisher that it was late Saturday night, to be followed by a Sunday and then a Labor Day, and all the liquor joints were shut down, and no beer or spirits could be sold to the committee, Missouri being one of those odd semi-dry states. So they had the extra money and didn't know what to do with it.

Now the next complication happened out of my earshot, so I can only report what I was told. I presume it to be correct, as the principals involved have corroborated the story on separate occasions.

One of the Clarion students, Glen Cook (whose first novel, *The Heirs of Babylon,* was published in 1972 by New American Library and whose stories have appeared in both *Clarion* and *Clarion II*), approached Ray Fisher to see if the unneeded contributions could be donated to the Clarion Workshop. It should be noted at this point that Clarion State College had done a magnificent job of funding the Workshops till then, but at that point in history *every* college was feeling the financial crunch of reactionary backlash, and it appeared the state of Pennsylvania might not be willing to pony up the necessary wherewithal in 1970. So many of us were scrounging for aids and donations. Ray told Glen he thought that would be a splendid way to put the extra cash to good use, and he dug me out of my conversation there in the crowd to ask me if I would do the thing for a third time. Just a bit wearily, I took the mike and explained about no beer in Missouri during a holiday and that the money was going to be given to Clarion.

The huzzahs were somewhat less unanimous than for the beer bust, but it seemed to go over okay, and, fearing some new call on my messianic talents, I fled the ballroom with my date.

Dissolve now to the next day, after a night of partying and bonhomie from everyone I encountered that night. I was to be master of ceremonies at the big Hugo Awards banquet. As I started to mount the speaker's platform, resplendent in tuxedo and overweening ego that I would win the Hugo for best short story, I was stopped by a Los Angeles fan who shall go nameless, as I've since discovered he is an unregenerate swine and troublemaker. He confided, strictly *entre nous*, that many of the fans were upset at what I'd done the night before. I shook my head as if trying to clear my ears of water. *What* had I done the night before?

Well, he said, the fans had been, uh, er, talking . . . and the word going around was that I had cavalierly appropriated monies donated for the fans' revels, to line my own pockets. I didn't quite get that, so he ran it past me again. But how, I asked, was donating the money to Clarion going to line *my* pockets? Because, he explained from what he assured me was the muddy logic of fannish thinking, I was to be one of the guest lecturers at the next Clarion, and the money would be used to pay me the staggering teaching fee *everyone* knew I was getting. I didn't bother to tell him that all of us who taught at Clarion worked for short line (not a pittance, you understand but far less than any one of us could have earned had we stayed at our typewriters). I merely assured him I'd "take care of it" when I was doing my emcee chores.

Then I sat down and had my dinner at the speaker's table. I must confess the entire rumorous affair distressed me. I like to think of myself as an ethical person, and though it is an unfounded conceit on my part, at least I am cunning enough to know one can't steal openly like that and hope to get away with it. Not even from fans.

So when the time came to commence the festivities, I stood up, took the microphone, and began doing the prelims. And in the middle of my pungent and hilariously incisive comments I said, "Oh, by the way, it's come to my attention that some of you who donated a dollar last night to repair the movie screen are upset that the excess collected is going to Clarion. Don't be dumb. Clarion is a great thing, it's part of our little world of science fiction, something that establishes lines of communication between the eras and generations of the genre, something that will feed our constant need for new writers, something worthwhile . . ."

To demonstrate just how untuned I was to the vibes in the banquet hall at that moment, I continued babbling my heroic platitudes even when they could not be heard over the shouting. I didn't realize that the few fans at that convention who cared more about intramural politics than the real problems of the field had built from whole cloth and a burgeoning hatred of the entire Clarion concept a paranoid pre-continuum in which I was fleecing them of . . . one dollar. So oblivious to what was happening was I that even when the shouts and catcalls began coming from odd corners of the room I didn't realize what trouble I was in. To my mind, I was once again facing the isolated stupidity and provincialism of a few hidebound old-line fans who dreaded the opening of sf to the world . . . an enclave in which they'd been able to huddle, balming themselves with the delusion that "fans are slans," special and chosen and better than the rest of the world that sneered at their fantasies of space travel and time machines.

It was that, of course, that lay at bottom. But it was more. And it is that "more" that concerns me here, for it speaks directly to the hairline fractures in the structure of the Clarion experience. And I'll address myself to it in a moment, as soon as I tie up the ends of the St. Louis debacle, if only as an interesting historical footnote to the special wonder Clarion has become.

The rantings and screamings grew more pronounced and now people were leaping to their feet, shaking their fists at me. I had gauged the mood of the crowd with unerring inaccuracy. There I stood, microphone in hand, shouting back at the few loudmouths I recognized, castigating them for their narrow vision in denying a project as worthy as Clarion, while *they* were denouncing me as a thief and self-server. At no time did they or I understand we were talking at cross-purposes. In the words of Strother Martin, "What we have here is a failure to communicate."

Fist fights broke out in the back. Someone threw a dinner fork at me on the platform. I flipped. Now I was cursing them in my best rodomontade, damning their parents, their sexual proclivities, their aspirations, their ethics and their pitiful descent from their ape ancestors to their present amoebic incarnations! Tables were overturned. Men were screaming across the room at women, women were hurling food at men standing on chairs, shouting. In a matter of moments the room had turned into a brawl.

Robert Bloch took over, things quieted down somewhat, and the banquet continued apace. Later, I won the Hugo (to a very strange crowd reaction: half the throng applauded wildly, standing and cheering; half sat silent or booed openly; it was not, as they say, an entirely popular decision). And when the awards dinner was ended, as I was about to stalk off the stage, the most vociferous of those fans who had pilloried me for misappropriation of funds came up and thrust into my hand a check . . . made out in the name of Clarion. A donation.

If you feel confused at that item, think how I felt.

I went straight to my room, to try to piece out with some delayed logic *just what had happened down there.*

A few friends came up, and we sat quietly talking. Then, as andy offutt and I tried to reason it out, an explosion outside the door to my suite set pictures on the wall to rattling. I dashed to the door and threw it open, but all that remained in the hall was the stench and smoke of the massive firecracker blast that had blackened the wall and door.

At that point, I said goodbye to science fiction fandom.

It was not till many months later that I perceived what all that had been in aid of. And how it would apply so directly to Clarion. It has taken me four years to put it all together, but I think I now understand, and I hope you will forgive me going on at this length to set it all down, but it was the start of the gargoylization of the Clarion experience, and the tones of dismay that trembled in the voice of that banquet crowd have now, in some ways, become my own tones. I only hope that what I set down here will be taken as constructive warnings, cautionary notes, as opposed to the hysterical paranoia of those who have feared and denigrated the Clarion Workshops since their inception. This has been the past and, as said, the past is merely prologue.

Were Clarion students not so uncommonly successful, had the "Clarion teaching technique" not proved so effective, had all the ballyhoo promises of Clarion publicity not been fulfilled many times over . . . these cautionary lines might never have had to be written. But they are, it is, they were—and they have had to be.

As Von Runstedt said, "Victory has many fathers, defeat is an orphan." The "victory," if you will, of the Clarion experiment has many claimants to the reasons for its success. I am one of them, and while I am under no illusions about my minuscule part in the overall program, I have trumpeted the glories of Clarion from books, magazines, writers' journals, speakers' platforms, radios and television sets. I have been unstinting in my praise, profligate in my compliments, even effusive in my critical judgments of the writers who have come out of the various Workshops. In plain terms, I have hardsold shamelessly. I won't apologize for it; at the outset, it was necessary.

The necessity arose because of the first shadowy anti-Clarion comments that went flittering through the science fiction world. Traditionally, fans and readers and writers and editors were prepared to accept the emergence of talent from the ranks of fan writers. Bradbury, Silverberg, Carr, Benford, Lupoff, Hoffman, Wollheim, Ted White, Wilson Tucker, Pohl and Asimov, to name just a smattering, were all fanzine-publishing, letterhacking, convention-going dyed-in-the-hekto-ink fans before they outgrew the amateur ranks. It was tradition. And it went hand-in-hand with the almost pathological position most professional writers hold, that you can't be *taught* writing, only craft. It's a position I subscribe to myself, in the main, though Clarion has managed to ameliorate considerably the rigidity of my thinking in that area. Silverberg, for instance, when I spoke to him about this article, and that philosophy, said that the current "hot" new writers—Gordon Eklund, Gardner Dozois and Geo. Alec Effinger—are autonomous, self-directing and self-programming; that they could learn very little at a Clarion Workshop.

I pointed out to Bob that Effinger had gotten his first big ego-boost as a writer from his attendance at the 1970 Clarion Workshop, that though he was very much a talent of his own making his personality till that time had been a very unsure, retiring one, but that his overwhelming acceptance at Clarion had given him the push to go forward, culminating at an early point-of-assay with his first novel, *What Entropy Means To Me,* a very strong first effort, a 1972 Nebula nominee.

Bob countered with the absolutely accurate reminder that neither he nor I (both out of fandom) had been told we were any good but that didn't stop us. We continued banging away at our craft and, though neither of us may be Stendhal at this stage of the game, at least we have become successful at what we enjoy doing. I agreed that the "born writer" will write no matter what blocks are thrown in the path and the best they can get from a Clarion Workshop will be some help with the plumbing, but that a borderline case can be helped over the first hurdles by group acceptance and the serious attention of professionals the amateur may consider authorities. It is a nebulous problem, and one that has much to be said on both sides.

The core of it, however, is that those who've made it on their own tend to denigrate and dismiss formal teaching methods when it comes to writing. It is a widespread and generally held conceit. And that, linked with the fans' distrust of successes rising out of the mainstream, venturing occasionally into "their field"—Herman Wouk, John Hersey, Michael Crichton, Allen Drury, to name two good and two bad examples—made for a subterranean rumble of negativity where Clarion was concerned.

In no small part, the St. Louiscon horror was prompted by that negativity. Fans who had been slaving away in the amateur ranks for years and had not been able to break into professional print wrote sneering and uninformed analyses of what went on at the Workshops. (One young lady, who had been a friend of a Clarion student at Tulane in 1971, wrote a piece on how it seemed to her that it was all fun-and-games and no one did any work. This despite the fact that she was not around during the endless hours of solitary writing the students did, nor was she an attendee at more than one class session, and was permitted to romp as groupie only during their off-hours when they were relaxing. Of *course* it looked like a pajama party to her. But it was typical of the gossipy fanzine reportage by outsiders.) Highly respected writers like Lester del Rey, wholly unfamiliar with the specifics of Workshop rigors, but judging the entire program from the weary position of "writers are born not taught" and using as evidence the contents of one Clarion anthology, expressed grievous doubts about the viability of the program. Those who were ineligible for the program, for one or another reason, vented their animosity and frustration with endless stories of how the instructors were in collusion to publish Clarion students even though their writings were abominable. It went on and on, and in retaliation, in self-defense, for better or worse, many of us oversold the product. We took it as a holy crusade to keep Clarion in the limelight and its graduates free of the brickbats of the jealous and ill-informed.

Hence . . . the St. Louiscon massacre.

And the promulgation of some traditions and bad habits that now emerge as very definite threats to the Clarion Workshops and all the good works of which they are capable.

It is my intention to speak to these flaws in an attempt to warn those who will be conducting Clarion/East and Clarion/West sessions this year and in years to come, as well as others adopting the Clarion "method" for their own seminars and workshops in other collegiate settings.

First, and most dangerous, is the overrating of writers who come out of the Workshops. There have been some outstandingly successful and original talents, to be sure: Ed Bryant, Geo. Alec Effinger, Gerard Conway, Robert Thurston, Vonda McIntyre, Glen Cook, Lisa Tuttle and others. But they are all young talents in terms of experience, and promoting them as this season's saviors can only harm them. There is a brutality concomitant with elevation to godhood that has stunted writers far better than any of those named.

There's really no excuse for the overblown praise, but there *is* an explanation. It's called the Besieged Citadel Syndrome.

Fly in the face of all that homegrown rustic philosophy that avows it's impossible to produce good sf writers from a structured academic situation, go against all those years of new writers coming from the recycling of fanzine fiction contributors, defy all the tenets of the discipline that say a good sf writer *must* have a sound grounding in the physical sciences, ignore any liaisons with the fan world . . . and very quickly one senses beady little eyes staring from the underbrush. Even paranoids have enemies: witness Dr. Richard Kimble, the Fugitive.

Witness the St. Louiscon, the cornucopial flow of badrapping "analyses" in fanmagazines, the disdain of professionals who sensed some obscure threat to the art-form that had nourished them, the animosity of self-styled sf historians and pedants who resented their territory being usurped. The Besieged Citadel Syndrome set in.

And young writers who should have been permitted the same ripening time as those who had gone before were denied that necessity. They were suddenly totems. They were held up as vindication of the Clarion method and the miraculous laying-on-of-hands of the visiting lecturers. By hurling them into the arena, against writers who had honed their talents through thirty and more years in the pulps, the slicks, paperback originals and hardcover *succès d'estime*, they were done a terrible disservice; all in the name of proving the worth of a small cadre of professional writers-turned-teachers. That writers like Bryant, Effinger, Thurston and Busby have been able to stand the gaff, to move forward with their careers in a dignified and wholly commendable fashion, seemingly oblivious to the waves they've created, is testament to their personal integrity as writers, and no credit attaches to those of us who've made figureheads of them.

But the warning is there. If another Geo. Alec Effinger comes out of the ranks of Clarion graduates, we must restrain our impulses to carol his or her genius from the pages of scholarly journals or from speakers' platforms. We must permit the talent to ripen at whatever rate the individual demands. If we don't, we will stunt the talent before it has a chance to fully flower. I cannot express strongly enough my fears in this area. I've seen at least two better than average Clarion writers turned into ego-dripping, strutting martinets because they were lauded too highly by a few of us, before they'd learned how to handle quick acceptance and praise all out of proportion to their gifts.

Second are the evils attendant on the alleged status of *being* a Clarion graduate.

The mythos that has grown up around the Workshops has slowly concretized into a kind of secret society. On numerous occasions during question-and-answer sessions at colleges and universities, I've been asked (in all seriousness) if it's possible to break into print in the sf world without the Clarion cachet. When some earnest young student asks me that, I feel a sinking in my stomach. It means one more artificial barrier has been erected between those who desperately want to write in the medium, and the easy routes they can take to achieve that goal.

Selling to the sf magazines and anthologies is hardly a difficult task, if one has talent. Virtually every issue of the magazines and every edition of the anthologies include stories by unfamiliar names. All they had going for them were good stories, well written and originally conceived. They submitted them even as I submit my stories, and the editors judged them solely on the basis of what came off the typed pages. No magic. No special cachet. No secret handshake, no old school tie, no connections . . . just good stories.

But to amateurs, looking in from the outside, unfamiliar with even the basics of how to submit a story, Clarion has become yet another physical manifestation of the paranoid delusion of the "closed conspiracy." That such a tight little society does not, in fact, exist is beyond their comprehension. Or more accurately, beyond their trust. They see the same names, month after month, in the magazines and books, and so they *must* believe it's all nepotism. And when a new name appears, if they can find a linkage with the sf "establishment," it only serves to shore up their conspiracy theories. Clairon has become another node of the sf orbit for them. Even granting it is the attitude of the uninformed, the hopeless amateur or the disgruntled loser, it is a hideous concept that must be exploded. Merely to say it isn't so, however, will not serve the purpose.

It must be chaptered-and-versed for the uninformed. They must be shown that *anyone* with talent can be a Clarion student, and that not all Clarion students immediately and without travail become selling writers. They must come to understand that the few Clarion writers who have drawn praise and continuous publication since their attendance at the Workshops would very likely have done so *without* the Workshops, that the Clarion cachet is more myth than reality.

Further, the air of exclusivity that has come to surround Clarion graduates is of the students' and teachers' making; it is not a free pass into print; it is almost one of Vonnegut's "false karasses." It is a clubbiness at once real and rewarding, imaginary and hurtful. Because of the sense of *belonging* that comes to all but the most retiring and hebephrenic members of a Clarion Workshop, there is a residual sense of *family* that is a valuable and viable serendipity to the actual writing lessons learned. I would not demean that sense of belonging; it is a lovely thing to behold. But from the outside it looks like clique and conspiracy. Clarion administrators, apologists and students must come to realize this sad fact. And they—we—must go out of our way to de-fang it for all those who could benefit from the Clarion experience, were it not made to seem so formidable and inaccessible.

Which leads me to my third warning: the cliques.

As I reported in an essay in *Clarion II*, there have been Workshops where the repeaters assumed the attitudes of old summer-camp buddies, playing fraternity actives to the newcomer pledges. They have clubbed together, roomed together, dined together—have formed, in short, ingroups within the ingroup. Granted, those cliques eventually break up under the merciless assault of having their individual writer-parts exposed day-in-day-out to the glare of personal and literary criticism. Even so, the week or two it takes to produce a homogeneous "class" are partially wasted weeks. They produce anti-groups among the newcomers, who cleave to one another in another Besieged Citadel setting. Not only is it wasteful of potential friendships, but for the first few weeks of a Workshop it produces comment and criticism in the critique sessions that can be clouded by personal animosities. Such criticism is, of course, useless to all concerned.

Another facet of this cliqueishness is the inevitable seeking-out of a hate-symbol. Because of the ineluctable development of the group toward unity, the students *always* find one among their number behind whom they can unify with loathing. Usually it's the one whose personality flaws are too bizarre even for the tastes of a group notable for their endless weirdnesses. Not unexpectedly, it is also usually one whose talent is minimal. It offers an unquestioned rationale for making the poor slob a pariah. I've seen it at every Clarion I've taught. One year it was a barely teen-aged boy whose credentials were so shaky he should never have been admitted to the Workshop. Another year it was a man in his late thirties whose psychoses were by turns pathetic and terrifying. A third year it was a girl who had always been the brightest in her school but who, when thrown in with others equally as bright, or brighter, grew vicious or sullen or whimpering and who, finally, was sent to a sort of Coventry by her fellow Workshoppers, even to having her roommate move out on her, leaving her the only one at that Clarion who roomed alone. I wish my conscience were clean enough to say I tried to stop the ostracism of those various students, but on several occasions I let it slide. Not only because the hate-objects in question were eminently detestable—several of them rejected even the most open-handed of attempts at friendship—but because I chose to see the putting of those students beyond the pale as ultimately "in the greater good" of unifying all the others into a productive group. On several other occasions I did reach the hated students and they came into the group, but that is hardly expiation for the sin of allowing even one to remain the brunt of such massed hatred.

Were the cliques to be broken up immediately, this recourse to scapegoat would not occur, I believe.

The memory grows painful. I'll move on.

Fourth, even the forming of a class gestalt has its drawbacks. Chief among these is the inordinate amount of time and energy that is wasted writing "in-group jokes" as stories, for the private amusement of classmates and teachers. One year it was stories about green slime . . . the class had gone to a bad horror movie. Another year it was sex stories of an incredibly adolescent and banal stripe . . . one of their number had made the mistake of handing in a male-chauvinist tract. Still another year it was kaka stories . . . someone had written a story about walking turds.

Naturally, there is no way to repress the high spirits of a monkey-barrel of wild talents, nor should such attempts be made, I venture. Sophomoric private jokes serve the worthy end of releasing tensions, of letting off steam; and occasionally a workable story idea emerges from the green slime. But in my experience at the various Clarions (and I've taught them all, every one, on both sides of the country), I've seen the jokes permitted to run on too long. Perhaps a fourth of the output of any given Clarion class during the first two weeks of a session is made up of such flotsam. It should be brought to an ass-grinding halt as soon as it's provided the release of the built-up steam. This is a responsibility of the visiting instructor, and I won't go into it at this point because I'm dealing with the misdemeanors of the students here; a little further on I'll get to the felonies of the teachers, greater by far than those of their students.

But before I get to those of us lofty and immortal pros who sit and pontificate, I'll get off the students and talk about the administrations of the Workshops. There are flaws in the mechanics of the Clarions that need illuminating . . . and setting to rights before another year passes.

Understand one thing, please: when I speak of the administrations, I do not refer to the academic institutions that have subsidized, hosted and nurtured the Clarion Workshops. The sponsoring of various Clarions by Clarion State College in Clarion, Pennsylvania, Tulane University in New Orleans, Michigan State University in East Lansing, and the University of Washington in Seattle has been, down the line, supportive, sincere and even courageous: in a time when anti-intellectual/anti-collegiate feeling has run high in this country, wiping out entire activity budgets for some colleges and universities, the institutions that have sponsored Workshops have stood by their commitments. Where other writers' gatherings have been nixed, the Clarion Workshops have not only continued, they have split to bring forth *two* self-contained, wholly autonomous Workshops, one on either coast.

No, when I speak of the "administration," I speak of those

dedicated and talented amateurs who've done the line producing job: the paperwork, the arrangements, the admissions, the ugly scutwork. Robin Scott Wilson was the first administrator, followed by James Sallis and Dr. Joseph Roppolo at Tulane; and Vonda McIntyre at the University of Washington, and Leonard N. Isaacs and R. Glenn Wright of Justin S. Morrill College at Michigan State University. In largest part the Clarion experience and the Clarion success are the realizations of their dreams. Their job is a seemingly endless and frequently thankless one; often onerous, always exhausting, and hardly commensurate in remuneration for the donkeywork months of aggravation, hassles and simple physical effort to the point of breakdown they pour into the project. They are nobler than mere words can convey, and they will punch me for deifying them thus.

But they are only human—to cop a fresh phrase—and they have allowed some bad organizational habits to creep into an otherwise intelligently and expeditiously run operation.

First of these is the screening procedure whereby a scattering of no-talents manage to gain acceptance to the Workshops every year. At the outset, in the early years of the Clarion thing, it was excusable because a certain number of students *had* to be enrolled just to make financing the Workshop feasible. Below twenty-five full-time enrollments, it was financially a losing proposition the college could not support. Above twenty-five it became unwieldly. So at first there was considerable scouring and in perhaps one or two cases the level of talent was not as high as the class average, which was usually incredibly elevated.

But, interestingly, the number of duds in the classes of those early years, before Clarion became a catchword and a cachet, was considerably lower than currently. Perhaps it was because Robin Wilson was doing the screening and he insisted on actual *work* being submitted; as opposed to the present method (which I find disastrous) in which applicants for admission to the summer workshops are merely required to fill out an application form that includes space for a very brief essay on *why* they want to come to the Clarions. Well, hell, friends, who gives a damn *what* demons drive people to want to come to Clarion? The operable question is: *Can they write?* Have they talents that can benefit from a six-week crash program in writing sf professionally?[1]

In discussing this element of the gargoylization of the Clarion experience with Robin Wilson, and with particular reference to the post-1968 sessions, Robin told me endless tragic stories about what he has come to call the Wanda Blunk Letters.

Wanda Blunk is a mythical name for a composite creature whose letters of application read, in part:

"Dear Dr. Wilson, I am a sophomore at the University of Chicago and I became interested in sci-fi [sic] last August when I read 'The Stranger from a Strange Land' [sic]. Now I'm ready to go into *seriously* writing sf. I don't have many friends and I feel that writing sf will bring me the touch with the world I need . . ."

The letters go on, Robin reports, with a lonely, plaintive trembling that can only be compared with the lovelorn letters received by the protagonist of Nathanael West's *Miss Lonelyhearts*. "They are letters from bright, alienated, desperately lonely kids who want to join the club," Robin told me. "They've read three Heinleins and a Vonnegut, and they're sold on the life of a science fiction writer. But they have no discernible abilities in that area."

Because of the admission prerequisite of submitting actual writings that could be evaluated, Robin was able to screen out most of the Wanda Blunks. Not so in subsequent years with the Why-I-Wanna-Be-a-Clarion-Writer essay as the only guide to an applicant's talents.

Look: let me pause and take a sidetrack here, for a moment. To the casual reader, it may seem that all this disparaging talk about Wanda Blunk and others of her ilk is terribly cruel and chill and anti-human. Perhaps it is. But there are some very real *de facto* considerations that must be understood.

Almost *every*body thinks him- or herself capable of being a writer. People who wouldn't for a moment think they could be a plumber or a brain surgeon without long years of study and practice think they can sit down and write as well as Joyce Carol Oates. How wrong they are: great Art looks simple because it *is* great. If you doubt it, watch Fred Astaire dance. See how simple it looks? Now try it. Right . . . you understand now. Understanding is the issue here.

It's a question of perceiving the differences between unknown writers and amateur writers. An enormous gap. I've had some things to say on this point elsewhere, but a recent exchange between myself and Ruth Berman, a very talented newer writer who publishes a fanzine called *No*, speaks directly to the point and explains, in detail, why it is absolutely imperative to be as uncompromising with the Wanda Blunks of the world as one can be, without being brutal.

It begins with an introduction I wrote for a story in an anthology I edited, *Again, Dangerous Visions*. It reads:

> **There is a vast difference between being an "unknown" writer and being an "amateur" writer. It is hardly a subtle difference, yet most unpublished pencil-pushers find it impossible to understand the distinction.** ***Not*** **understanding is pernicious. It leads people who might otherwise be utterly happy as shoe clerks or computer programmers or dental technicians to wasted lives of unfulfilled dreams, pounding typewriters and scribbling in journals, and never** ***ever*** **finding the right words. The words that make a story or a screenplay or a play something special. So someone will want to buy it and stake an editorial reputation on it, and pay the highest possible compliment for the use of it: a check of money. That says, "You may be 'unknown,' but you are not 'amateur.' You have a talent, and your talent has created a thing of special properties that takes the reader somewhere he has never been before. I love it, and I want to publish it, and I want to be associated with it; I want to let some of the magic of this special thing rub off on me by my act of presenting it." That is the compliment, and it is hard-won. Failing to receive that compliment, thousands of amateurs every year send their amateur stories to magazines and anthologies, send their amateur plays to producers, send their amateur teleplays to agents and studios . . . and die when rejection follows. They have failed to perceive the disparity between amateur and unknown. They believe that being the latter is inherently noble, somehow umbilically linked with greatness, never realizing that if the linkage exists—*if* it exists, and not for a moment will I admit it does—but *if* it does, never understanding that being** ***amateur*** **severs the umbilicus. To be unknown is simply to be unknown. To be an amateur is to be tone-deaf, without rhythm, color-blind. It is as far from the state in which the compliment can be won as the chicken is from the eagle. Both are fowl, yet one will forever peck at the dirt, and the other will soar to mountaintops. They scrawl their dreams in journals, they pound on into the night behind typewriters, and they die when their dreams are rejected, never un-**

derstanding that the amateur is doomed *never* to find the words.

The second phase of the discussion—which I hadn't known would become a discussion till Ms. Berman's magazine, *No,* crossed my desk—took form as a short essay titled "That Only an Amateur." I enter it here, with Ms. Berman's permission, to pursue this matter to a (hopefully) logical conclusion:

"There is a vast difference between being an 'unknown' writer and being an 'amateur' writer." So Harlan Ellison begins his introduction to Greg Benford's "And the Sea Like Mirrors" in *Again, Dangerous Visions.* Somehow, as I think about it, the distinction Ellison is drawing strikes me more and more as invalid. Not that there aren't plenty of awful writers who love the idea of writing so much that they won't give it up and keep on wasting the time of editors like Harlan Ellison with their awful manuscripts. But:

"To be an amateur is to be tone-deaf, without rhythm, color-blind. . . . The amateur is doomed *never* to find the right words." What, never? Well, hardly ever. The unknowns start out as amateurs——or so I would expect. Ellison claims that Benford "was never an amateur. He was unpublished, but he was ready. He wrote for fan magazines and he sent off manuscripts to the professional journals, but for a long time he was unpublished: he was unknown. But he was no amateur."

The fan activity is something of a red herring. Fan magazine writing is mostly assorted kinds of essays, and it's quite possible to be good at writing essays without being able to write good stories (or vice versa). The facts that Benford was writing for fanzines and collecting professional rejection slips don't in themselves mark him off from the amateurs who are doomed *never* to find the right words. Some of them write for fanzines, too, and *all* of them, as defined by Ellison, collect rejection slips. (There are some amateur writers——a lot of them in fandom——who write purely for an audience of other amateurs who share their love for the field. And there may be a few amateurs who write for themselves alone and feel no urge to share their results. For obvious reasons, neither of these groups is included in Ellison's discussion.)

Well, then, how *do* you tell an amateur from an unknown? By the quality of the writing? Can't be. Writing is partly a craft, a skill that must be learned, and everyone starts out writing badly. And even at advanced stages, that particular test is no use to the amateur-or-unknown himself or herself, because writers are rarely good judges of their own work. How about the length of time a subject has been writing badly without showing signs of improvement? It's a good indication, no doubt, but it's not a definitive characteristic; people don't all learn at the same rate.

No, finally, the only way to tell the difference between the two is in retrospect. A new writer is an ex-unknown. Oh, there's usually an intermediate stage when an unpublished writer can be identified as non-amateur by a collection of handwritten rejection slips saying things like "not this time, but try us again," but sometimes the subject jumps directly from printed "no thanks" to sales without any in-between stage.

And in the meantime, before reaching the "try us again" stage or actual sales, the unpublished writer has suffered considerable embarrassment at the idea that he or she *may* be a hopeless amateur wasting the editor's valuable time. I used to agonize over John Ciardi's approximately once-a-year columns in the *Saturday Review* devoted to the subject of what rotten poems people submit to him for SR. I'd comb the description, trying to see if there was any hint that he was thinking specifically of One of Mine. Eventually, I was lucky enough to get two poems accepted, after about five years of trying, so I was able to stop cringing. But I still think he gave me (and his other would-be contributors) unnecessary pain in writing those columns——I doubt that the subject interested his noncontributing readers very much, and it obviously didn't discourage the rotten writers from continuing to send him their work.

Complaints about the awfulness of amateurs are probably about as likely to discourage the "unknowns" as the amateurs. In fact, Ellison claims in introducing one of the other stories in the book ("Harry the Hare" by James B. Hemesath) that "many fine stories by unknowns languish for years and eventually go into the trunk as the

writer goes into plumbing or CPAing." The authors of some of those languishing stories may have been scared off by editorial complaints.

And one other point. Ellison says that amateur writers think that being an unknown writer "is inherently noble, somehow umbilically linked with greatness." I'm not sure what he means by that. If he means that unpublished writers frequently salve their egos by claiming that greatness is uncommercial, publishers take only mediocre work, and their own work is too good to be accepted——well, certainly some do just that. But I doubt that "hopeless amateurs" do it any more than "promising unknowns." On the other hand, if he means that amateurs think that there is something innately noble about trying to write, that it is better to try to express one's feelings in writing (or painting, sculpting, composing, etc.) than to let them disappear——aren't they right?

Of course they're right, and so is Ruth Berman.

But neither of us, in limited space, had really gotten down to the core of the issue. And it's the issue that burns at the core of the Clarion experience, its current flaws, and its ultimate success or failure over the long haul.

I hope that in my response to Ms. Berman in a subsequent letter, I touched the core of that problem . . . the reason for my dogged pursuit of specifics in what may seem to be a sidetrack to this essay's main thrust.

The problem—if there is one and I suspect we are talking about the same thing in different agreement—is that the subject is a big one and, confoundingly, one that seems to defy definition without deep and extensive examination of terminology. It's like defining sf—what Bogart might have called, as he called acting, a "mug's game"—and by the very defining, exclude so much other. The best definition of sf is "anything I point to and say that's sf." Likewise, the only satisfactory definition of "amateur" is what we would both point to and say, "that's amateur."

Amateurism, I suppose I meant (and probably should have stated more clearly), is a state of mind. In a surreal way I typify it, and identify it with the state of mind of

TV viewers who think the actors actually dream up the words they speak or, even more horribly (and I've encountered this on several occasions), they think Leonard Nimoy *is* Mr. Spock or Dan Blocker *was* Hoss. It could be categorized as a lack of basic understanding of the *realities* of writing and/or selling.

For instance: there are writers who come to the Clarion Workshops whom you can take aside and work with line by line on a defective story, point out why the syntax is prolix and broken-backed, the language unpretty or vague, the grammar clearly "schoolgirl," the plot illogical and hinged on random circumstance that does happen in real life but is unacceptable in fiction, the characterization shallow and cliched . . . and they will go right back and do it again, with no comprehension of what they've done wrong, or how it can be set to rights. And if pilloried repeatedly for these same crimes, they will retreat into an amateur's arrogance that what they're doing is "experimental" and "fresh," when the truth is simply that they don't *understand* how to write.

On the other hand: there are unpublished writers whom you can read and even with all the flaws noted above present, see in their work the spark that says they understand—on some cellular level perhaps—the art of storytelling. For those people, even comments as vague as "Make your characters more real" suffice. They go back to the work and their native understanding urges them to find the truth in the work, to peel away the falsities, to write the story more muscularly.

Recourse to authority is easily the cheapest way to win an argument and I assure you I won't do it here, but I merely offer as some validity of my position the knowledge I've gained in having read perhaps two thousand manuscripts for the *Dangerous Visions* books, the hundreds of stories I've had to analyze and critique in writing workshops, and the vast total of letters I've received from people who want to write, sillily asking me for advice or instruction or agenting services. It *is* possible, within proscribed limits for there are always exceptions, to tell an amateur from a potential professional. Every editor can do it. Silverberg and Terry Carr and I have sat and talked about how it's possible to tell if a story in submitted manuscript form is of interest or simply the work of a dub, by reading the first page and the last. It may seem

chill—to the kind of mind that thinks one should love *all* members of *all* minorities simply because they are members of a minority rather than judging each individual on his or her own merits and defects—but that editorial method is used by *every* editor I've ever talked to about the problem. There are simply people who will *never* be professional in their writing habits or abilities, and to waste time with them is to steal it from those who have the talent and *need* the attention.

As for scaring off those with talent . . . it can't be done. Ciardi may have made you quiver, but he made you examine your work and yourself, and he didn't scare you off . . . you sold to *Saturday Review*. It didn't scare me off when my college English professor told me I had no talent and should forget writing as a career. It didn't scare off *any* of the writers who understood that writing is a holy chore and they had been touched with the gift. It only scares off dilettantes and amateurs whose abilities are tiny or nonexistent, or whose lack of ego and feelings of self-worth would doom them much more quickly than the harshest words a critic could employ.

Your sentiments do you honor, Ruth, but as a woman who clearly has writing ability and talent, you should toughen up. To be so all-inclusively Florence Nightingale about the talentless and amateur will serve you ill in years to come. The amateurs will descend on you and waste your time, drain your resources, nickel-&-dime you to tears with their endless demands, their silly letters, their vague dreams and desires. The ones who are *not* amateurs will understand that only they, themselves, can bring those dreams and desires to fulfillment, that there are no magic shortcuts or arcane rituals proffered by writers who *have* made it. They are realists—even if they are dreamers—and they are professional—even if they've never sold—and they will find their own paths.

Somehow, somewhichway, the random elements have come together correctly, to make the Clarion Workshops an unqualified success at a task most of us thought was impossible: training unknowns to be producing, often selling professional writers of the most difficult literary form extant—speculative fiction. How it happened we're only beginning to comprehend: each year we learn a little more. But one thing we know for certain, and it returns me to the jump-off point before my digression, we must be as tough in *whom* we admit to the Workshops as we would be in accepting writers to a professional writers' conference.

We deal with *unknowns,* but we've GOT to eliminate the few *amateurs* who manage to creep in every year. They waste the time of the classes, they learn nothing useful really, and while I suppose a humanitarian case could be made for providing Wanda Blunk and her no-talent kin some human companionship, love, warmth, self-esteem and sense of belonging . . . however briefly . . . *that is not the proper business of the Clarion Workshops!*

Clarion is not a breeding ground for social workers, it is a relentlessly demanding arena in which the weak are supposedly made strong and the strong made tougher. The writing game is not one well suited to weaklings. It can crush a talent that hasn't learned to discipline itself and direct its energies.

This I believe with all my soul and heart and blood.

And for those who select the students to attend each year to permit less than the best in, either because they fear the rolls will not be sufficiently filled, or because they feel some commendable but misplaced compassion for the Wanda Blunk letters, is to do a disservice to those students who *need* the Workshops to learn the basics for their future lives, to do a disservice to the readers of sf who look to Clarion for fresh voices, and ultimately to do a disservice to the genre as a whole.

Screening methods *must* be tightened, to sift out the no-talents before they spend their not inconsiderable admittance fees and best efforts must be expended on their behalf. Toward the end of this piece I'll detail how I think these methods can be beefed up. (While I generally contend it is not incumbent on those who sense and explicate a problem to have ready solutions, in this instance I have a few thoughts, and I'll lump them all together at the finale.) I'd like to go on here to enumerate the few other flaws in the Clarion system promulgated by the administrators.

The second serious flaw is the encroachment of sf fandom, an encroachment unwittingly abetted by those who handle the admissions. At the beginning of this article I dealt with the highly vocal opposition to Clarion by some segments of old fandom. But the lavish adoration of *new* fandom is almost as horrifying. Many younger sf fans, thinking Clarion is some sort of exclusive club, a way to make themselves Bigger-Name Fans, have attended Clarion Workshops not because of a deeply rooted desire to become writers, but because they want to build a rep. A few have discovered it was no picnic, and hardly a sorority picnic. They have found something greater than the need to be large frogs in the tiny pond of fandom, and their writing has become the centerpost of their lives. But others have merely used Clarion as semi-cachet to enmesh themselves more completely in the incestuous fan magazine/convention/letterhacking circle of the fan world. Tighter admissions methods would tend to cut down the appearance of such types in classes where there is little enough time to accomplish the important chores of crash-learning.

Third, and this problem slops over into the flaws of the guest teachers, there is virtually no integration of teaching methods from week to week. Each of the professional writers who sallies in for seven days of instruction teaches in his own way. Which is fine. Except. Much ground is covered several times, with often conflicting data being passed on to the bewildered students. Whole areas are left unexplored. No forceful direction is shown to the students. Time is wasted. Problems that arise go unsolved for several weeks before one of the mid-session teachers finds him- or herself facing an ingrained bad writing habit. A course plan needs to be worked out pre-Workshop, with definite areas (programmed to the teachers' particular strengths) set out for each instructor in addition to anything else needing to be taught. Without such a course plan, it remains haphazard and repetitive of effort.

And fourth, guest teachers are frequently chosen on their name value in that field, rather than on the basis of their ability to teach well, their ability to relate to the students without being absorbed in their gestalt, their ability to make maximum use of the time for which they're being paid without playing Big-Time Author.

This last problem I lay directly at the feet of the administrators, some of whom have felt Big-Name Writers would cause the Workshops to fill up more quickly, some of whom have been *themselves* impressed by a writer's work and reputation, but who have failed to research the writer's potential in this very special Workshop situation. As a result, during at least four Workshops, to my certain knowledge, entire weeks have been a washout to the students. I'll name no names: there are those who contend *my* weeks of teaching were washouts. Much of what I say, consequently, is strictly personal opinion, based on what I've seen and heard . . . mostly from students. But with potentially sensational Clarion instructors like Thomas Disch, andy offutt, James Sallis and Roger Zelazny left untapped, some of the professionals who've gone on the Clarion ego-trip stack up inadequately. To be polite.

The essence of the problem, as far as the administrators are concerned, is that they got into it sidewise, without really understanding how enormous were the problems of running a Workshop this complex and successful.

But the flaws they've permitted to go unchecked are minimal compared to those fostered by myself and my compatriots brought in ostensibly to pass on the accumulated wisdom and perceptivity of years of professional work.

And here is where the bulk of the blame belongs.

Understand: though some of us will insist this aspect of the Clarion experience is a minor consideration and *hardly* the reason we sweat our asses off every summer . . . teaching at Clarion Workshops is a massive ego-trip.

Academically, sf has only lately been recognized and accepted. Lecturing at colleges, speaking to attentive crowds of people who treat one the same way they would treat Mailer or Nabokov or Dickey, is a heady experience. Receiving that cachet of legitimacy bestowed on those who "speak at universities" is a kind of honor many of us in the ghetto of sf have long sought. And to be affiliated with a project like the Clarion Workshops makes it that much more potent a credential.

So many of us come with our images already in residence. For a kid from some small Midwestern town who has been reading Sturgeon and Knight and Delany and Russ with wonder and admiration to suddenly find himself in their company is a monumental experience. (Let's deal with realities here, not false humbleness. It's irrational for *any*one to equate the writer with what the writer writes, and to be in awe of the mere vessel for the talent, but that's the reality. At least half the newcomers in every Clarion Workshop are awed by the "stature" of their teachers. I can understand it: were I to study under Paolo Soleri or Bucky Fuller, I'd be in awe, too. But it's a deadly evil to permit continued life.)

And many of us go to pains not to dispel that hero-worship. We operate like Delphic Oracles, uttering our *dicta* from the mountaintops, and woe to the snotnosed punk who dares to offer us less than worship and adoration.

The gossip that is passed from room to room before some of the guest instructors arrive is so out of proportion to the dimensions of the myth-object in reality, it can only be compared with the legends of Paul Bunyan or Mike Fink.

And, as I have found out to my dismay, this dealing with the myth-image rather than the reality puts the teacher out of rapport totally with the students. Their reactions to criticism, their feelings of freedom in approaching the teacher with writing problems, their freedom to disagree . . . all are warped and curtailed.

Naturally there is no way students can be expected to deal rationally and maturely with a human being they've known only as a famous name on books and magazine covers, unless the "famous name" defuses him- or herself. But by playing to that adoration, by accepting it and often wallowing in it, we have done our students a terrible disservice. And robbed them of what they came to Clarion to find.

But beyond the horrors of the myth-image, many of the Clarion teachers have committed the sin of not being themselves. They have swallowed all that guff about the nobility of the younger generation and they have tried so hard to be one of the kids that their credibility and value have been destroyed. We Clarion instructors must realize that yes, Clarion has a fun side as well as a work side, but that by joining the kids in totality we become ludicrous, suspect and less effective in the classroom. To relate to the students, to get it on with them on their terms, is absolutely necessary, but we must hold back a little. We must perceive that while they may adore us personally, because we're "into it" with them, we diminish our critical faculties, tend to soften our criticism, spend too much time trying to be in the gang with them. It is our very distance from their world that makes us valuable. Allegedly, we know something they don't. But if we're no more removed from their circle than a charming beer buddy, why should they listen to us?

It is a dichotomous situation, at best. On the one hand I seem to be saying we cannot stay on so lofty and mythic a plane to awe them into rigidity, but at the same time we musn't get too close. The two positions are hardly mutually exclusive, however. There is a place in between, a place best inhabited by Joanna Russ, it seems to me, who has struck a balance that serves herself and the students best all around.

And then we are responsible for puffing up many of the students, out of all proportion to their talents *at that time*. We are responsible for permitting the time-wasters in the class to lure us into discussions that are unproductive. We are responsible for not assaying the manuscripts with a more critical eye. And one of us was responsible for being a snob, for locking himself away save for classtimes, making himself unavailable to students who needed private consultation. And several of us have entered into personal relationships with students that weakened our positions as teachers.

Well.

I've gone on at three times the length assigned for this essay. Much of it is sidetrack. All of it has been boiling around in my gut since St. Louis. Now that I've gotten most of it off my chest, I'll try to capsulize what corrective measures can be taken, in my lone opinion.

• There are students who are making full-time careers out of being Workshop attendees. They must be thrown out to fall or fly in the professional world. No student should receive more than two invitations to Clarion.

• Cliques are divisive. Administrators, returning students and particularly teachers should work diligently to integrate them into one class.

• Returning students should be billeted with newcomers for a full flow of ideas and procedures. Old buddies should not be allowed to room together.

• A preliminary study course program should be set up with the cooperation of the visiting teachers and the administrator, with definite assignments stressed. Week-to-week continuity is a worthy goal to pursue.

• Teachers should be rotated. New minds and new voices are desperately needed. Robin Wilson has written, "My own role in the Clarion experiment is now drawing very much to a close. I may lecture occasionally, but I think I will be making arrangements for another editor for the *Clarion* series; it is time for fresh minds and hands. It has been a good experiment, I think, but I hope very much it will not become frozen in *any* mold; vitality is movement and change, and I hope others will give the experiment new direction."

• We professionals must cease our overblown praise of what Clarion is all about. The period of oversell is ended. And students must be more reserved in this area.

• No student should be permitted into the Workshop without having submitted at least seven thousand words of written work. To admit applicants merely on the basis of an essay is insanity. No potential artist gets into an art institute without a portfolio. If the chore of reading these submissions is too tough for the administrators, they should farm them out to the teachers who will work that year's Clarion. Two opinions on each student would be even better.

• There should be refresher sessions post-Workshop.

• Admission information should be more adeptly disseminated to colleges and universities during the year preceding a Clarion.

• Admission requirements should be stiff. Since what we can teach, *de facto,* is limited, the hopeless (but not the marginal) should be eliminated at the outset.

• Periodic reports on what Clarion is doing, with chapter and verse on which students have sold and where, should be released to fan magazines and other journals, to minimize the animosity of paranoid fandom.

• Guest instructors must become sensitive to the ebb and flow of writing in their week of instruction. In-group or private-joke stories must be channeled before they become a time-wasting spate. Students must have impressed upon them the briefness of time allotted for a Workshop, and must be made to understand that nights learning how to create a living character are better spent than those in which the typewriter produces something to make one's classmates snicker.

• The actual *mechanics* of the Workshop—Xerography, billeting, air conditioning if necessary, dining accommodations, blackboards, comfortable chairs during the critique sessions—must be considered *before* the sessions begin. And most important, the guest instructor *must* be billeted in among the students' rooms, available at all hours for consultation. If not immediately in the clump of student rooms, then certainly within a two-minute walk.

• Individual consultations with the guest instructor *each week* should be scheduled for *every* student. And students should come to these private rap sessions with specific problems. The instructors should read as much of the work that has already been produced as possible on the very first night of arrival, instead of partying, so they can go into classes on Monday morning armed with the data on as many students as possible.

• Guest instructors must cease being "kind" about the work produced or the student's potential for making it as a professional. We do them no kindness when we lie to them about their chances. We must be ready to lobby on the side of harshness, as opposed to easing difficult situations by glossing over inadequacies and murmuring false encouragement. But those who *have* the talent and fritter it away must be clubbed into understanding that theirs is a special gift and it takes clean hands and composure to employ it properly.

• Administrators must not admit students for considerations outside talent. No matter how politically or financially expedient such admissions may seem. Clarion is the semi-pro league and only the hardiest and most talented should be given access to that league, for they are the ones who have the best chance of making it into the majors. For the others it is hobbyism.

• A bad or inept instructor should have his or her covers pulled by the students. Publicly. If we fuck up, it's not patty-cake time. We are diddling with the minds and abilities of potentially fine writers and that is a sacred trust. And if the instructor doesn't shape up . . . *out*!

• More "hard science" writing should be taught, and less dilettante experimental bullshit. We are *sf* writers as well as fantasists, and we ought to be able to direct our students in that area as well as in technique and theme. (With Ben Bova teaching at MSU this year, part of this problem has been solved.)

• Guest instructors have to keep a sense of proportion in their relationships with students. We're teachers, not playmates.

• Guest instructors must work their asses off to burst the "myth-image" bubbles in which many students float. And students have to get hip that those Big-Name Pros are just people with a talent better developed than those possessed by the people they're teaching. We ain't gods, for Christ's sake! So the less naive students should actively work to burst the bubbles *before* the myth-object arrives for his or her week.

• Students must be encouraged from the outset to be unstinting in their analyses of submitted work. They must be as tough as they would want others to be to them. Mild "I didn't care for this story much" comments are virtually useless in a critical situation.

Clarion Workshops have become household words in the sf world. Clearly, they have done much good. There are good writers whose names appear on tables of contents regularly who, five years ago, were unknown; they got that necessary push at Clarion. A tone of literacy unknown to the sf field before Clarion has made itself clear, due in some part to the literary and academic backgrounds of this new breed of college-spawned writers. It's all healthy inflow. It makes the soil richer. But if Clarion is to thrive, continue to be a viable part of the sf experience, watchful and loving eyes must be cast on it from here on out. It should be permitted to develop like Topsy, clearly, but when flaws reveal themselves . . . they must be set to rights.

In the seventeen years I've spent as a professional sf writer, and the twenty-three years total as part of the sf world, I conceive of my affiliation with the Clarion Workshops as one of the most rewarding and valuable interludes.

You may guess what's coming next.

And it explains, I suppose, why I've gone on at such interminable length.

This will more than likely be my last year as a Clarion teacher. I think my time is at an end with the project. The "myth-image" has become too tangible to kill, my value as a teacher is no longer what I would want it to be, and so I—like Robin Wilson—pass the Clarion experience on to newer and fresher minds and hands.

May they become as enriched by the association as I have been. Take care of yourselves. I'll see you around.

[1] While there is great merit in Harlan's thesis (p. 209), it contains a minor error in fact. I did not require samples of applicants' work during the first three sessions, much as I might have wished to; I was too desperate to fill the class. I *did* reject large numbers of applicants because they (a) could not write a clear English sentence, (b) appeared uncertain in motivation, or (c) seemed motivated only by a passionate desire to meet Harlan Ellison (or some other staffer). Perhaps the pool of potential Clarion students is now large enough to provide a class full of people who are *both* talented and motivated, but when the management passed from my hands, I urged my successors to rely more heavily on motivation than anything else. Submitted manuscripts, after all, may not be entirely the work of the applicant. Further, great motivation—even if talent is marginal—can make the workshop a valuable educational experience. The institutions sponsoring Clarion are in the education business. So am I. We have responsibilities beyond literature.—R.S.W.